Too LETHAL TO Love

A MILITARY ROMANCE BY

KRISTIE WOLF

Editing by Jen Graybeal and Kimberly Hunt of Revision Division
Proofreading by Rosa Sharon at Fairy Proofmother Proofreading, LLC
Cover and Interior Design by Laura Hidalgo of Spellbinding Design
Paperback ISBN: 979-8-9887850-6-4
Special Edition ISBN: 979-8-9887850-7-1
eBook ISBN: 979-8-9887850-8-8

For Linda — my beautiful forever friend with a heart so big, so pure, she attracts angels. Love you!

A NOTE FROM THE AUTHOR

Yay! Project VIPER is officially a series now. I had a blast writing about another one of my super soldier heroes and the smart, badass woman he falls for. I hope you enjoy reading Kane and Beth's story as much as I loved writing it.

Like *Too Dangerous to Love*, *Too Lethal to Love* is near and dear to my heart. As the granddaughter and daughter of veterans, the wife of a Marine, and now the proud mom of a Navy recruit, I have deep and sincere respect for the brave and selfless men and women who protect our country.

As a marketer in government technology, I feel the same about the folks who dedicate their careers to federal service.

The inspiration for Dr. Beth Parker came from the super smart, dedicated women I've met who are leading innovation at federal agencies.

To everyone working in the public sector, thank you from the bottom of my heart.

To all the active military and veterans out there—thank you for your service. To the folks at the Veterans Administration—thanks for taking care of our vets.

Veterans Affairs Veterans Crisis Line: Call 988 and select 1 or text 838255.

AUTHOR'S DISCLAIMER

Too Lethal to Love contains swearing, sexually explicit language, sex on the page, and fight scenes.

ONE

First Lieutenant Kane Darren launched himself and the DEA agent in his arms toward the hovering helicopter. Bullets pinged off the bird's tail in rapid succession. One hit his stronger-than-steel bionic leg as the whir of the blades drowned out his curse. He didn't feel pain, but the agent whose cover had been blown was barely breathing, thanks to the Diablo drug cartel.

Kane handed the unconscious woman to his teammate and climbed in. He flipped his middle finger at the machine-gun-toting herd of mercenaries barreling through the tree line. Adrenaline roared in his ears as he thought the command to blow them sky-high.

Fire!

His lips twitched into a feral grin as an electromagnetic current pulsed like a live wire from the chip implanted at the base of his neck down his spine. The deadly tide flowed to his bionic leg, weaponized with technology courtesy of Project VIPER. Less than a heartbeat later, a V-Strike streamed from the center of his kneecap. The deadly, invisible laser traveled through his pants without leaving a trace and struck the ground with the force of a lightning bolt.

The impact shook the Mexican jungle. Flames erupted in the tall grass. A wave of heat penetrated his thick helmet and the high-tech gear protecting every inch of his body. His skin nearly melted from his bones, but he snarled with satisfaction as the explosion sucked a dozen of the bastards back into the bowels of the Yucatan Peninsula.

The helicopter pitched to the right as it rose from a clearing barely big enough for the bird to have landed in. He grounded himself with the enhanced strength in his steel leg as he and his brothers-in-arms picked off the unending force of mercenaries dodging the flaming trees.

Fire! Fire! Fire!

V-Strikes shot from the center of his quad and the juncture of his shin and ankle. His targets fell to the charred jungle floor, but fuck, cartel goons with machine guns kept coming like a plague of locusts. VIPER's mission was to extract the agent and her valuable intel, not eliminate the devil's right-hand men in one day. But if a bullet hit the helicopter's fuel tank, they'd all be burned to hell.

He was a super soldier for God's sake. A lucky shot wouldn't be the cause of his demise, but the heat might.

Even though his head throbbed like he'd snorted half the opioids in the compound they'd infiltrated, he poured gallons of wrath into his command to fire. The intensity of his V-Strikes was controlled by his thoughts. Dialing it back from killing to incapacitating might get the job done, but these savages who manufactured deadly drugs and beat women didn't deserve mercy, even if it was almost Christmas.

His teammates showed no mercy either as V-Strikes pulsed from their super limbs. Their combined force sucked the last of the Diablo army back into the underworld like the devil had called them home.

Kane yanked off his helmet and whipped his head to Dr. Hudson Langley, VIPER's trauma surgeon. "Is she alive?"

Hudson shined a penlight into Agent Jenna McKinney's bloodshot stare. "Barely."

"We're clear," Linc shouted from the cockpit as he flew them away from the burning jungle.

Kane scrambled the few feet to Jenna, his super leg jittering beneath him, and sank to his knees above her head. Her sweat-soaked body shook as they rapidly ascended into the air.

"Fuck," he muttered as he grabbed a silver emergency blanket and tucked it around her quaking body. There hadn't been time to fully assess the extent of her injuries when they'd found her tied to a chair in a dilapidated barn a few feet from the main building. Rage sped up his breathing as the helicopter's dim light revealed how she'd been tortured.

Bruises, some greenish blue with age and some fresh and angry, showed through the bloody sweat dripping down her cheeks. Her lower lip bled from a jagged cut. Even her nose, which had a spray of freckles across it in the photo he'd seen during this morning's briefing, had been busted. The freckles were nowhere to be seen under the bruising and blood. God knew what other damage hid beneath her crimson-stained T-shirt and filthy jeans.

His teammate Chris crouched beside her and gently opened her eyelids. With care, he peeled contact lenses from her corneas and dropped them into a case as Hudson readied a syringe.

Kane cradled her head in his lap and brushed blood-soaked hair away from a knot on her forehead. His other teammate, Nic, dropped to his side next to her. He traced the edges of a days-old bruise on her bicep with his black, steel fingers. "*Dios mio.*"

My God was right.

Kane glanced at the fire-tinged smoke choking the early afternoon sky. Before he'd lost his leg to an IED in the Middle East, he'd witnessed plenty of gruesome sights with Marine Corps Force Reconnaissance. This level of brutality had him wishing for thirty seconds with the deviants holed up in the Diablo cartel's stronghold. He'd only need a second to obliterate them with a V-Strike. The first twenty-nine he'd use to unleash the strength in his super leg on their unholy asses.

His gaze fixed on a cut in Jenna's lower lip. "How is she alive after what they did to her?"

"Because she's higher than this helicopter." Hudson glanced at her track-mark-riddled forearms as he jabbed a syringe into her chest.

Her eyes shot open.

"Hey." Kane braced her head with his hands.

She lashed her fingers around his wrists and stared up at him. The glassy defeat in her gaze almost made him vomit. "Stay with us, Jenna. You're safe."

"Please." Sounds as ragged as her tormented flesh grated from her throat. "Tell Greg no…no regrets."

Kane held his breath as everything, from Jenna's swollen lips to her shuddering body, stilled. He didn't need Hudson to confirm she'd said her last words. And he didn't need to reread her file to know Greg was the husband she'd never go home to.

"Fuck." Hudson sat back on his haunches.

Chris sighed as he patted the pocket holding the valuable intel Jenna had uncovered.

Nic made the sign of the cross with his steel hand. "Thank you for your service."

Kane echoed his words as he stroked Jenna's swollen cheek. Tears stung his eyes, which felt as bloodshot as her lifeless gaze. Yeah, they'd retrieved the intel they'd come for, but in a few hours, someone would knock on Jenna's door. Only one glance at the person's stiff posture and somber expression would be needed for Jenna's husband to know his wife was never coming home again.

A memory of two men in uniform, another doorstep, crept into Kane's mind. Futile wishes that they'd gotten to Jenna earlier mixed with his past. He swallowed the bitter concoction along with his waning adrenaline. It erupted in his gut like one of the explosions he'd caused in the jungle. Jenna's last words whispered through his mind as he closed her eyes and covered her face with the emergency blanket.

No regrets.

Would her husband think that when he learned about her brutal demise? Fuck, no. She'd been scheduled to be permanently extracted tomorrow, alive and well, and in time for the holidays, with critical information that could help save millions of lives. Now, her husband's Christmas gifts would be a bottomless box of jagged pain, soul-slashing torment, and the regret Jenna thought he shouldn't have.

But he would have regrets. Kane knew firsthand that grief was the gift that never stopped giving. Closing his eyes, he sent up a silent prayer for Jenna's soul and for her husband who was about to have his world blown to smithereens. He glanced at his teammates as he fought to wrangle his spiraling thoughts, but the super strength VIPER had engineered him with only applied to his leg, not his psyche.

Would Chris's fiancé, Scarlett, think "no regrets" if the love of her life died on a mission? The genius who cybernetically engineered their brains with their prosthetics may have a mind like a machine, but she was still a woman in love. And what about Hudson? His role as medical support didn't totally shield him from gun-toting mercenaries and other hostiles. And unlike Kane and his VIPER teammates, he didn't have a weaponized limb to shoot lasers from. Kane doubted Hudson's pregnant wife would find comfort in "no regrets" if her husband came home in a coffin.

So far, Kane and his VIPER brothers had returned from their handful of missions in one piece. Even though their super soldier capabilities increased their chances of survival a hundredfold, death could still find them.

And grief would overtake the ones they left behind.

He held on to Jenna's body as he succumbed to his memories that raced faster than the helicopter. Unlike Chris and Hudson, he didn't have a wife, a fiancé, or even a girl-friend to mourn him if he died protecting his country. He only had Gran and his sister, and now his VIPER family. He didn't intend to add any more to the list of loved ones who would grieve if he didn't come home.

Serve first. Love Later.

He'd been born to serve. Duty to his country was woven into his DNA just as tightly as his love for his family's land in West Virginia. At thirty-two, he still had plenty of military miles in him. Those miles would lead him to situations where the chances were high of winding up dead, like his buddies who hadn't survived the IEDs that took his leg. Or Jenna, who risked her life to save others.

He'd learned long ago that relationships and the military didn't mix, especially for someone who pledged to fight the worst of the worst. Loving a woman—even the one he couldn't get off his mind—would have to wait until he parted ways with Uncle Sam and the dangerous existence he'd committed to.

A few hours later, Kane followed his brothers out of the conference area and into the hall at VIPER headquarters. He didn't break his stride toward the locker room as he looked at the comms unit strapped to his wrist. "That was the shortest debrief ever."

Nic checked the unit embedded in his steel arm. "Thank God, because Scarlett will have our balls if we don't get Chris to his engagement party on time."

Chris chuckled. "And Beth will have your ass."

Beth.

An image of Scarlett's best friend danced in Kane's vision. Everything about her shimmered, from her long, dark-brown curls to the colorful, sparkly clothes she wrapped around her sweet curves. Even the tight smiles she sporadically offered him beamed with an inherent, vivacious spark he itched to ignite. The man in him ached to learn why that spark didn't awaken into a flame. His training demanded he know why she never sat with her back to the door and why she hid a gun in her giant tote bag. The super soldier he'd become needed to eradicate whatever gave her nightmares.

Nic nudged him in the arm. "Beth put me in charge of beer and making sure the happy couple gets to the party on time. What did she put you in charge of?"

"Nothing." The petite research scientist whose head barely reached his chin had made it clear she didn't welcome his attention. At least not the kind she knew about. He may not be able to get her out of his mind, but he'd damn well protect her from whatever she feared.

TWO

Beth Parker braced her hands on the glass bakery counter. "You gave my cake to someone else? It's only a half hour past the time I said I'd pick it up."

Well, it was ninety minutes past the time Beth had *wanted* to pick it up, but the network in her lab at the National Agency for Health had been down half the day—again—and had royally screwed up her schedule. She needed that damn cake, but yelling at the teen behind the counter who kept glancing at her phone wouldn't do any good.

Counting to five in her head, Beth clung to the last of her patience. "Maybe there was a mix-up. I'm here to pick up a vanilla pound cake with strawberry filling, red flowers, and silver-dusted buttercream frosting. It's for an engagement party."

More like a let's celebrate your impending nuptials while the groom-to-be is between deadly missions kind of celebration.

Beth shivered. The sudden chill had nothing to do with the deep freeze blanketing the Washington, DC area and everything to do with her best friend marrying a literal super soldier. Scarlett, and Beth as her supporting bestie, didn't take a full breath whenever Chris and his Project VIPER teammates deployed. Today had been a hard-to-breathe kind of day until they'd gotten word that the VIPER boys had returned safe and sound from their latest assignment.

What kind of assignment, she had no idea. Scarlett knew most of the details since she used to be Project VIPER's chief information security officer and now headed up technology innovation across the military. She wasn't at liberty to share what the guys did when the Department of Defense called them away at a moment's notice, and Beth didn't want to know.

The military hadn't given them sleek, black artificial limbs that looked like they belonged on sci-fi superheroes for goodwill reasons. According to the public, the Department of Defense established the Veterans Integration Placement and Recovery Program to give special forces amputees a second chance at their military careers in security detail roles.

Security detail, my ass.

Last week, when she'd met Scarlett and the VIPER boys for dinner, the waitstaff was scrambling to move a massive table set for twelve. Chris and Nic had lifted it like it was a piece of children's furniture set for a tea party. The waitress had been so appreciative of Nic's bionic arm, she'd slipped him her number.

No, super arm. Super is what Scarlett said the VIPER boys liked to call the technological marvels they'd been outfitted with. And damn, they were a marvel to witness. They moved their enhanced parts more gracefully than she managed her flesh-and-bone ones.

According to Scarlett, the bionic limbs were permanently attached to their bodies. No straps. No harnesses. A seamless melding of steel and flesh that was beautiful and tragic at the same time. Beth spent many nights wondering what the marriage of man and machine looked like underneath their clothes.

Well, what it looked like under the clothes of one VIPER boy in particular. That had to stop.

The teen chomped on her gum as she opened a binder on the counter and leafed through it. "Red flowers, you say?" She eyed Beth's glittery silver nail polish. "And metallic dusting because you obviously like bling. And I love your coat. It twinkled like fifty shades of purple under the streetlights when you walked in."

"Thanks." Beth ran her fingers over the faux fur cuff. "Now, about my cake."

"Oh, I remember now. How could I forget? My boss gave it to your husband a few minutes ago."

Beth slammed her palms onto the glass countertop. "My *what?*"

The color drained from the teen's face as she retreated. "You, uh, didn't send your husband to get it?"

Unease skated down Beth's spine as she swung her head to the door.

He's not here. I'm safe.

The emptiness and her affirming mantra didn't stop anxiety from rippling toward full-blown alarm. "I don't have a husband. I don't even have a boyfriend. Who the hell did you give my cake to?"

The teen backed through a door. "Uh, let me get my boss."

Beth nodded, afraid if she opened her mouth, she'd beg the teen not to leave her alone in the empty storefront. "He's not here. I'm safe." She whispered it again as she dipped her hand into her enormous tote bag and wrapped her fingers around the small pistol at the bottom. The security of the warm metal grounded her but didn't stop the past from hammering at her resolve not to hide behind the counter and cry.

Fighting the rising panic, she scanned the small bakery.

The busy sidewalk.

The crowded parking lot beyond.

Nothing out of the ordinary. Just shoppers and a weary donation-collecting Santa.

Pushing trapped air out of her lungs, she trained one eye on the entrance, the other on the door the teen had disappeared through and sang along with the Christmas song playing overhead. Her grip on the gun didn't lessen any with the distraction technique she'd learned from her therapist.

A chorus later, a woman who appeared to be around the same age as Beth emerged from the back of the bakery. "Hi, I'm Angie." She dusted her hands on her apron and smiled. "I'm the owner. My apologies for giving your cake to the wrong person. The man knew your name, though."

Beth's pulse pounded as fast as the sweat forming on the back of her neck. The lack of an imminent threat didn't stop her fears from vaulting her into the past.

No. She tugged at the ends of her curls. He'd never shown himself before. Why start now? This was just a misunderstanding. Or maybe the bakery's computers had been hacked by a criminal trying to steal credit card information and someone took a liking to her cake order.

God, that last bit sounded stupid, but she couldn't live with the scenario she feared. There had to be a reasonable explanation. "Did my alleged husband know anything else about me?"

"He knew what type of cake it was. The occasion. The names on the cake. The address and the phone number on the order form. He even mentioned that you'd gotten a cake here a few months ago for your twenty-eighth birthday."

Beth's pulse rang in her ears like a gunshot with every

piece of information Angie rattled off. She clutched her gun tighter. "What did he look like?"

"Tall, dark, and sexy, from what I could tell underneath his sunglasses and ski hat. And he thanked me in the sexiest Spanish accent."

Beth relaxed her grip on the gun a smidge. Could it have been Nic? He fit Angie's dark and handsome description and excelled at making women blush when he spoke Spanish. She'd asked him to pick up beer for the party. Maybe he'd decided to grab the cake too. "Did you notice anything unusual about the cake stealer? Anything identifying?"

Like a black bionic hand?

"No, nothing unusual."

Beth tightened her fingers around the gun again. It couldn't have been Nic. His mechanical fingers were hard to miss, and he wouldn't have said he was her husband and missed the chance to hit on the gorgeous redhead.

Angie pointed to the glass-front refrigerator on the far wall. "I'm happy to give you a full refund and a new cake free of charge, of course. I'm afraid it will have to be a plain white sheet cake because that's all we have left, but I can decorate it with the flowers and sprinkles that you ordered."

"Fine." Beth eyed the binder on the counter. "Do you always keep that out in the open?"

Angie picked it up. "No. It belongs underneath, but sometimes, if we're busy, like today, it doesn't get put away."

Beth let go of the gun and pulled her hand from her bag. Some cheapskate must have peeked at the order forms in the binder and randomly chosen her cake to swipe. She clung to that explanation. Considering the other scenario wasn't an option.

It had been two years of silence from the man who'd terrorized her. Two years of fighting for control. The affirming words she repeated helped when she felt threatened but didn't completely ease her anxiety. Nothing ever would.

As she pulled up the messages on her phone, tension ebbed from her body.

No disturbing texts.

No threatening emails.

Nothing to indicate he was back.

The hum of an engine snapped her head up. A black SUV backed out of the parking spot directly in front of the shop. As it drove away, her compact sedan came into view.

The phone slid from her grip. She clamped her other hand over her mouth, but the terrified edges of her scream tore through. The cake she ordered sat on the top of the hood. Its silver-dusted frosting twinkled under the streetlight.

Angie ran to her side. "Are you okay?"

Beth ignored her as she picked up her phone. Her fingers trembled as she dialed the second person who came to mind who could help. She had to stay far, far away from the first.

THREE

Kane leaned back into the jewel-toned throw pillows on Scarlett's, and now Chris's, couch since they'd recently moved in together and tipped his beer bottle toward Nic. "Are those gingerbread cookies on your ugly-ass Christmas sweater going at it?"

"Even cookies have needs." Nic rose from the couch and glanced at the stairs. "Based on how long that shower has been running, I'd say Chris and Scarlett's needs are being satisfied too."

"They'd better hurry up. It's almost time to go."

"Can't rush love." He started for the kitchen. "Want a beer?"

"Nah, I'll save it for later." Unless he was on official leave, as Chris was for the next couple of days while he and Scarlett were on their "engagement-moon," two drinks were his limit. He'd need them later to dull the pain in his hip where VIPER's surgeon had attached his super leg. After the Mexico mission, he'd received a special concoction to help heal the bumps and bruises he'd sustained. The aches were nearly gone, but the wonder drug did nothing for phantom pain.

His leg ached like it was still made of living muscle and nerves instead of an indestructible alloy invented in the VIPER lab.

Nic appeared back in the doorway, his phone to his ear. "I'll meet you there." He hung up and motioned for Kane to follow him as he strode to the front door.

Kane stood and pulled on his leather jacket over his navy-blue button-down. "What's happened?"

"Someone stole Beth's cake and scared the shit out of her."

"What?" Kane sprang from the couch. Confusion about the first part and anger about the second raced through his mind as he scooped up his cowboy hat from the coffee table and jammed it onto his head.

Nic gave him a rundown of the incident at the bakery as they jogged down the steps. "Sounds like some asshole is fucking with Beth, and not in the way *you* would like to."

"Shut up." Who knew that when he'd signed on to be part of the nation's first generation of super soldiers he'd not only gain his career back but also get a bunch of busybody brothers? Nic wasn't wrong though. Beth starred in his fantasies.

Kane opened the door of his pickup truck and pulled his handgun out of the glove box. He couldn't utilize his V-Strike technology if they encountered hostiles at Beth's place. His weaponry was only active when VIPER headquarters gave the okay. He didn't mind reverting to good old-fashioned firepower, though. Sometimes he missed the weight of a gun in his hand. "How far out is she?"

"Fifteen minutes." Nic closed the door of his SUV and slipped the weapon he'd retrieved inside his coat.

"Good." She lived around the corner from Chris and Scarlett in an identical townhome in Alexandria, Virginia, just outside of Washington, DC. There was plenty of time to secure the place before she arrived.

"Beth made me promise not to tell Scarlett. She doesn't want her to worry during her engagement party. She also told me not to bring you."

Nic's words nearly tripped him up but didn't slow his stride. "She what?"

"What did you do to piss her off?"

"I did nothing." Well, nothing since a few weeks ago, and nothing she knew about recently. "We all can't be Casanovas like you."

"Someone in this *familia* has to be the charmer."

Kane snickered as he secured his gun inside his jacket. "Whatever, brother." He didn't have to act like a ladies' man with Beth. He'd only known her a couple of weeks, but enough chemistry naturally kindled between them to start a fire. But even if she hadn't been giving him the cold shoulder lately, Beth wasn't a one-night stand kind of girl. Until he got out of the military, he was a no commitment kind of guy.

He pulled in cold air as he picked up his pace. "Feels like we just did this a few weeks ago."

"We did. Let's hope tonight's drama doesn't send anyone into hiding. Or the hospital."

"Let's hope." Although taking Beth to the ER after she'd hit her head during a break-in at Scarlett's townhome less than a month ago had been one of the best nights of his life. At least up until their impromptu not-quite date went to shit.

Kane forced the memory from his mind as they approached Beth's place in the middle of the well-lit block. All looked quiet from the inside. So did the neighborhood. Once he made sure her house was secure, he'd have a conversation with the pretty research scientist. She may not like him, and God knew he couldn't pursue anything more than friendship, but she'd damn well tell him why Nic had been the one she'd called.

Beth glanced in the rearview mirror as she pulled into the parking spot in front of her townhome. One hand clenched the steering wheel. The other fisted the gun by her side. She hadn't been tailed as far as she could tell, but what did she know?

She turned her attention back to the windshield. A familiar figure in a black cowboy hat and dark jeans that hugged his body like a sin jogged down her steps.

Kane.

As she switched off the engine and disengaged the door lock, she cursed. Heat flooded her cheeks, half from embarrassment that hadn't abated from their first encounter and half from anger at his appearance. Before she could reach for the handle, he opened the door.

With one arm braced on the roof, the other on the frame, he leaned in. "Are you okay?"

She met eyes the color of a summer sky as she slipped her gun into her bag. "What are you doing here?"

The clouds shifted as if disturbed by the ire in her voice. A sliver of moonlight beamed from the heavens. The scant glow highlighted the hardness in his cerulean gaze. He cocked his head as if his question about her welfare was obvious. And it *was* obvious. She'd been hurt again. This trauma wasn't physical like when he'd been tasked with taking her to the hospital after the break-in at Scarlett's, but she'd been injured just the same.

No, worse. Physical pain went away. Tonight's ordeal would leave scars that would plague her forever. Worse than that, it had stolen the precarious sense of safety—of normalcy—she'd struggled to attain.

There was nothing normal about living in fear, and certainly nothing normal about asking for help from some sort of super soldier trained to protect and fight.

Or die trying.

"You shouldn't be here, Kane. Where's Nic?"

Annoyance flashed in his gaze, half-hidden by the brim of his cowboy hat.

He straightened and held out his hand as he backed up a few steps. "We'll talk inside where it's safe."

The only place she felt safe was in her lab at work. Armed guards, metal detectors, and access granted by biometric verification had a way of making a girl feel secure. The runner-up was her home with its top-of-the-line security system. Her holiday plans didn't allow her to take refuge in the first. Tonight's events compromised the second.

Ignoring his outstretched hand, she grabbed her bag and exited the car. The crisp night air did nothing to cool her aggravation. She'd worked hard to learn how to take care of herself. Relinquishing control over her safety meant she'd regressed to being a victim. She'd spent too much time in that role. A bizarre cake stealing wouldn't banish her back, but the incident had scared her.

She wasn't naive enough to turn down protection; she just couldn't accept it from Kane. But Christ, the hard set of his jaw and the tension radiating from his wide shoulders blanketed her with the same sense of safety she felt at work. The gun she spied under his faded black leather jacket helped too.

He ushered her up the stairs and into her house, his head on a swivel, all business and coiled energy. This shift to protector, so at odds with the easygoing country boy who cracked jokes with a twang and talked about his horses back home like they were his babies, unnerved her almost as much as the mysterious cake stealer.

In a flash, he shut the door and locked it. She stared at him as memories of the last time he'd walked—no, carried her over the threshold—engulfed her brain. Clearing her throat, she shoved that night aside. "Where's Nic?"

"Getting his laptop so he can check the security feeds from the bakery and the shopping center. We secured your house and the backyard. No sign of a break-in or any surveillance equipment. Whoever threatened you hasn't been here."

"I wasn't threatened, just…" She crossed her arms over her chest.

Violated. Again. Although her fight-or-flight response agreed with Kane.

He peered through the light-up snowflake hanging in her window. "Someone arranged an incident to let you know you're being watched. That's a threat in my book."

God, she wanted to tell him he was overreacting. Perhaps some weirdo really had scammed her cake, put it on the hood of a random car so he could check his phone, and then forgot it.

And maybe Santa will come down my chimney tonight.

Kane tipped her chin up with his fingers. "Do you understand that this is serious shit?"

"Yes." *All too well.* "I also understand guests will be here soon." She hung her bag on a hook by the door. As if remembering his manners, he removed his hat and handed it to her. A lock of sandy-colored hair fell onto his forehead.

She squeezed the brim of his hat to stop herself from brushing it back. "I need to get ready for the party."

"Not yet, sugarplum." He took the hat from her and hung it over her bag. On the hook next to it, he hung his jacket. "You're going to tell me what happened back at the bakery."

She shrugged an arm out of her coat and raised her brows. "Sugarplum?"

He winked and smiled as he slid the coat from her other arm and bunched the faux fur in his hands. "This coat reminds me of the sugarplum candy Gran makes at Christmas. A decadent treat rolled in purple sugar crystals."

The silly nickname shouldn't sound so familiar or so sexy, coming from his full lips in that West Virginia twang. Nor should his hat resting on top of her bag look so intimate. The worn black felt glowed under the white lights intertwined with garlands of fresh pine hanging over the doorway. Matching decorations on the stair rail, on the hearth on the adjacent wall, and on the Christmas tree next to the fireplace bathed the room with the scent of pine and a warm glow. The place looked as festive as she'd be feeling if tonight hadn't gone haywire. "Is the 'sugarplum' thing going to go on all night?"

"It will. At least until you tell me what happened."

She stared at his large hand and studied how it contrasted with the softness of her coat. Hell, all six feet of him was a study in contrast with his warrior-hardened face one minute and his easy, dimpled grin the next. She could imagine him on his family's farm in West Virginia, riding horses in his cowboy hat and jeans as easily as she could picture him wearing a uniform and shouting orders. Even the rich, earthy scent that clung to Kane, like the land he left behind to join the military would always be woven into his fiber, hinted at a patient side that handled skittish horses and a fierce side that protected what was his.

She avoided his gaze and looked past the living room and into the kitchen. "Tonight is about Scarlett and Chris, not about my drama."

"You call what happened tonight drama?" He fisted his hands around her coat. "I call it scary."

His grave tone deflated her denial about the gravity of the situation, but she held on to the one thing she could control. "Please, Kane, let me focus on the party. Nic knows what happened and is looking for clues. You made sure my house is secure, and I appreciate it. I'll tell Scarlett everything when she gets back from her engagement-moon."

"She needs to know now."

"She has enough to worry about with her stepfather. I don't know everything that went down when she was kidnapped a few weeks ago, but I do know it involved terrorists. I know Project VIPER was almost disbanded. And I know she worries about Chris each time you guys are called on a mission." Beth cocked her head to the side. "Did I miss anything?"

He held up his hand. Something flashed in his eyes as if her rambling dredged up painful, maybe sorrowful, emotions he didn't want to address. She'd seen that look flicker before but didn't have time to search her memory for when and where.

"That about sums it up, sugarplum. In fact, it borders on divulging classified intel."

"Scarlett's like my sister." She fiddled with the tips of her curls that cascaded past her shoulders. "Of course she told me everything she could."

He narrowed his eyes. "What else is wrong besides the obvious?"

"Isn't the obvious enough?"

"When you play with your hair, your mind seems to go elsewhere. Based on the pain in your eyes, it doesn't look like you're in your happy place."

His accurate assessment jabbed her in the heart. They'd only spent one evening together, which ended in disaster.

And when she met Scarlett and the VIPER boys for dinner, she sat as far away from him as possible. How had he picked up on her nervous tic so quickly? "Please, Kane. Give me a few hours to pretend I'm a normal maid of honor giving her bestie an engagement party. When it's over, I promise I'll tell Scarlett and call the police."

He shook his head. "First, nothing about you is normal, Dr. Beth Parker."

Oh, buddy, you have no idea just how abnormally screwed up I am.

"And second, no police. If we can't identify the culprit on the surveillance feeds, the local PD certainly won't be able to. They're good, but our technology is far superior to theirs."

"Fine." She waved her hand, refusing to admit she agreed with his logic as she stepped around him. "I have to get the cake from the car."

He clamped his fingers around her arm. "You didn't bring home the stolen cake, did you?"

"Of course not. I'm stuck with a boring replacement, not the masterpiece I had custom made." Her lower lip trembled. She captured it between her teeth and stared at the white and green plaid pillows on her red couch until her tears stopped threatening to spill. Scarlett's night would not be ruined by some creep with a cake fetish.

Kane slid his hand up to her shoulder and squeezed. "Hey, it's just a cake."

Beth shrugged him off. "It's not just a cake. Tonight is my best friend's engagement party, which I've been envisioning since we were kids. I should have had months to plan it, but no, Scarlett needs to get married quickly because she fell in love with a super soldier who might not come home from dangerous missions nobody can talk about. Forgive me if I want to make tonight perfect."

He flinched as the pained, sorrowful look flared in his gaze again.

"You're right." He dropped his hand from her shoulder and stepped back. "We need to make tonight perfect for Chris and Scarlett. They…" His gaze trailed to the door, along with his thoughts. "I'll go get the cake."

Beth stared at him as she concentrated. She still couldn't place where and when she'd seen that look in his eyes. Although it had lasted less than a second, it managed to break her heart. Abandoning her effort, she sighed. "Thanks. I'll get the food out."

"No. I'll take care of that too." He placed his hand on the small of her back and nudged her to the stairs. "Go get ready."

"I got it. The eggnog needs rum and cinnamon and there are certain bowls things go in."

"And I saw earlier that you have sticky notes on each of them. If the government can trust me enough to attach millions of dollars' worth of technology to my body, then you can trust me with the food." He tapped his super leg and winked. "Although I might need some help figuring out the pasta salad goes in the Santa dish labeled 'pasta salad.'"

She couldn't help but smile at his sarcasm or those damn dimples. "Fine, but don't eat anything until the party starts. I want everything to look perfect when Scarlett gets here." As she turned to leave, her gaze landed on the security console by the front door. "How did you get in my house?" She'd made sure to engage the system before she'd left.

He shrugged. "You have your secrets; I have mine."

FOUR

Kane eyed the spread of food on the table in Beth's brightly lit kitchen like it was a strategic battle plan. Should he group all the snowman-themed dishes together or intermingle them with the Santas, reindeer, and gingerbread men? And what about the lone angel dish?

The security system signaled movement at the front door. Kane checked the video feed. A few moments later, Nic sauntered into the kitchen, a grin on his angular, too-handsome-for-his-own-good face.

"Channeling your inner party planner?" Nic set a case of beer on the counter. "I met one last week I could persuade to help you decorate."

"Screw you, Romeo. Where do you think the angel should go?"

He tapped his sweater. "By the gingerbread men, of course, so she can get some action tonight."

Linc pushed Nic aside and stalked into the kitchen. "Who the fuck cares about angels and gingerbread men?" He eyed the cake sitting on the black countertop. A small

Christmas tree decorated with scarlet, silver, and gold balls sat next to it. "That doesn't look like the stolen property on the surveillance feed."

"It's a replacement." The video Nic procured from the shopping center showed a man coming out of the bakery and placing the stolen cake on Beth's hood. His face was obscured, and the black sedan he'd climbed into had bogus plates, but at least they'd gotten something to work with.

Linc shrugged. "Looks just as sparkly, like this whole damn house. Where are the plates? I'm starving."

Kane slapped his hand away from the divine-smelling crab dip that bubbled with gooey melted cheese on top. "Don't touch the food until Beth gives the okay." The aesthetic of the spread didn't matter to Kane, but it did to Beth.

Linc held up the bottle of amber liquid in his hand. "I did my job. I brought my cousin's moonshine that I can't drink in case we're needed to take care of whoever fucked with Beth. I deserve some damn food."

Adrenaline surged through Kane. While the missions they'd completed so far were the get in, get out, quick kind like in Mexico, they could be assigned to protection duty, like the public thought they'd been established for.

Nic waved him off and looked at Kane. "How is she?"

"Shaken, but she won't admit it." Kane set the angel down next to a snowman. "Maybe she'll feel better knowing you got him on video."

"Piece of cake, pun intended." Nic snickered at his own joke as he opened a white cabinet and found a glass. "I sent the surveillance footage to Ryan. He's examining it to see if we can learn more about the mysterious cake stealer before he comes over."

"Good." Kane trusted Ryan Bradley, VIPER's new chief information security officer. He had been instrumental in helping recover Scarlett from her kidnappers. "Did you tell anyone about what happened?"

"Scrooge over there." Nic nodded toward Linc as he grabbed a can of soda from the refrigerator. "And Chris. He promised not to say a word to Scarlett."

Beth's security system beeped another alert. Kane checked the video feed and smiled as he Chris lead his bride-to-be through the front door.

Scarlett took off her coat as she waved from the threshold. "Where's Beth?"

Kane directed the slim genius in the pretty red dress to the stairs.

She lifted to her toes and kissed Chris's cheek. Something heavy settled in Kane's gut as Chris wrapped his hand around her long, blonde ponytail and kissed her like she was the sustenance he needed to survive. The boulder in his gut grew heavier as he watched Chris track his fiancé up the stairs with a lethal blue gaze. With her safety still at risk from the terrorists who tried to kidnap her, Chris didn't let her out of his sight. When he deployed on missions, a VIPER support team member was assigned to protect her.

How did Scarlett and Chris smile, fuck in the shower, and enjoy life, knowing happiness could end tomorrow?

He thought of Jenna's last words to her husband.

"No regrets."

Kane knew from experience regret could consume even the strongest person. Once it gnashed its poisoned teeth into a heart, drank from its soul, and spit it out, nothing but a shell remained.

Chris strode into the kitchen. "Whoa! That's a lot of Christmas creatures." He reached for a cracker with his steel hand.

Linc slapped his arm away. "Don't touch that. The party-planning elf upstairs made Kane her bitch. He'll have a hissy fit if you touch the spread."

Chris flipped up his middle finger. "Where's your Christmas spirit?"

"Left it back home in Alaska with the rest of Santa's Eskimos."

"Santa has elves, not Eskimos, you bah humbug."

"Whatever." Linc headed for the living room. "Let me know when we can eat."

Nic followed. "Fucking moody pilots."

Kane watched his two brothers sit on the couch and stretch out their super legs. Two on Linc and one on Nic. Four deadly limbs in total when you counted Nic's arm. While Kane didn't like that the cake stealer knew where Beth lived, the asshole wasn't getting past those two.

Or any of them.

He may have one super leg, and Chris only had one super arm, but they were plenty deadly, even when their weaponry wasn't activated. He'd only need the enhanced strength engineered into his body to neutralize a threat in an instant.

A smile tugged at Kane's mouth as he rubbed the seam on his hip where steel met flesh. He knew it sounded childish to refer to their cybernetically engineered appendages as super. Scarlett usually rolled her wide green eyes when they said it, but the weapons seamlessly melded into their bodies were scientific miracles. They had every right to call themselves and their awesome-as-fuck appendages whatever they wanted and to use humor as a coping mechanism, considering the trauma that preceded their arrival at Project VIPER.

Their wounded warrior status also came in handy when they went out for a drink after a long day at VIPER headquarters, at least for him and Nic. Now that Chris was engaged, he went home to Scarlett. Since meeting Beth, Kane had ditched the bar scene too, but for a very different reason. And when Linc decided to join them for a drink, he typically sat in the corner with a scowl on his face.

Kane turned to Chris. "Linc's moodier than usual."

Chris stared into his bottle of water. "Can't say that I blame him."

Neither could Kane. He knew what happened to Linc in the Middle East during the holidays. The Alaskan with the spiky platinum hair and glacial blue eyes that matched his bristly, cold demeanor had every right to want to ride out the season piss drunk on his cousin's moonshine, but he abstained for Beth because he considered her family.

The reminder that Kane should consider her family too should stop visions of sugarplums from dancing naked in his head. So should the glares she'd been sending his way each time they'd been in the same space since their not-quite-date.

As if on cue, the sugarplum floated into the living room. This vision didn't look like a sweet fairy though. She looked more like a lush strawberry with decadent whipped cream on top in her red, sparkly miniskirt and white fluffy sweater. Wondering how sweet she'd taste hardened his cock quicker than it took Santa to get down a chimney.

The security system beeped as guests approached the house. Kane glanced at the video feed on his phone.

Chris eyed the device. "Dare I ask why you have access to Beth's security system?"

"Nope." He wasn't even sure of the answer himself other than the fierce need he felt to protect a woman he didn't want a future with from a threat he knew nothing about.

"She's vulnerable, you know."

"I know." But vulnerable wasn't a word he'd use to describe Dr. Beth Parker. Contagious energy, like a burst of positive, glittery vibes, detonated when she walked into a room. Whatever scars she had, she hid them well, but he'd endured enough trauma in his life, the worst of it before his leg had been blown from his body, to recognize the signs in someone else. And tonight, he'd seen the gun in her hand when he'd tapped on her window. "Are you ever going to tell me who she's afraid of?"

"I've already told you; it's her story to tell. And don't go turning on the wounded warrior country boy charm you wield like a superpower. She's off-limits."

"Got it." As much as his body wanted to argue the point, he couldn't. He'd witnessed the pain and fear that clouded Beth's eyes. She needed someone stable in her life. Not a human weapon made to kill or die trying.

FIVE

Scarlett breezed into the kitchen, a plate of crumbs in each hand. "Beth, this cake tastes as divine as it looks. Thanks for throwing me an amazing party."

"Anything for you." Beth beamed the maid of honor worthy smile glued to her face. Her lips hurt from forcing it to stay there.

Linc sidled up next to her. "How about some ibuprofen for me? All this festive shit is giving me a headache."

"Sure." She could use some herself. "It's upstairs. Be right back."

She weaved through the living room and waved to the few remaining guests. At her front door, she said goodbye to Hudson, VIPER's trauma surgeon, and his pregnant wife, Tessa. She smiled at Dr. Patience Fairbanks, the orthopedic surgeon responsible for attaching the prosthetics to the VIPER boys.

The brunette with the glossy brown hair and eyes to match had her head bent to Sergeant Gage McAllister's. Unlike the VIPER team he supported, Gage possessed all the limbs he'd been born with. If the hard gleam in his gray eyes and those muscles that nearly tore the stitching on his long-sleeve polo shirt were any indication, the lack of a super limb didn't make him any less dangerous. If tonight's events hadn't left Beth so shaken, she'd engineer more than a conversation between the two. Just because post-party sex wasn't in Beth's cards didn't mean she couldn't help others enjoy holiday cheer.

She trudged up the stairs. The throbbing in her head increased with each step. At the top, she leaned against the wall. The cake-stealing incident compounded her apprehension about going home tomorrow for her town's annual Christmas party. Last year, she'd let nerves rob her of the annual tradition. She wouldn't let that happen again.

As she pushed off the wall, her phone buzzed with a text alert. She pulled the device from her pocket and looked at the message.

Pain, as raw as the day a pair of savage hands broke her wrist, seized her breath. Her vision blurred as the message jumbled into nonsense. She barely made out the sound of heavy footsteps rushing toward her as she dropped the phone and lunged for her bedroom door.

Strong, real hands, not the remembered kind from her nightmare, grasped her upper arms from behind.

Not again. Not again.

She ducked her head and twisted like she'd been trained to do. An insistent voice saying her name froze her midmotion.

Kane. It's Kane. Not him. He's not here.

Kane spun her to face him. "What's wrong?"

Laughter from the partygoers tunneled into her ringing ears. Remembered pain zipped up her arm. Fresh fear raced to catch up.

He's not here. I'm safe.

Kane picked up her phone, his other hand securely on

her hip, and backed her into the bedroom. His scowl deep-ened as he looked at the message. The sprinkles on the cake froze into tiny ice shards that pricked her gut with each frightening word he read.

"Is this from the dickhead who hurt you?"

She dropped her gaze and stared at her feet. Curling her toes inside her heels, she closed her eyes and willed her legs to stop shaking. "The cake stealer didn't hurt me."

Kane closed the distance between them in two long strides. "But someone did. The terror on your face is the same as when I took you to the hospital and you made every excuse not to go in. And it's the same as when I watched you have a nightmare in my truck on the way home and then later in this bed." He nudged her hand with his. "Come on, Beth. You can tell me what haunts you."

She jerked back from his touch. Panic vibrated under her skin like a thundercloud about to burst into a Category 5 hurricane. Wrapping her arms around her middle, she fought the urge to launch herself into Kane's strong arms. Unlike the last time they were in her bedroom, she wouldn't put herself in a position to be pushed away again. "Some guy stalked me online a couple of years ago."

Kane didn't need to hear the entire twisted tale, and she didn't trust herself to tell it without breaking down. She was a master at pretending everything was okay, at least on the outside. She'd worked her ass off to manage her fears enough to be a functioning member of society, but all the training and preparation in the world couldn't stop the message from pulsing in her vision.

> Your cake was almost as pretty as you, querida.

Memories careened from the cage where she'd impris-oned them. Like rabid dogs, they pounced as brutally as if her fears were slabs of raw meat. Her breathing sped up along with her heartbeat as she fought to control her spiraling thoughts.

He's not here. I'm safe.

But even as her brain battled to believe the words, her body retreated until her knees hit the bed.

Kane glanced at the message again. His chest rose and fell as he studied the single sentence. "You said that the cake stealer spoke to the owner in Spanish. *Querida* is Spanish for sweetheart, darling, and all sorts of other things a creepy stalker might call you."

"I know what it means." But she wasn't letting her trauma take the spotlight. Tonight was about Scarlett. Straightening her spine, she pulled in a slow, fortifying breath. When the house was empty, she'd sit on the couch with the lights on, her eyes on the front and back door, and her gun in her hand. Right now, the urgency to go back to doing something normal, like giving Scarlett an engagement party without the past crashing the festivities, shook her harder than her fear. "I've got to get back downstairs."

He blocked her escape. "Who texted you?"

"Move, Kane. Linc needs something for his headache and Scarlett and Chris are leaving soon and…" She looked away from the indigo flecks in his eyes. The determination in their depths matched the intensity of her fears.

He clamped his hands on her shoulders and seated her on the bed. Dropping to his knees, he caged her in with his body.

She tried to rise, but he shielded her like an impenetrable wall. "None of this is your business, Kane." Hell, none of it should be anybody's business. She'd hoped this twisted chapter in her life was over. She'd even begun to believe it. But deep down, she'd known her stalker would return, just as she knew Kane would protect her from him.

She couldn't let him.

She shoved at his chest and met solid muscle that didn't give an inch. His strong, steady heartbeat, so unlike the rabid rhythm of hers, pulsed against her palm. "I mean it, Kane. Move."

"I'm not leaving like the last time you were upset in this bed."

Mortification—and another kind of heat she didn't want to feel—spread across her cheeks. "I've forgotten all about that night."

"That's a load of horseshit. You know how I can tell?" He dropped his hand to her thigh. "Because you're shaking, and your cheeks are redder than your skirt. Later, we'll discuss the night you claim to have forgotten. Right now, you are going to answer my question."

Her breath stuttered as he fiddled with her sequined hem. "I thought you were some sort of cowboy, a country gentleman."

He smirked. "See what I did there? I annoyed you so you'd forget about being scared for a minute and think clearly enough to understand that I can help you."

She huffed out a curse. Score one for the cowboy. His play had worked. The knot in her belly loosened a little. "I *am* scared, but I'm not helpless. I know how to use a gun, and I study martial arts."

"Good to know." He clasped her chin in his hand. "But know this about me. I'm part of an elite special forces team. I'm literally built for danger and intrigue."

That she didn't doubt. She wasn't stupid enough to turn down help from a legit super soldier, but accepting it from the genuine hero kneeling before her like a knight offering fealty was a deadly idea.

She wouldn't let another man die protecting her again.

Damn. Kane had broken horses less stubborn than Beth. She'd been testing his patience and his resolve not to get involved with a woman beyond a one-time fling for weeks. Turning down his offers to help with the party. Avoiding eye contact when they ran into each other at Chris and Scarlett's house. Sitting on the other side of the table from him when she met up with Scarlett and the team for dinner. Yeah, she'd been polite, but he didn't want courteous. He wanted the feisty woman he'd taken to the hospital who had argued with him about getting a CT scan and only agreed to the test after she'd bargained for ice cream afterward.

"Tell me who sent that message so I know whose ass to kick." He held her gaze and itched to get his hands on the motherfucker who stole the dazzle from her eyes and replaced it with stark fear.

Sighing, she slipped her chin from his grip. "I wish I could give you the name of the stalker who made my life hell, but I don't even have a face."

She rose from the bed. He inhaled her lilac scent as she brushed past him. The enticing essence didn't mask the fear etched in her features. She may have learned to live with whatever went down with her stalker two years ago, but the present appeared to have shattered her reconciliation with the past.

A few steps brought her to the window. Without looking back at him, she toyed with the lavender cord holding the white gauzy curtain back. "Two years ago, my friends at work created a profile on an online dating site behind my back. I agreed to meet a guy who seemed normal, mostly to shut my friends up, and I made them promise to come along. When I canceled because my fiancé Danny and I had gotten back together, the guy started harassing me."

Fiancé? Kane flinched as he followed her gaze to the nightstand. A framed photo of Beth and a handsome blond-haired guy sat next to a lamp with a beaded shade.

Lucky bastard.

"How were you harassed?"

"He sent me messages indicating he knew my whereabouts. Sexually explicit texts threatening in detail what he would do when he finally claimed me."

She wrapped her arms beneath her breasts and tucked her hands under her armpits as if talking about what happened chilled her to her core.

"I'm so sorry that happened to you." He knew the words didn't make it any better. He'd been hearing similar condolences since he'd lost his leg, but he'd signed on for a lethal job. She'd merely signed up for a dating site, for fuck's sake. "How long did the harassment keep up?"

"For six months. He stopped after he attacked me and Danny while we were walking back from a late Christmas movie. We..." She swallowed. "We'd taken a shortcut down an alley. We'd always felt safe on that route even though it wasn't the best area in town, but..." Her arm trembled as she slid her hand to her wrist.

His steel leg vibrated beneath him. Scarlett called the reaction to excitement or stress a glitch in his neurotransmitter. The team called it his "tell" when they played poker. The fucker who hurt Beth would soon call it his worst nightmare.

"He grabbed me and threw me against a brick wall. I tried to catch myself with my hand. The impact snapped my wrist." She ran her finger over a long scar. "I needed surgery to repair the breaks. I got a concussion from when my head hit the ground." She pressed her fingers into her temples and dropped her gaze. "After that night, I swore I'd never go back to a hospital."

And he'd been the one who'd convinced her to go the ER and relive the fucked-up experience again.

"Shit, Beth. I'm so sorry." He crossed the room and landed inches from her. Gently, he sketched the pale scar with his fingertip. He'd spent so much time wondering about the emotional wounds she hid beneath her shine that he'd missed the physical one she concealed under sweaters. Hiding his tangible scar was easy to hide under clothes too. He muzzled the urge to tell her about the internal ones that kept him from wrapping her in the safety of his lethal body and protecting her forever. "Did the cops catch the guy?"

She shook her head as she sniffed. Kane wasn't sure if her actions were an answer to his question or a refusal to cry. The first scenario had his fists clenching. The second broke his heart.

"Scarlett tried to find him…" Beth looked toward the window. "But if he could elude her…"

He followed her gaze to the darkness beyond the curtains. "That means we're not dealing with some amateur, horny dude." If the guy had better skills than Scarlett, he was either one of the best in the world or working with the best, and that made him dangerous as fuck.

Running his hand through his hair, he fit the pieces of what he'd learned together. One by one, the events clicked into place and made sense of their not-quite-date.

Her hesitancy to go to the hospital.

The nightmare she'd had in his car on the drive back to her house.

The way she'd clung to him when he'd carried her upstairs. Like he'd helped her find a sweet spot in her dreams, and if she let him go, she'd fall back into her nocturnal hell.

The way she'd cried, "Danny," and screamed for help in her sleep after he'd tucked her into bed, and the terror in her eyes when she'd awoke.

He'd thought Danny was a guy who hurt her somehow, not the man she'd loved. Envy panged in his chest. He shut it down. "What happened to your fiancé?"

Scarlett appeared in the doorway. "What about her fiancé?"

Beth stiffened. Kane ignored Scarlett's concerned tone as he dipped his head to Beth's ear and whispered, "I know this is hard, but it's time to tell her and the team. We need their input."

Beth wrapped her hand around his wrist. "No. I don't want to…I can't do this now."

The tremor in her hushed voice strengthened his intentions to find the bastard who made her shake in her sexy-as-fuck heels. "It will be okay, I promise."

"It hasn't been okay for a very long time, Kane. You can't make it better."

He could. If only for tonight, he could kick out the guests, take her to bed, and prove he could make her feel more than better. But he wouldn't. She was Scarlett's best friend. And he'd promised her she'd be okay, which meant offering protection from anything that could hurt her, including the potentially lethal events in his future that could leave her with more scars.

SIX

Beth sat ramrod straight in the wooden chair at her kitchen table. Kane flanked her, his steel leg pressing into hers like an immovable security blanket. With faces as hard as stone, yet with a river of anger and empathy coursing beneath their tough exteriors, the VIPER team listened to her account of what happened since she'd gone to the bakery. Nobody needed to know her whole twisted saga. Tonight's events had rattled her enough.

The arrival of Ryan Bradley, VIPER's chief information security officer, and Admiral Edgar, VIPER's director, should have made her feel even safer. Ryan was former military. At thirty-five years old, he held as many degrees as Scarlett. He radiated the least amount of alpha hormones, but the outline of muscle under his tailored white dress shirt suggested the time he spent in a uniform wasn't solely in front of a computer.

He shot her a smile from across the table. Sympathy brimmed in his kind gaze. She managed a weak grin. When she'd met him and his uncle, the governor of Maryland, a few weeks ago at the Army vs. Navy football game, she'd sensed strong convictions and good hearts inside both men. She'd been glad a man like Governor Bradley held a seat in Congress. Now she was thankful his nephew—with thick, wavy blond hair and an authoritative, sexy professor kind of look that merely hinted at his brilliance—sat in her kitchen.

Beth figured Admiral Edgar must also have formidable skills if he'd been chosen to lead Project VIPER. The tall, lanky sixty-something-year-old stood at attention by the sink, his big fists clenched at his side. The impeccable neatness of his starched red western-style shirt, dark, pressed jeans, and shiny black cowboy boots paraded his military background. His penetrating gaze and the hardness in his square jaw embodied his commitment to truth and justice. Add spurs and a six-shooter, wrinkled clothes and a cloud of dust, and he could be a sheriff from the Wild West.

He touched his palms together in prayer. "I am deeply sorry for your trouble tonight. Please tell us more about your initial contact with the stalker."

Beth sat up straighter. Even though her kitchen nearly busted at the seams with testosterone, she still felt vulnerable. "I agreed to meet the man I met on the dating site at a local bar for a drink. His profile said his name was Bobby Collins."

Edgar's bushy eyebrows furrowed. "This contact was made on the site's page, not through your personal email or via text or phone, correct?"

"Yes." If anyone else in the room had asked her that question, she'd shoot them a snarky comeback about not being too stupid to live. Edgar, however, wasn't in her kitchen for the beer and cake. He'd declined the party invite because of a prior commitment. Someone alerted him about tonight's events, and he thought it was serious enough to drop whatever he was doing and come.

"What happened next?"

"After Danny and I reconciled, I sent Bobby a message

via the site and took my profile down. The next day I got a pleading text message to meet with him. I blocked his number, but similar texts, and then messages to my personal email kept coming. I got a new phone number and shut down all my email and social media accounts, but he kept finding me."

"According to police reports, false accounts with the dating site had been established during that time frame." Ryan stroked his trimmed goatee. "The hackers were never identified."

Beth eyed his laptop. "Did you just hack into the police department?"

Scarlett raised an eyebrow from across the table. "You act like that sort of thing has never happened in your kitchen before."

"Point taken." She'd sat at this table many nights watching Scarlett try and locate the stalker. If she couldn't find him, Ryan wouldn't either.

She turned her attention back to Edgar and reiterated what she'd told Kane about being ambushed in the dark alley.

"I tried to fight." God, she'd tried. Her vision dimmed as the crack of her skull against the ground reverberated in her head. She blinked a few times to refocus. "I blacked out, but I remember hearing voices. I heard the stalker say something in Spanish but couldn't make it out as Danny screamed my name."

Those voices she heard nearly every night in her dreams keened through her mind. She clenched her fists in her lap to stop herself from plugging her ears.

Kane covered her hands with his and squeezed. "Take your time."

His strong grip belied the patience in his tone. She welcomed both. Pulling in a breath that did nothing to untwist her insides or calm her frantic heartbeat, she forced herself to speak. "Then I heard a gunshot. Then nothing. The next thing I remember is waking up in the hospital and learning that Danny was…"

She dropped her head and closed her eyes. Tears she didn't want to spill in front of everyone bullied their way past her lids. Kane's grip tightened as he muttered a curse. She heard a chair scrape across the floor. A moment later, Scarlett stood next to her.

Beth's shoulders shook as a sob gurgled up her throat. She forced it down. Crying didn't change a goddamn thing. Every day since the attack, she'd pushed herself to leave the house, to go to work, to live a normal life and not hide in fear or wallow in sorrow. Yet right now, the final word of not just the sentence she couldn't finish but Danny's life was stuck on the edge of her tongue.

Scarlett stroked Beth's hair. "Danny didn't make it."

Beth nodded, half in thanks for the intervention, half in silent affirmation, as another tear slipped past her defenses. Kane unlaced her clenched hands and slipped his fingers into hers. His hold was as fierce as his unspoken support.

"*Dios mio,*" Nic said.

"My God," Chris echoed.

She opened her eyes. Both men stared at her from across the table, their lips pursed in horrified, livid lines and their lethal bodies tensed to fight. Ryan sat between the two, his hands speared into his wavy blond hair. Something akin to the strength emanating from the VIPER boys flashed in his gaze. A half second later, he banged his fingers on the keyboard. "We'll find him."

Linc slid behind Ryan and clamped a hand on his shoulder. "Work fast so I can filet the fucker with my fishing knife."

"Not if I get to him first with my shotgun," Edgar said.

Kane's leg vibrated against hers like a ticking time bomb. "Get in line."

The hard-core support surrounded Beth like a fortress. Her tears retreated as she pressed her palms onto the table to ground herself. For the past two years, she'd lived on edge. Yes, the police had investigated, and Scarlett had done her deep-dive cyber thing, but outside of her federally protected lab, she'd been solely responsible for her safety. Now, the nation's most dangerous assets stood in her kitchen, vowing not just to protect but to avenge.

Little did they know she was the most lethal person in the room.

She slipped her hand from Kane's. Getting too close to the sexy-as-sin super soldier put him in danger.

Ryan glanced up from his laptop. "The surveillance feed from the shopping center is too grainy to get an ID. The bakery's video feeds were a dead end, so I called the shop and spoke to the teenager who helped you. Turns out, she took a photo of the cake stealer with her phone because she thought he was 'smoking hot.' The image is only a profile and it's blurry, but I ran it and got a potential match."

Beth shot from her chair so fast she swayed. "You know who he is?"

"Potentially." Edgar cleared his throat. "While you were enjoying the festivities, Ryan and I were busy looking into your background."

Eggnog curdled in Beth's belly.

Oh shit. He knows.

She swayed again. Kane grabbed her elbow as she readied herself for what would surely come out of Edgar's mouth.

"Dr. Parker, I need you to tell us about the drug you are working on at the National Agency for Health."

The hurricane in her belly settled into a thunderstorm. He didn't know about her past, thank fuck. As she sank into her chair, she sent up gratitude for keeping her ghosts where they belonged—dead and buried. "I can't talk about my work. It's classified."

Ryan handed her a file with the VIPER logo stamped on the cover. Trepidation skittered up her spine as she opened it.

Edgar slid next to her. "Your director confirmed all this information. You've been cleared to tell us everything about this project. This is groundbreaking work, Dr. Parker."

Pride fought for space in her emotional whirlwind. "Thank you, but what does my work have to do with what happened tonight? And how did you get these details so quickly?"

"Because"— he took the file from her and tucked it under his arm like he was packing away a weapon—"I'm Admiral Edgar."

"Okay." Who was she to question a man who could circumvent bureaucratic red tape? "For years, since I started at the agency as an undergrad, I've been working with a team developing a promising cancer drug. We discovered it has applications in other areas, not as a treatment, but as a..."

She glanced at Scarlett. Despite the night's events, a grin spread across Beth's face. Permission to share this news with her bestie and the VIPER team, to tout the groundbreaking work she'd been sworn to keep classified, trumped the squall in her belly. "We found the drug could cure opioid addiction."

"Holy fucking shit." Kane spun her chair to face him. "Are you working on Triple X?"

She blinked, not at the awe in his gaze, which did a weird thing to her heart, but his knowledge. "You know about it?"

"I can't pronounce the wonder drug with the three *X*'s in it, but we know intel agencies have been tracking the Mexican cartels' interest in Triple X for months."

"Drug cartels?" A bead of sweat dripped from her hairline down the back of her neck. "No. The cartels can't find out about Triple X. If they get the formula…" Goose bumps pebbled on her skin and burned like toxic rain as she scanned the grim faces in the room. No, not just grim, but… concerned. "Wait, do the cartels know about my involvement with the drug?"

"It appears so." Ryan spun his laptop to face her. "The man who stole your cake, as far as we can tell from the photo, is Enrique Chavez, son of the Diablo leader, Maria Chavez."

Beth jerked as if she'd been stabbed with a cake fork. She knew about the notorious cartel and its ruthless leader.

Kane cursed under his breath. The rest of the VIPER boys chimed in with equal vigor.

"He knows my name." The man on the screen the bakery owner described as tall, dark, and sexy instead of big, evil, and scary knew everything about her. She whipped her head to the front door. "He knows where I live?" She wasn't safe here. She hadn't even been safe in her… "Oh, God. The network in my lab. It's been down a lot lately." She fixed her gaze on Edgar. "It wasn't maintenance like we'd been told. The Diablos were trying to hack us. Did they breach our firewalls and get the formula?"

Her shoulders relaxed as he shook his head no.

"Thank God."

"But they've amassed enough data to know the drug works. They're scrambling to counter before it makes an impact on their operations."

"They can't get it." She clasped her shaking hands under her chin as she looked at each super soldier in the room. "Triple X is on the FDA approval fast track. In a few days, it will be available to thousands of people in drug trials across the country. So many lives could be saved."

Edgar nodded. "And that's too many addicts to lose for

the cartel's bottom line. Intel we recently uncovered indicates that the major players in the Mexican drug trade are in a race to get the Triple X formula. Maria Chavez has set a midnight Christmas Eve deadline for her son and his team of enforcers to deliver it. Enrique is her only living child. She lost her twins when they were twelve years old. The loss reportedly hit the thirteen-year-old Enrique hard, and he became quite the mama's boy. If his mother wants the formula, and the bragging rights that she got it first, he'll go to any lengths to get it."

Any lengths? She pressed her fingers against her lips to stifle a gasp. "Oh God, what if Chavez stole my cake to lure me outside? If I'd run out when I spotted my cake on the hood or hadn't let the owner carry the new cake to the car, I might have been taken." The terrifying what-if scenarios mushroomed up her throat like a nuclear blast. "And if Kane and Nic hadn't secured my house, an enforcer from the world's most feared drug cartel might have been waiting for me."

Scarlett appeared at her side. "Breathe, Beth."

"No." Her voice hitched as more goose bumps exploded on her skin. "I can't be a target for some sicko again."

Scarlett linked her arm with Beth's. "Let's pivot from Enrique the Enforcer for a minute. I want to hear everything about this wonder drug you've been working on that will change millions of lives."

Beth nodded and sniffed. Bless her bestie for the much-needed diversion. "Well, the chemical compound of…" Her heart rate slowed as she talked about Triple X. One glance at Kane had it racing again. Scarlett was the only one in the room who likely grasped much of what she was saying because of her scientific background, but Kane? The way he gazed at her, with those full lips partially open and a reverent look in his eyes, skyrocketed her pride and melted her heart.

God, that second bit had to cease.

He slid a bottle of water into her hands. "If you could explain all that to us, then you could explain it to the cartels. And much more if under duress."

"Duress?" Her voice squeaked as his features shifted from awed admirer to no-nonsense warrior.

Edgar cleared his throat. "Enrique Chavez is known for extracting information in unsanctioned ways. His father, who was killed along with the twins in a skirmish with a rival cartel two decades ago, was a brutal bastard. Enrique's mother is reportedly worse and raised him to show no mercy. If you're on their radar for whatever reason, you're in grave danger."

An image of Jenna's mutilated body slammed into Kane's mind, but it wasn't her lifeless eyes staring back. He spun Beth to face him. "Did you hear Edgar? Tell me you heard him."

The stunned fear in her gaze assured him she understood.

He didn't stop her when she turned away, but he kept his hold on her hip. Her body shook beneath his hand, but she was tough. She had to be tough if she'd held down a demanding job and completed her PhD while looking over her shoulder for the past two years. Pretending everything in her sparkly life was alright while she lived with the grief of losing her fiancé and the fear of a stalker—no, a murderer—reappearing took a lot of strength.

Strength his mother never had.

His own grief, decades old but still raw, submerged the hollow place in his chest. Closing his eyes, he tried to drown the impending memory, but it surfaced anyway.

"What do you mean you aren't coming to my track meet? It's the state championship."

His mom stared at him from her bed, which hadn't been made in weeks, through bloodshot eyes. "I'm sorry, honey. I'll try and make the next one."

He yanked on the hem of his team jacket and blinked back frustrated tears. "I'm a senior, Mom. This is your last chance to see me win gold and beat the school record."

"I…" She looked away. "I just can't do it without…" A tear slipped down her cheek as she pulled the neckline of his father's Marine Corps sweatshirt up to her chin. "Gran and your sister will be there to cheer you on. Good luck, honey. I'm sorry."

Kane opened his eyes and shook off the memory plagued with things he should have said, should have questioned, but didn't. His gaze landed on Beth. Damn, he admired her for finding the mettle to put her emotions on hold and be there for the people she loved. Still, tonight's events were a lot to take in.

Hell, it was a lot for him too. After the Mexico debrief, he'd caught a quick nap. Instead of his typical nightmares that alternated between memories like the one he'd just shut down and painful replays of the explosion that took his leg, he dreamed of Jenna. Her bloody face. Her last breath. Her final words.

No regrets.

Chris pulled Scarlett into him like his memories from Mexico created a need to be close to the woman he couldn't live without. Flexing his super arm, he looked at Edgar. "Why would Chavez go through the trouble of stealing Beth's cake when he could have simply abducted her?"

Beth leaned into Kane's side. "And why target me? There are plenty of other research scientists with more knowledge. I'm the baby on the team since I was in accelerated programs that helped me complete my PhD earlier than others. And why not go all the way to the top? Director Sable knows everything. I think she's been with the agency since the invention of penicillin."

Kane nudged her to face him. "Your work on Triple X, the intel we have about the Diablo's deadline, and a known enforcer messing with you adds up to no good. Not to mention the timing of your stalker's return. He could be working with the Diablos. They have accomplished hackers on their payroll. And you can be sure Chavez has a motive for his actions. You need protection while we uncover more intel."

Edgar nodded. "One of you needs to be her security detail."

Beth held up her hand. "Does anyone care what I have to say on the matter?"

Scarlett touched Beth's arm. "Of course. Chris and I will cancel our trip so you can stay with us."

"No way." She waggled her finger between the bride and groom-to-be. "You two can't cancel your engagement-moon because I'm in trouble again."

"They won't." Kane knew how important it was for Beth to give her bestie a perfect engagement experience. "Admiral, I'll stick with Beth until we get more information."

"No." Beth backed up a step. "That won't work. I'm going to a Christmas party tomorrow in my hometown. I won't be back until the twenty-fourth."

"Then I'll go with you." He turned on his grin that charmed women from West Virginia to Washington, DC. "I love a good party."

"You can't come to North Benson with me."

He shrugged. "Then we'll stay home."

"No way. I missed the party last year and won't miss it again."

"A word in private, please." He nudged her to the back

door. To his surprise, she obeyed and let him lead her outside. His earlier search of the property revealed high fences and a large awning. Both created a space safe from anyone watching. The barriers, however, didn't block the view of her bare legs as she jutted her hip and glowered at him.

"I don't want you as my bodyguard. Nic or Linc can do it."

He backed her into the wall. "You barely know them." And no way was he giving his brothers the opportunity to get to know her better. Hell, *he* shouldn't want to get to know her better, not when he couldn't offer anything beyond protection. If a relationship was in his immediate future, he'd already be a dozen dates in with the brilliant, beautiful scientist, who he found even more attractive since learning she'd been working to save millions of lives. But their timing sucked and his scars ran too deep to alter his life plan. Besides, he'd promised Chris he wouldn't act on his filthy fantasies.

She jutted her chin up. "I barely know *you.*"

"You know how I taste."

Her soft hiss escaped through her gritted teeth. "You're a bastard for bringing that up."

Maybe it did make him a bastard for discussing their ill-fated kiss in her bedroom during their not-quite-date. But watching the gold flecks in her eyes ignite into flames set his adrenaline racing faster than a dangerous mission.

Stepping back but still close enough to shield her from the cold wind, he eyed her from head to toe. Despite his timeline to serve in the military first and settle down later, thoughts about making Beth *his* raided his mind. All night, he'd been fighting the urge to unwrap the pretty package before him, starting with her soft sweater and slowly working his way down to her red shimmery heels. Feeling them dig into his ass while he filled her topped his list of things he shouldn't want for Christmas, along with visions of enjoying future holidays together.

He took her hand and turned her wrist. With his fingertips, he brushed her scar. "You're Scarlett's bestie, which makes you part of the VIPER family. Accept my protection, sugarplum."

She waved her finger at him in a circle. "You're doing it again. I can see it in your eyes and it's not going to work."

He stepped closer until the tips of his worn cowboy boots hit the toes of her dainty heels. "Doing what?"

"Switching from charming and sexy but sometimes annoying cowboy to intense, sometimes scary, but always bossy warrior."

He winked. "I knew you liked me."

She pressed her fingertips into her temples. "Have you heard anything I'm saying? I agree protection is warranted, but it can't be from you."

No, it shouldn't be from him. She was a danger to the life he'd built around not falling in love until it was time, but even that cold truth wouldn't stop him from convincing her that he was the super soldier for the job.

Beth speared her hands into her hair and tugged. Her scalp stung from the pressure. "I don't want your protection."

"Why?" He seized her chin in his big hand. The hardness in his gaze sharpened to icicles.

A chill seeped from the brick and permeated her thin sweater. "You know why."

"I have an idea, but I want to hear it from you."

The words wouldn't form on her tongue. Plenty of tingles did, even though she didn't want to talk about the humiliating, post-nightmare kiss that had left her aching for more. Biting her lip, she willed her caution tape not to unravel around the tempting super soldier.

Soldier.

She eyed the man whose job was to run into danger on a regular basis. "I'm a target. There's not just one, but two potential threats in my life. Leave it to me to be an over-achiever with not just a stalker but a cartel member after me. Whoever protects me is a potential target too."

Well, there were three potential threats if she included herself. How could she not? History didn't lie. Neither did numbers.

"Don't worry about me." He took her hand and placed it on the front of his thigh. "Feel that?"

"Yeah." The confession skated out on a harsh breath.

"Your tax dollars literally made me for this shit, Beth. Take advantage of it."

The back door slammed open. "Get your asses in here."

Kane muttered a curse as Edgar barked at them from the doorway. "We aren't done with this discussion, sugarplum."

The cold air hit her like a ball of ice as they separated.

Edgar scowled at them as they entered, a cup of coffee in his hand. "Are you two done arguing?"

"Yes, Admiral." Kane wrapped his arm around Beth's shoulders. "She's decided to accept my help."

She opened her mouth to say she'd never said such a thing, but Scarlett blew out a long sigh. "Good. I'll worry so much less while we're gone. But I'll stay if you want me to."

"No, I want you to go." Scarlett had missed so much growing up under her stepfather's iron rule. The boarding schools he'd sent her to didn't have football games and school dances. She'd never even gone to a prom. What kind of friend would she be if she asked Scarlett to miss her first vacation with her fiancé? "Enjoy your trip and don't worry."

Kane squeezed her shoulder. "Looks like we're a couple for the next few days."

She scurried from under his arm. "Couple?" Oh, hell no. She was already North Benson's biggest source of gossip. She didn't need to add fuel to the yule log. "I never agreed to that."

He tapped his chest and winked. "I have it on good authority that I'm an excellent date."

"The party is a fundraiser. It's black tie. There's no time to get you a tuxedo."

"I've got a dress uniform. That's better."

Dear Lord. Kane in a dress uniform might be the death of her. Or him, if she couldn't keep her hands—and her heart—to herself.

Edgar tipped his coffee cup toward Beth. "Dating isn't a bad idea. We can be sure the Diablos did their research and know your connection to VIPER. They don't know the team's full proficiencies, but they know what the public does. If Kane acts solely like your security detail, they might think we've uncovered Chavez's identity and task someone else we know nothing about to abduct you."

"But if they've been watching me, they would know Kane's not my boyfriend."

Scarlett picked up discarded plates and cups. "But it makes sense he could be. You've been spending time with him, me, and the team for several weeks now. There's a history."

"Your bestie is right." Kane nudged Beth under the mistletoe above the door and brushed her ear with his lips. "Ready to deck the halls with me, sugarplum?"

<h1 style="text-align:center">EIGHT</h1>

eth stomped out of the kitchen. Kane watched her perfect sequined ass until she turned out of view.

Scarlett sighed. "Give her some space until she wraps her head around all this, okay?"

Kane nodded. She could have all the space she needed in this house, but once they left for her hometown, he'd be glued to her side whether she liked it or not. As VIPER's therapist liked to point out, his past didn't just leave him with a responsibility to protect those he might leave behind but also those he cared about.

Edgar pulled his keys from his pocket. "My gut tells me this is just the beginning of her troubles. Keep her safe until we figure out this cake stealer, stalker, cartel mess."

"Yes, sir."

"Thank you, Admiral." Scarlett clasped both of her hands around his. "I appreciate you taking the threat seriously."

"Anything for my favorite genius. For now, we're working under the assumption the stalker and Chavez are operating independently."

Nic grabbed a handful of chips. "So even though we

have no idea why Chavez didn't steal Beth instead of the disco ball cake, we can assume the stalker watched it go down. Either that or Chavez's been her stalker since the beginning."

Chris shook his head. "But that doesn't add up. The cartels aren't into psychological warfare. They strike fast and draw blood."

Kane agreed. It didn't add up at all.

Ryan looked up from where he typed at the table. "You're all set for pre-activation."

Kane thought the passphrase to bring his weaponry online. Prior to a recent fiasco that almost caused VIPER to be disbanded, his weaponry could only be made live by head-quarters. New protocols gave him the ability to bring his weaponry online quicker. If he was in a pre-activated state, all he needed to do was simply repeat his unique passphrase in his head and V-Strikes were at his command.

Seconds later, the chip at the base of his neck pricked and he twitched.

"Still sting?" Scarlett asked.

He gave her a side-eye. Fuck yeah, it still hurt to have a powerful current triggered in his body. Not as much when he was fully activated in phase two, and the current pulsed from his neck, down his torso, and into his leg, but enough to still cause a reaction.

Edgar pointed his key at him. "You only activate phase two if it's life or death."

"Understood, sir." He prayed Beth's situation wouldn't come to that.

Scarlett tugged him down the short hall to the pantry as Edgar and Ryan packed to-go containers with leftovers. "You'll take good care of my friend without taking her to bed, got it? Succumbing to what I see in your eyes when you look at her could be a matter of life or death."

"Jeez, when did you become so intense?" And when had he let his feelings for Beth become so transparent?

From the moment I met her.

When he'd run into Scarlett's house after her townhome was breached, her gorgeous friend with the bag of ice on her head, fear in her gaze, and her chin up in the air had stopped him in his tracks. Despite the pain from Beth's head injury and the scare from the break-in, the anti–damsel in distress with the defiant nature clearly was just as attracted to him as he was to her.

Scarlett giggled. "How could I not become more intense when I'm surrounded by super soldiers?"

"Glad to see we've been a good influence, but your delivery would have been better if you'd thrown in a few swear words."

"Fine. I'm *fucking* serious."

"Ah, there's the potty-mouthed genius I've come to love." He tapped her nose. "I already had this conversation with Chris. The only reason I'll touch your friend is to push her out of danger."

Scarlett stood on her toes and kissed him on the cheek. "Don't die, okay?"

"I'm a super soldier. You and your techy magic made me nearly invincible, remember?"

"Yeah, but there are some things science and technology can't protect you from."

Beth perched on the edge of her bed. "Kane cannot come home with me."

Scarlett stood in front of her. "Why? Are you planning on falling in love with him?"

"You know I can't do that, but if I could, it wouldn't be

with someone like Kane. He's pigheaded and bossy and thinks I'm helpless."

But you are.

For the last two years, she'd armed herself with defensive techniques in case her stalker returned. She'd installed a top-of-the-line security system that was even more secure since she'd won a free upgrade a few weeks ago. All her precautions might be enough for a lone stalker, but an enforcer from a Mexican drug cartel?

"Overbearing and protective are VIPER prerequisites. Chris is the same way. I can't wait to watch Nic and Linc fall for someone and get all caveman on them."

"Kane isn't my someone."

Scarlett sat next to Beth on the bed. "He is for the time being."

"But he can't be." Beth dropped her voice to a whisper as if Kane could hear from downstairs. "He's bound to hear people talk about my curse."

Scarlett grabbed Beth's hands between her palms. "And he'll think it's nonsense, just like you should."

"I do think it's nonsense."

"No, you don't."

A familiar sense of shame crept through Beth. She was a scientist, for Christ's sake. She, of all people, should know better that curses didn't exist. It was ridiculous to believe God or the powers that be had said, "Hey, this Beth Parker chick is a bad person, so let's punish her." But that's what North Benson's gossip brigade whispered behind her back. Even though Beth had no idea what grievous sin she'd committed, the doubt her hometown's resident gossips planted had taken root so deep into her psyche a part of her believed it.

Beth sighed and stood. "You're my best friend. You're supposed to be on my side."

"I am on your side, but I agree with the plan."

"What, you work for the Department of Defense, and now you're an expert on strategic planning?"

Hurt clouded Scarlett's green eyes. "That's not fair. I want you safe, and I trust Kane. Besides, all you talked about when I started working with VIPER was meeting the 'hot vets.'"

Obsessed with meeting them had been more like it. She may not be on the hunt for love, but that didn't mean she couldn't discover if the nation's finest on the battlefield were good in bed. And then Kane sauntered into Scarlett's house in his cowboy hat and that dimpled smile. A dozen ways he could heal her had come to mind, and none of them included going to the hospital.

Yet, she'd gone with the hot, strong vet. Even though she'd fought going, he didn't press for a reason why. Instead, he'd used his cocky charm to get her seen quickly. Made her laugh while she fought memories from the last time she'd been in the ER.

And he'd taken her for ice cream.

She sighed as she turned to her dresser and inhaled the lingering fragrance of her lilac-scented perfume. Scarlett always said the VIPER boys were more than hot vets. By the time she'd left the ER, Beth understood Kane Darren really was more than muscle, dimples, endless blue eyes, and the tightest ass she'd ever seen. He was the kind of guy a girl could fall in love with.

She liked him too much to sentence him to that fate.

Scarlett sidled up to her side. "What's this?" She picked up a silver chain with a shiny medallion about the size of a nickel hanging from it. A heart gleamed from the center.

Beth smiled. "It's a gift from the North Benson hospital for my fundraising services over the years. They presented it to me at the last meeting when we finalized details for the Christmas party. I attended virtually, but Evangeline was there, so she sent it to me."

Scarlett placed the medallion back on the dresser and brushed her palms together as if they were dirty. "I hadn't realized she was back from Dubai."

Beth picked up the necklace and clasped it around her neck. "She got back a couple of months ago. Her three-year contract was shortened to two for some reason."

"Are you sure the board didn't make her send you the gift? Doing something nice doesn't sound like her."

Beth shrugged. "Maybe she's trying to make amends."

"Maybe. Either way, she's going to be green with envy when she sees you with Kane. You'll need to guard him like you're *his* protection detail." Scarlett opened the jewelry box on the dresser and riffled through the earrings. "I know I don't know Evangeline that well. Maybe I'm jealous because she became your best bud after I was shipped off to boarding school. Or maybe I don't like her because she worships my stepfather, which is a giant red flag, but she always seems like she has to one-up you. And I haven't forgotten about the cruel things she said after Danny's funeral."

Beth hadn't forgotten either. She hadn't seen Evangeline since she'd moved to Dubai days after Danny's burial. They'd only spoken in the last couple of months because Evangeline joined the fundraising committee at the hospital.

"Wear these to the party." Scarlett handed Beth a pair of silver hoops encrusted with delicate crystals. "And look on the bright side. At least you don't have to introduce Kane to your mom and dad."

"There's that." Her parents were embarking on an African safari first thing in the morning. She'd already been warned communications would be spotty, thank God. If her mom got wind she'd brought a guy home for Christmas, she'd be on the first flight back with the wedding halfway planned. "I do have to contend with the gossip brigade though. They're almost as scary as the Diablo cartel."

"You handle the dumb gossips. Let me and the VIPER team handle the stalker and drug lords." Scarlett swiveled her head around the room as if to make sure nobody was listening.

"Don't worry. Kane and Nic swept the entire place for surveillance equipment." Beth's gaze darted toward her bathroom. How thoroughly had they checked? Earlier, she'd put her vibrator into her toiletry bag on the sink. God, she hoped she'd zipped it up.

Scarlett closed the jewelry box. "Of course they secured your place. They're professionals. And the way they refer to themselves as *super* isn't an exaggeration."

"Can you elaborate on these superpowers?"

"No, I can't. Just know you have four loyal, dedicated men on your side and the best technology in the world at their disposal. You'll be safe while they work to end this."

But would Kane be safe? While his leg felt strong enough to repel a bullet, and he looked like he could take on a gang in a dark alley with one hand tied behind his back, he was still vulnerable to forces out of his control.

The forces she shouldn't believe in but stupidly did.

NINE

Beth dropped the secure phone Kane gave her this morning into her tote bag as he settled next to her in his pickup truck.

He took off his cowboy hat and tossed it in the back seat. His black leather jacket shifted. The shoulder holster he'd slipped on over his white Henley shirt before they left the house came into view. A bit of tension released from her neck, knowing the gun in her bag had a friend. She prayed they didn't have cause to play together.

Reaching for the seat belt, she pulled it across her body. It clicked into place along with her gaze on his jean-clad thigh.

The side of Kane's lips tugged up in a smirk. "In case you're wondering, yes, it is."

She snapped her head up. "Huh?"

"My leg. It's just as spectacular as you're imagining it."

Heat crept into her cheeks as her gaze fixed on his dimple. "I wasn't imagining anything of the sort." More like imagining what it felt like under her touch. Against her own thighs as he… "I've seen Chris's and Nic's arms. I know what your steel, or super, or whatever you want to call it, looks like."

And that knowledge gave her plenty of material to work with when she fantasized about what other wonders awaited under his pants.

After she'd said goodbye to Scarlett and Chris last night, she hadn't argued when Nic and Linc stayed so Kane could go home and pack. As Linc sat on her sofa and watched a football game and Nic helped her clean, she wondered what horrific events had brought the two of them to VIPER. When she'd finally laid her head on her pillow, she wondered the same about Kane. The thought still occupied her mind when she found him in her kitchen this morning with coffee and bagels from her favorite deli.

He took her hand and placed it on his knee. "You have no idea how hard my steel is. Or how super I can be."

Warmth radiated through his jeans. "I expected it to be cold." Last night it hadn't felt cold when it vibrated against her under the table, but she figured that was her own body heat.

"Scarlett worked some sort of magic to make it feel like flesh and blood. It's all networked with my brain."

"Can you feel me? I mean my hand?" She pressed the pads of her fingers into his steel as he backed out of the parking spot. The questions—and the contact—felt more personal, more intimate than any encounter she'd ever had with a guy.

"Yes." He placed his hand over hers. "I can feel the pressure. It's hard to explain, but I can feel you. Your heat."

She swallowed a squeak as his leg vibrated beneath her palm. "Can you feel pain?"

He shrugged as he pulled out of her neighborhood and onto the main road. "It's hard to tell. I feel phantom pain all the time. My brain still thinks I have a biological leg attached to my hip, so actual pain and phantom pain are indistinguishable. It mostly aches where my leg is cut off, and the steel is attached. It hurts today. The warmth is helping."

Knowing she could make him feel better shot heat from the corner of her smile into her cheeks. "So, I'm a human heating pad."

"Yup. And I'm a human weapon." He glanced at her and winked. "Looks like we both have superpowers."

If only her superpower would incinerate the ridiculous notion that she was cursed.

"You okay?" Kane squeezed her knee.

"Yeah." She pulled her hand away from his steel. The list of things she needed to discuss with him stretched for miles, but she couldn't help but ask what had been on her mind since the day they'd met. "How did it happen?"

She studied his profile, his jaw moving from side to side as he maneuvered the truck through Saturday morning traffic. The silence, save for honking horns, lingered for what felt like an hour. "Forget it; you don't have to tell me. It was rude of me to ask." She didn't like to talk about her trauma. What made her think he wanted to share his?

He stopped at a light and looked at her. "No. It's okay. You told me what happened to you. It's only fair I share my story."

Guilt settled in her chest. She hadn't told him everything, only what he needed to know.

He hit the gas as the light turned red. "I was in the Middle East on a routine maneuver when we came upon a mess of IEDs. You'd think the *improvised* in improvised explosive device would mean it was built half-assed, but every device worked perfectly. Too many of my team, men and women with families back home, lost more than a leg."

An image of Kane as he lay in a fiery field with burning

debris raining down on his broken body had her hand slip-ping back to his thigh. "I'm so sorry."

He glanced at her. "I survived. I'm grateful for that, and grateful VIPER offered me a second chance at my military career. I don't take that for granted."

"I'm glad you survived." Clearing the emotion from her throat, she drew her hand away from the impossibly hard steel under his jeans and focused on her own situation. "We need to set some parameters for our pretend rela-tionship."

He smiled. "Lay it on me, darlin.'"

And like that, sunshine burst through the clouds in his eyes. Pleasure at being able to bring him out of the dark rippled through her.

"Here's how I see it, cowboy. There's no need to be all sugarplum and couple-like unless we're in a public place where someone might be watching. Traveling and staying together sends the message I'm living my life oblivious to the threats hanging over me. That's what we want, right? To make them think we're not on to them?"

Kane grinned. "First, I'm never going to stop calling you sugarplum. Second, I agree we don't need to be couple-like when we're alone. But we do need to let everyone we meet think we're together because one, maybe two, murderers are watching you."

She shot her gaze to the rearview mirror.

He looked too. "We're not being followed, but that doesn't mean someone isn't monitoring us. Cameras and satellites can track our location just fine." He checked the mirror again. "Scarlett mentioned your parents are in Africa on a safari."

"Yes. Their plane took off about an hour ago." And they didn't expect to hear from her until Christmas Day, when this cartel crap would hopefully be over.

"Then we only need to worry about your friends. Why aren't you spending Christmas with your parents?"

"My dad was a firefighter. He spent many holidays working, so we've always celebrated on our own schedule. We did our Christmas festivities a couple of weeks ago. When this opportunity came up, I encouraged them to take it. I can only stay away from the office for a few days anyway and want to be back in DC for Christmas Eve mass."

"Don't they have churches in North Benson?"

"Not a fabulous old stone church with a view of the Washington Monument from the steps." A smile lifted her tense lips. "I don't typically go to mass, except on holidays, but I teach a science class there for the youth group kids a couple of times a month. What about you? Do you mind spending the holidays alone?"

"Actually, this will be my first Christmas not spending it with Gran. She's going to visit my twin sister Livvie and her boyfriend in Atlanta."

"Twins? That must have been fun growing up."

"Yeah, she was a lot of fun to tease. Despite being annoying, she turned out pretty okay. She's an orthopedic surgeon now." He blew by the entrance to the beltway. "We have to make a quick stop to see Gran and say Merry Christmas before she leaves for the airport."

The way he said *we* felt way too comfortable. Like she could get used to spending holidays with Kane and Gran at the house they shared. "When we get near my parents' house, we need to stop for a bottle of wine." She rattled off the name of a liquor store. "I drank the last of my favorite when I visited a couple of weeks ago."

"Got it. Remember, when we are in public, you treat me as your charming, handsome boyfriend."

She rolled her eyes. Her arrival in town with a man on her arm would be like a Christmas gift for the gossip brigade.

Except they'd have the added fun of speculating how long he'd live.

As Kane took the next exit, Scarlett's words repeated in her head.

Kane will think your curse is nonsense, just like you should.

She should think it was nonsense. Time was supposed to heal her morbid thinking, and yet here she was, too afraid to fall for the guy sitting next to her and too afraid to tell him why. Maybe she should have stayed home and went to work where it was safe and Kane-free. Between the gossips who reveled in rewriting her past into a fractured fairy tale, the stalker who wouldn't go away, and the new uninvited cartel characters in her story, North Benson felt triply unsafe.

"Wait." She touched Kane's arm. "What if my parents' house is bugged? What if Chavez or—"

"Relax. Nic had a couple of his ex-military buddies sweep the place. It's clear."

Telling her to relax in his country twang had the opposite effect. So did his explanation. "They broke into my parents' house?"

"No. One of Nic's friends owns the security company they use. He sent them a message late last night saying someone was coming today to fix a broken camera your dad had reported. He and his team did more than a simple repair."

"You could have asked me first before you did that."

"You were asleep, and it needed to be done to keep you safe."

"I may not be a super soldier, but I know how to protect myself." For two years, she'd controlled every decision to ensure her safety, from choosing the best defensive driving course to which martial arts school to attend to which brand of Mace to put on her key chain. Control kept her from taking permanent residence in her secure lab. Since Chavez stole her cake, she could feel in her gut, in her heart, that hard-won power unraveling thread by thread. She held on to the flimsy pieces and rattled off everything she'd done to take command of her life.

"Remarkable work, Dr. Parker." Kane stopped at a traffic light. "What you have done may be good enough if a lone stalker attacks you again, but Chavez and his associates will outnumber, outgun, and outmaneuver you before your brain has time to tell your muscles to move. Now, tell me about your parents in case they come up in conversation."

She pursed her lips together as her last scrap of control flew out the window. He was right. All her work would amount to a swat on the kneecap if she met Chavez and his men face to face. She stifled her frustration as she stretched out her legs. "My mom's a retired nursing professor. Now, she heads up fundraising for the local hospital. I'm on the board, which is why I want to be at the party tonight. All proceeds go to the new cancer wing."

"So, you're both smarty-pants that give back to the community?"

"Yeah, we're pretty amazing." Her voice flattened out as she toyed with the medallion hanging in the *V* of her sweater. "I spent a lot of time at the hospital when I was in high school with a, uh, friend of mine who had cancer. I wanted to give back to the people who helped him." She glanced at Kane. Respect glimmered in his gaze. She fed off that and forced a spark in her voice. "My dad retired from the North Benson Fire Department. Now he takes do-it-yourself classes at the local home store. He just renovated the kitchen himself and did a great job."

"Maybe he can give me tips on how to renovate mine and Gran's place. The kitchen is too small for us to cook together."

"That's…sweet." She chewed on her lip instead of asking

a dozen more questions about his life with Gran beyond what she knew already. After he'd lost his leg, Gran came East to take care of him and now they shared a house. She had a feeling the rest of the story would make her like him even more. "What about your parents?"

"My dad was an Air Force pilot. He was killed in action when I was seventeen."

"Oh, Kane."

He shifted his jaw as he glanced at her. The glint of sorrow she'd seen in his eyes earlier flickered.

"After my dad died, my mom struggled with taking care of herself and the house, so we all moved in with Gran and Gramps. A few months later she…"

Beth stared at his white-knuckled grip on the wheel. Holding her breath, she prayed the dip in his voice and the hint of anguish in his tone didn't mean what she feared.

"She died after Livvie and I left for college."

"I'm so, so sorry." A memory from two weeks ago when she'd met Scarlett and the VIPER boys for dinner popped into her mind so suddenly she flinched.

"I thought you weren't coming," Kane said as Nic slid into the vacant seat next to him at the table.

Nic scrubbed his hands down his face. With a sigh, he looked around the Italian restaurant like he wasn't sure if he wanted to be there.

Beth leaned closer from her spot several chairs away. "Are you okay, Nic?"

"No." He shook his head. "I was on a date when I got a call about my buddy. He was one of the guys on my team when everything blew to hell." He dropped his chin to the spot where his steel arm met his flesh-and-blood shoulder. "He survived the blast. Got married. Had a few kids." He stared glassy-eyed across the room. "His wife was…" Nic's voice broke. "She was

killed in a drive-by last night. I still can't believe it. My buddy was tough enough to survive a fucking ambush, but he's such a mess right now he had to send the kids to his parents because he can't take care of them."

Beth glanced at Kane's profile as he steered the pickup truck into the next lane. She didn't know why she'd pivoted her attention from Nic to him that night at the restaurant as the tragic story unfolded. She did remember the barefaced torment in his eyes when Nic spoke about his buddy being so distraught he couldn't take care of his family.

Kane's similar words rippled through her ears.

"Afterward, my mom struggled with taking care of herself and the house, so we all moved in with Gran and Gramps."

Kane had quickly masked his reaction at the restaurant just as he did now, but she'd seen enough to know that the wisecracking cowboy had a big heart that had been broken.

Now she knew why, and it broke hers too.

"I'm so sorry about your parents." She tried to search his gaze, but he kept his eyes on the road.

He nodded, his grip loosening on the wheel as his body relaxed. "If my dad were here, he'd kick my ass because I chose to serve with Marine Corps instead of the Air Force."

His wide grin and deep laughter lightened the grave mood.

She smiled too. "Did your dad encourage you to be in the military?"

"Every man in my family has served for generations. I never thought of doing anything else but committing my life to protecting my country."

She wanted to ask if that existence was as lonely as it sounded, but the tense set of his jaw indicated he wouldn't be receptive to her questions. The nostalgic edge to his voice said the memories were bittersweet. "Do we need to pretend in front of Gran?"

"No. That woman can smell bullshit from a mile away. And we don't have to worry about my house being bugged. It's as secure as VIPER headquarters. There are cameras in every room, except the private areas, but even those have listening devices I can tap into if I sense something's wrong, like if Gran isn't returning my messages or something."

Beth giggled, half at his acute vigilance and half at herself for liking him even more because he watched out for his grandmother.

"Hey, don't laugh. I look out for those who are important to me." He pulled into a driveway in the middle of a quiet suburban street. "Don't tell her. She'll have my ass if she finds out. Hell, she may already know. You remind me of her sometimes. Smart, with a respectable, yet annoying, 'I got this' attitude."

"I'm going to take that as a compliment. And your devotion is sweet in an over-the-top sort of way." Pulling off her seat belt, she took in the long ranch house the color of Kane's eyes as he came around to open her door. He really needed to stop being so chivalrous. So attentive with his domineering, sexy brand of charm. So adorably dedicated when he talked about his grandmother. And he needed to stop calling her smart. She was far from it. Smart people didn't believe in curses.

TEN

Kane took Beth's hand and helped her out of his truck. Not that she needed his help, but she'd accused him of being over the top. And sweet. Why not live up to her expectations?

"Oh my God." She pointed to the classic baby-blue Buick parked in Gran's driveway.

Kane tugged her up the walk. He pulled her against him as she reached a hand toward his grandfather's car. "No touching. I polished her a couple of days ago."

"Sorry." Beth rolled her eyes. "She looks like a movie star should be driving her with those sleek lines and sexy curves."

No, Beth looked like a movie star in her sugarplum coat and oversized sunglasses. And not just any movie star. The kind who took control of her career, didn't let anyone stand in her way, and used her stardom to help others.

And the kind who needed protection from a crazed stalker who wanted to claim her as his own.

Not going to happen, buddy.

He couldn't blame the guy who knew everything about Beth for being infatuated though. From the moment they'd met, he'd thought she was like his grandfather's Buick—a classic beauty with sleek lines and sexy curves. But the more time he spent with her, the more he learned there was more to Dr. Parker than a pretty exterior.

Beth ogled the car over her shoulder. "Can we take her for a drive with the top down?"

He placed his hand on her back and opened the door. "And while we're at it, we can fly a banner that says, 'Abduct Dr. Beth Parker here.'"

"I didn't mean now, wiseass."

He inhaled the smell of freshly baked apple pie as he ushered inside. "I'll make a deal with you. Stop arguing about your safety and I'll take you for a ride when it's safe."

"Deal, but only if I can drive."

He dipped his head to hers. The scent of lilac floated into his nose, and he inhaled. He heard her breath catch in her throat. Wanting more of a reaction even though he shouldn't, he grazed her ear with his lips.

"Not a chance, sugarplum. Gramps and I restored that baby. Before I left for my last deployment, he promised to give it to me when I got back. He died while I was gone, and then this happened…" He tapped his steel leg. "And then Gran drove the Buick out here to take care of me. Now I take care of her and the Buick, which means no one drives it but me and Gran."

He expected a snarky comeback. Instead, she breathed his name. He wasn't sure if the sound that turned his cock as hard as a candy cane was a reprimand or a plea. He went with the first. His grandmother's booming voice saved him from exploring the latter.

Kane stared after Beth as she walked out of Gran's kitchen and toward the bathroom down the hall. The dark jeans she wore with tall black boots hugged her perfect, heart-shaped ass to perfection. He couldn't even think about her red V-neck sweater showing a hint of black lace underneath.

As soon as the door closed, Gran clapped her hands together. "She's the one for you."

Kane snapped his gaze to her. "Wait. What?"

"That girl you've been looking at with puppy-dog eyes since you walked in. She's the one for you."

Kane shook his head as he stabbed his fork into the warm apple pie. He should have known better than to think Gran wouldn't pick up on the feelings for Beth he wasn't ready to have. Since he was a kid, his grandmother swore she could sense when two people were destined to be together. "I don't believe that nonsense, Gran."

Total nonsense. It had to be.

"Pay attention to me, boy. I've been right about all my brothers and sisters; God rest their souls. And I was right about every one of your cousins."

"And what about Livvie. Is her boyfriend right for her?"

"That girl has a habit of jumping in headfirst with her wild heart. It's one of the things that make her special but it's also reckless. This is one of those times she's going to wind up hurt. She needs to listen to me before she marries that whiny bitch."

Kane choked on his food. "Gran." He took a big gulp of milk. "I can't believe you just said that."

She shrugged as she sat down in the chair across from him. "I've learned a few things from hanging out with you and your VIPER friends."

"We don't say shit...I mean stuff like that when you're in the room."

She tapped her hearing aid. "I can hear you guys

perfectly from the kitchen when you sit around the dining room table, eat like you haven't seen food in days, and curse like sailors. And whiny bitch describes your sister's man perfectly."

"Are you going to tell Livvie your opinion? That should go over well."

Gran waved her hand. "She won't listen. Nobody believes I can predict these things until they're madly in love or their heart is broken. She'll have to learn the hard way. Don't be stubborn like your sister. Listen to your grandmother. Those quickie booty calls of yours are a waste of time."

"Gran." His ears turned red, but she wasn't wrong. He didn't even stay the night when he had a hookup. Hell, he didn't even fully get undressed, let alone spend time with the same woman twice. "You know I can't think about settling down until I'm out of the military."

Gran wagged a finger at him. "I know what's keeping you from settling down."

"Yes, you do, and you of all people should understand what happens when the love of your life doesn't come home." He glanced at the framed photo of his parents on the windowsill above the sink. At seventeen years old, he hadn't understood. He'd been a kid who got angry each time his mother missed a track meet. Each time she'd passed him off to Gran when he needed something. Maybe if he'd taken the time to understand the gravity of her grief, to step out of his own and realize she was drowning and needed help, she'd still be alive.

But she wasn't. A distracted driver may have killed her, but grief was the reason all the joy inside her died long before. He'd never forget how losing the man she loved had siphoned her will to live or the toll her defeat had taken on him and Livvie. The thought of risking a fate like that to a woman, to someone passionate like Beth who hurt as deeply as she loved, tore through his heart with a punch stronger than his steel.

Gran pointed to the bathroom. "I do understand. More than you think. Don't regret not putting a ring on that girl's finger while you have the chance."

Beth woke as Kane's truck came to a halt outside the liquor store. She'd only meant to close her eyes to ease her headache. That had been two hours ago.

"Did you have a nice nap?" He parked in front of the double doors covered in whiskey and beer ads and cut the engine.

"Did I look like I was?" Yawning, she stretched her arms forward and released the tension her shoulders. She never fell asleep in the car, but this had been her most decent slumber in a long time.

"You were out cold."

"Good." That meant she hadn't talked, cried, or screamed in her sleep.

He scanned the parking lot dotted with half a dozen vehicles. "We're still ten miles from your parents' house. Don't they have liquor stores in North Benson?"

"Yes, but I like this one. It's never crowded." And it wasn't owned by the brother of the biggest mouth in the gossip brigade. She bit her tongue and willed North Benson's notorious pack of judgmental housewives to do the same.

Now that would be a Christmas miracle. Maybe she and Kane should skip the party.

She eyed him as he grabbed his cowboy hat from the back seat and placed it on his head. With a smooth movement belying the metal attached to his hip, he slid out of the truck. As she stared at his ass encased in worn jeans, she wondered what he'd look like sliding off a horse.

Sliding into bed.

Sliding into…

She squeezed her legs together to quell the delicious flare between her thighs. Maybe her plan to skip the party wasn't the wisest idea.

She'd be alone with Kane.

In front of the fireplace with rum-laced hot chocolate and no willpower to resist the irresistible package by the Christmas tree.

Going to the party with him at her side might be like jumping in front of a firing squad, but she'd take the heat. Yes, she'd die from embarrassment if Kane found out about her cursed past, but it was better than risking his life if she got too close, like carnally close, and fell for him.

She was already halfway there.

Kane appeared by her door before she could open it. As he helped her out, he scanned the strip mall and led her to the entrance. "How many bottles of wine do you need?"

"Just a couple. I was going to get some after I picked up the cake last night, but—"

Kane stopped her from grabbing the door handle. "I go first."

She raised her eyebrows as he pulled the door open and peered around the space. A moment later, he pulled her inside. She eyed his broad back as he strode in front of her, somehow keeping an eye on her and their surroundings.

Following, she trailed him to the end of the aisle and touched his shoulder. "What I want is right here."

A car door slammed, followed by another. She glanced out the windows. Two young guys who barely looked legal threw up the hoods on their sweatshirts and hurried toward the entrance. A muscle ticced in Kane's jaw. Quickly, she yanked two bottles from the shelf.

As the guys in the hoodies approached the register, a new wine she'd never seen caught her eye. "This looks good. I should get one for…"

Kane shoved her behind a display of whiskey bottles. "Get down and stay put."

She gasped as Hoodie One, the shorter guy, appeared near the entrance. He raised his wild, bloodshot gaze. A gun followed. Déjà vu punched her in the throat as she jerked her head to his friend by the register. The weapon he pointed at the clerk behind the counter didn't waver. Neither did his unhinged stare.

Not again. Not again.

She reached into her tote bag.

"Don't even think about it," Kane growled at her from the corner of his mouth as he slowly positioned himself between Hoodie One and Hoodie Two. "Listen, guys. I'm not going to do anything stupid, but if you hurt my girl, all bets are off."

His girl.

Pain slashed through her arm as memories of a cold, dark alley overlaid with the present.

No.

Seconds seemed to stretch into minutes as she pulled the weapon from her bag. Kane wouldn't be the next man to die defending her.

Before she could raise her gun, Hoodie One, by the counter, shook as if waking up from a trance. Kane swung his leg in a wide, graceful arc. The steel slammed into the teen's midsection and sent him sprawling in her direction. Beth jumped back as he fell face-first into the whiskey display. The force shot her onto her ass as boxes and bottles crashed to the tile floor. Pain lanced up her spine. Fighting for breath, she sprang to her knees and trained her gun on the fallen guy.

A choked inhale lodged in her throat as she looked up. Kane, looking more commanding, more intense than any action movie hero, stood between the hooded assailants, a weapon pointed at each of them.

He shifted his gaze to her without moving another muscle. "You can put your gun down. I got this. Are you hurt?"

She shook her head, air heaving from her lungs in short, painful pants. Broken glass scraped under her feet as she pushed herself from the ground.

He's not here. I'm safe.

She repeated the affirmation. Her mind flashed back to that dark alley, but she didn't scream Danny's name in her head. She screamed Kane's. The switch rippled surprise through her tortured psyche.

Kane adjusted his stance to face her as she caught a glimpse of his weapon still in its holster. Her gaze ping-ponged between the pistols in each of his hands. In the seconds between her falling and sitting up, he'd disarmed two assailants without even drawing his gun?

How on earth?

The cocky dimpled grin he shot her as sirens approached said he knew exactly what she was thinking.

After the cops finished taking their statements, Beth followed Kane to the liquor store exit, still in awe at how quickly he'd neutralized the situation. He hadn't even been breathing hard, for Christ's sake. He'd kicked the bad guys' asses, his cowboy hat still perched on his head, and held them at gunpoint with their own weapons like it was any other day wine shopping.

But it wasn't just any other day. It was a day in her company. North Benson's infamous—

"You holding up okay?"

She glanced at Kane as she pulled the collar of her coat around her neck. "Yeah, just fine."

"Bullshit." He opened the door. "I can feel you shaking."

She was, but fear wasn't the only reason she trembled. "Do you really think those were just two local addicts looking to score drug money?" That had been the consensus of every officer who'd streamed from the three squad cars parked in the lot. But the guys in hoodies weren't just addicts. They were boys with families and friends who would care if they went to jail. Would mourn them if they died of an overdose. They were the embodiment of why the Diablos could not get the Triple X formula.

"I don't know." Kane paused in the doorway and scanned the parking lot. "Headquarters is looking into it."

She followed his gaze and searched the crowd of onlookers behind the police barricade for Chavez's face. "How does headquarters know about the robbery already?" She hadn't seen him make a call.

"Superpowers, sugarplum."

He shifted the wine bottles in his hand the owner had given her, free of charge. Kane had refused a pint of aged whiskey with a tip of his hat. "Just doing my duty, sir," he'd said in that country twang.

Christ. Duty had never looked so damn sexy. She should be terrified. Instead, exhilaration flowed through her veins like some aftermath aphrodisiac that urged her to convince

Kane it was his duty to do her. She twisted a curl around her finger. If only he could be a casual hookup. She'd enjoy that body over and over until the sun rose.

And she'd never see him again.

But he wasn't some guy she'd never cross paths with. He was Scarlett's colleague. Chris's friend. Her protector, and dammit, she liked him.

A lot.

She couldn't fall, not even if her heart did a little dance when he threatened the hoodie and called her "his girl." Not even if those powerful kicks and his graceful speed were sexier than an all-male revue.

"Beth."

She snapped her mind from her what-if party and yanked her gaze away from the crowd. As she faced Kane, he gently pulled her hand from her hair. Threading his fingers through hers, he guided her into his truck and shut the door. As he spoke to an officer, she searched the crowd for Chavez one last time.

TWELVE

Kane shook the officer's hand. "Thanks for your help. We'll be in touch if we think of anything you should know."

The officer inclined his head to his squad car parked haphazardly behind Kane's truck. "Give me a minute and I'll get out of your way."

Kane nodded as he shot a glance at Beth in his passenger seat. She seemed to be surveying the crowd, no doubt wondering if Chavez or her stalker, if they weren't one and the same, were out there.

"Degenerates," he muttered under his breath.

Last night after Nic and Linc had left Beth's house, he'd lain on her couch and read through the history of the stalker's communications. The things the fucker said had been so disturbing he'd gone up to her bedroom to check on her.

It wasn't the first time he'd watched her sleep, and it wouldn't be the last. He wouldn't stop watching, protecting Beth with his life until whoever scared her was behind bars or in the ground. He'd been trained to defend and built to kill. He didn't have a problem with the latter if it was justified.

Edgar had instructed him to only use his weaponry if it was life or death. Well, a gun pointed at Beth didn't get any more dire than that. If he'd been alone, he could have taken down both assailants without stunning them with a V-Strike, but he wasn't taking any chances with Beth nearby. He'd hit them with an intensity so low no hint of the powerful laser would show on their skin or in any medical test. It had been enough to get the job done though.

As soon as he'd sensed trouble, he'd thought his passphrase. In an instant, he'd catapulted into phase two. The passphrase not only activated his weaponry but also engaged his communications system. The team at headquarters saw and heard the whole incident go down via the cameras embedded in the comms unit secured to his wrist. As he'd talked with the cops afterward, his arm chimed like a Christmas carol with requests from headquarters to check in.

Keeping one eye on Beth and the other on the now thinning crowd, he spoke over the mind comms. The cybernetic enhancement translated thoughts into electrical impulses. It was damn cool how he and his brothers could communicate with each other and the team back at headquarters without speaking a word or needing an earpiece to hear.

"Just finished with the cops. Getting Beth to a safe place and will check in soon."

"Roger that," Ryan said.

The police officer nodded as he moved his vehicle from behind Kane's truck.

"About damn time," Kane muttered. The feeling that the robbery was some sort of sick taunt sat like a steaming heap of horse shit in his gut. He didn't like the taste, the smell, or the idea.

As he yanked open the door, he caught sight of Beth's pale face and froze.

The chilling text message Beth received moments ago blurred her vision as she held up her phone for Kane to see.

> Welcome home, querida. Excellent choice of wine, although you should be sharing it with me.

Kane read the message and swore. "Did you give this number to anyone? Or make any calls?"

"No. I haven't even given it to my parents yet. Who did you share it with?"

"Just Scarlett and the team." His jaw tightened as he threw the truck in reverse. "Fuck."

"I thought you said this phone was secure."

"No technology is impenetrable, but whoever sent that message is a damn good hacker."

The gravity of his words, and gravity itself, jerked Beth sideways. She grabbed the handle above the door and held on as Kane sped out of the parking lot. As soon as she let go, a beep sounded from the roof. She jumped and grabbed the handle again. "What the hell is that?"

Kane held up his arm with a black device strapped to it. "My comms unit is networked with my truck."

"Status." Edgar's voice cracked through the air.

"Secure." Kane glanced in the rearview mirror but didn't slow down.

Edgar cleared his throat. "I'm here with Nic, Linc, and Ryan."

Beth shot a look at Kane. "Tell them not to call Scarlett and Chris."

"We can hear you," Nic said. "And we won't call the lovebirds."

She didn't like the unspoken "Not yet" in his voice.

"Beth got another text from the stalker." Kane read the message aloud. "Anything on the two liquor store robbers?"

"A couple of addicts. Based on the live feed, they were not professionals."

"My guess is the stalker watched the show from the sidelines," Edgar said.

Beth studied the text message as if rereading two sentences would glean new information. "Do we think Chavez fits into any of this?"

"Not sure. We'll continue to operate under the assumption that the stalker and Chavez are separate threats until we learn more."

"Agreed. Call me when you have more information." Kane reached over and took the phone from her hand. "The message isn't going to change, so stop looking at it."

She glanced around the car. "Are we still online with headquarters?"

"No."

"I didn't see you end the call or even initiate it." She ran her fingers over the computer screen in the dashboard he hadn't touched. "How did you do that?"

He winked. Just like that, he flipped the switch from warrior to cowboy.

"VIPER gave me superpowers, remember?"

She waved her finger in a circle. "Scarlett is going to have a lot of explaining to do about these *superpowers* when she gets home."

"You could torture the secrets out of me if you don't want to wait." He eyed the neckline of her sweater. "I'm sure you could find creative ways to make me crack."

Beth's body tingled from the hint of cleavage he stared at down to her toes. If he was trying to distract her from the frightening message with his inappropriate charm, it was working. "If you tell me, you'll have to kill me, right?"

His playful expression sobered. "I'd die before I let anyone hurt you."

His statement fanned the irrational fears her mind wouldn't release.

Nobody is going to die because of me ever again.

Kane made a right turn. As if her life was a movie script, the North Benson Memorial Cemetery came into sight. One by one, she counted the graves she needed to visit before she left town. With her heart as heavy as the gray clouds above, she turned from her lethal past and faced Kane. "I don't think my stalker is Chavez."

"I don't think he is either, but what makes you say that?"

"Chavez is a professional. My stalker didn't seem very professional at times. Yeah, he had mad technical skills, but if he was a trained killer, he wouldn't have left me behind when he attacked Danny."

Kane slowed to maneuver the truck around a patch of ice by the cemetery gates. She stared out the window. Thick, sorrow-laden cobwebs filled her chest.

Kane touched her knee. "Is that where Danny is buried?"

She pointed to the gate. "Over there."

Kane turned the corner onto North Benson's main street. "Tell me. Dr. Parker, what do you do in your spare time when you're not raising money for hospitals or working to cure cancer or opioid addiction?"

She looked away from his profile and those infernal dimples that made her want to kiss him for somehow knowing when she needed to be saved from her thoughts. "Well, I haven't been involved in the cancer aspect for a while. A cure is a long way off, even though my colleagues are making inroads, but we really could cure opioid addiction. I mean, if the data from this round of trials is any indication…"

As she explained the promising trial data, Kane studied her from the corner of his eye. He not only listened with rapt attention as she buzzed with information and excitement, but asked thoughtful questions, nodded his approval, and said, "holy shit," and "that's incredible," several times. She didn't pause until he stopped at a traffic light a block from her parents' house. "What's so funny? Did I ramble? Scarlett does that when she's nervous. I do it when I'm excited."

He shook his head. His grin lit up her heart like the nativity scene in the center of town.

"Then what, do I have something on my face?" She pulled the sun visor down and flipped open the mirror.

He caught her wrist. "You're perfect."

She bit her tongue before she responded like a lovestruck teenager parked at the lake with her boyfriend. "Then why are you staring at me?"

He dropped his eyes to his lap and shook his head. When he raised his gaze, admiration shone in their big sky-blue depths.

"I thought Scarlett was the smartest, hardest working woman I've ever met, but I was wrong."

She stared at him for a long heartbeat, then another, suspended in a compliment that shouldn't feel so intimate. Finally, she looked away, afraid to let his high praise and the sincerity in his words sink too deep into her heart. "Thanks. The good Triple X will do for this world is immeasurable."

Reaching over, he gently nudged her chin with his fingers and tipped her head up. "Triple X will save many lives, but it's not the drug I find fascinating."

The heartfelt, sexy words stalled her heart.

He nudged her chin with his knuckle and dropped his

hand. "You still haven't told me what you do in your spare time. Spill the details."

His statement, delivered in that sexy twang with a good dose of gritty bossiness, amplified everything she shouldn't feel for Kane and spiked a desire to give him what he demanded.

"I like to teach my science class to the kids at church because science is exciting, and the kids are fun. I like to go shooting with Scarlett. I like to visit the museums and monuments in DC even though I've seen them dozens of times. I like to organize things because it helps me feel like I'm in control, and I love Christmas."

He smacked his hand over his heart. "Really? I would have never guessed."

She swatted his arm. "Shut up. Your house had plenty of decorations too."

"That's mostly Gran. Tell me more about what you enjoy doing."

"There's not much more to tell except I like to go dancing and take martial arts classes."

He quirked an eyebrow. "Lucky me. I'll be the only guy at the party with a woman lethal in a fight and on the dance floor."

"Yeah, you will." She prayed he didn't think she was lethal after she told him about her cursed past.

THIRTEEN

Beth motioned to the brick colonial two-story at the end of a cul-de-sac. "That's where I grew up."

Kane surveyed the quiet suburban street. "Your house has the best Christmas lights on the block."

"It does." Green garland with red berries outlined the porch and the garage. Two lit-up lofty pine trees sat on either side of the porch steps with large, colorful presents underneath. Lush wreaths with deep-red bows matching the red shutters and door hung from every window. She pointed to the sled and reindeer on the roof. "My father was pretty excited about those new additions."

"They are damn cool. My dad used to put a giant Santa on the barn roof when we were kids."

"Was the barn red?"

He pulled a photo from the sun visor and handed it to her. "Yup, and full of horses, including my sweet girl."

"Oh my God, Kane, she's gorgeous." Beth stared at the huge, glossy black mare standing in front of a red barn with a wreath around her neck and a Santa hat perched between her ears. "She's the prettiest animal I've ever seen. What's her name?"

His grin brightened the cloudy day. "Holly Jolly, because she was born on Christmas Eve."

"I knew you liked Christmas as much as I do." She wagged the photo at him.

He snatched it from her hand and tucked it into the visor. "Don't tell the guys I dressed up my horse."

"Ooh, Kane has a secret." She shimmied her shoulders in her seat. "I'll be keeping that tidbit in my back pocket for the next time you piss me off."

"Great." He rolled his eyes. "I'll make you a deal. You keep your mouth shut and I'll take you to West Virginia and give you a riding lesson once this is over."

"And let me drive the Buick?"

"Don't push it, sugarplum." He held out his hand. "Do we have a deal?"

She placed her palm in his and shook. Driving the Buick would be fun, but seeing him astride a horse in tight jeans and his hat under a big blue sky was worth conceding her request. "Did you ever ride rodeo?" Her mouth watered at the thought of him in chaps on a bucking bull.

"A bit, but not competitively." He pulled into the drive and turned off the engine. "I watched too many friends be taken away in ambulances. I played it safe and ran track."

And now a vision of Kane in running shorts, sweat pouring down his shirtless torso as he circled the red barn, had another part of her body wet.

He rubbed his thigh. "Good thing my bones were in one piece when they were blown to hell."

Pain flashed in his eyes as he scanned the street. Sometimes, like when he was talking about things that deepened his dimples so much they overflowed with joy, she forgot she wasn't the only one who'd suffered and been left with scars.

Following his gaze, she studied the area around her parent's place. Was her stalker lying in wait behind her neighbor's giant blow-up reindeer? Or maybe Chavez took cover on the other side of the house behind Rita and Jerry's life-size Santa village. Rita would have a fit if someone shot a hole in one of the jolly elves.

Kane reached into the back seat. "What's so funny?"

"Nothing." She eyed the gift bag in his hands. "What are those?"

He smiled and winked as he pulled out two red tins. "One is something for us to enjoy. The other is to thank your parents for having me. They can open it when they get home."

"That's not necessary." But damn, it was respectful and sweet.

He opened his door and slid his leg out. "Where I come from, it is."

Oh no, there was that country boy charm her parents would love. Good thing they weren't around to hear him compliment their Christmas lights and witness him acting all gentlemanly. They'd get excited she'd finally brought someone home and she didn't want to disappoint them.

She twisted in her seat to follow his movements. With efficient strides, he walked around to her side of the truck and opened the door. Cold air whipped in, and she shivered. The temperature had dropped considerably since they'd left the liquor store.

He held out his hand. "Come on. Let's get you inside before it snows."

She took it and sniffed the air. "It sure smells like it's going to snow but it's not supposed to start until later."

He cupped her elbow and guided her around the car. As they approached the steps, he dipped his head to her ear. "I bet when this place is lit up at night and the snow is falling, it's as sparkly as you are."

"I'm going to take that as a compliment."

"You should."

He nudged the collar of her coat with his nose as he lifted his head. She could swear he sniffed her hair.

"Beth, is that you?"

Kane tensed as she spun to the familiar voice. She laid her hand on his arm. "Relax, it's just my neighbor."

She waved to the elderly woman peering at them from the edge of the porch next door. "Hi Rita. Merry Christmas."

"Hi dear. Who's that with you?"

"I'm Kane, Beth's boyfriend." He tipped his cowboy hat. "Pleased to meet you, ma'am."

Rita's delighted laugh carried across the snow-crusted lawn. "The pleasure is all mine, handsome."

Sweet Jesus, that man could charm the pants off anybody. Except her. Her pants needed to stay buttoned up tight.

"Do we really need to pretend we're a couple in front of the neighbors?" Beth whispered.

"Yes." He dropped a kiss to her forehead. "Nic's buddies reported they didn't find any bugs earlier, but that doesn't mean someone won't try and tap into your parents' network." He waved to Rita once more as he guided Beth up the steps. "It's best if we make everyone in town believe I'm head over heels for you instead of here to protect your cute ass."

She tilted her head as she punched the security code into a console. "Cute ass? That's not very professional."

"Stop making my job harder by arguing and let us inside. And once we're in there, you don't leave without me, or I'll put you over my knee and make your cute ass as red as this door, darling."

She snapped her head so hard her neck twinged. "You wouldn't dare."

"Try me." Kane didn't wait for a response as he nudged Beth over the threshold. As he closed the door behind them, he blocked Gran's nonsense about Beth being the one for him and chalked up the inappropriate conversation he'd initiated to simple lust. Taking in the layout of the house didn't calm his throbbing need for a taste of Beth. Not when the place glittered as brightly as she did.

A tall Christmas tree with heavy boughs that jutted out at odd angles stood in the corner. Fragile-looking ornaments nestled alongside homemade treasures hung from the boughs. Piled logs in the fireplace hearth waited for a match.

Beth flipped a switch by the door. Just like in her town-home, hundreds of tiny white lights lit the room like a winter wonderland. The scent of pine and the warm, cozy glow whisked him away on a bittersweet sleigh ride back to his parents' house when he was a kid. His mother used to go all out with decorations too. In the days leading up to Christmas, she'd hide Gran's sugarplums around the kitchen for Livvie and him to find when they came home from school. Even as a churlish teenager, he'd appreciated her efforts right until the year her enthusiasm for anything, including him and Livvie, died along with his father.

Were Nic's buddy's kids enjoying Christmas in the wake of their mother being gunned down and their father too grief-stricken to care for them? Kane shook his head at the stupid question.

For years, *he'd* hated Christmas. Hated seeing his mother's decorations intermingled with Grans. But on a snowy December 24th, while he was home on leave, his father's mare gave birth to Holly Jolly. While Kane thought Gran's sixth-sense claims were ridiculous, he sometimes allowed himself to believe that the horse was a gift from his dad.

Maybe a message to stop being a surly Scrooge and enjoy the holidays with his family. Sometimes, he got angry his mom hadn't received a sign to help deal with her loss. Most of the time he didn't believe in gifts or signs at all. When someone was gone, they were gone with no way to comfort the living.

He looked at Beth, mumbling to herself about the ornaments being in the wrong place. An ache to be the family she enjoyed Christmas with thumped in the broken part of his heart.

"Stay here while I check the rest of the house." He didn't wait for a snarky remark as he ignored the surprising desire he wasn't ready to act on. With efficiency born from years of training, he checked the spacious kitchen in the rear of the house that he and Gran could cook in without bumping into each other, the small office, and the neat garage. All were clear, as were the three bedrooms on the upper level. He hadn't needed clarification about which one was Beth's.

As he jogged down the stairs, he spotted her on her knees in front of the coffee table, eyeing a shoebox-sized gift wrapped in shiny purple paper.

"What's that?"

"I told you my family didn't always celebrate holidays on the exact day because of my dad's schedule, but my mom always had special presents waiting for me on Christmas morning." She picked up the box and shook it. "Purple presents."

Skirting the low table, he sat on the couch across from Beth. "Open it."

Beth bit her lip. "I should wait until Christmas, but…"

"You won't."

"No. I won't." She giggled as she tore into the paper. As she opened the box, she squealed.

One by one, she pulled out bottles of lotions and gels, tubes of cream and lip gloss, and flower-shaped soap. "I mentioned to my mom I was almost out of my favorite shampoo, and she got me more."

"Looks like she got you the whole drugstore." He picked up a round container and read the label.

Lilac after-shower moisturizer. For use all over your body.

He dropped the container like it was on fire. Visions of burying his face between her lilac-scented breasts, her legs, and every other place on her body threatened his resolve to keep his hands off the forbidden scientist. A quick taste wouldn't mean he was ready to settle down. It would only mean his enhanced strength wasn't enough to stop himself from taking this gift thing a step further.

He pulled one of the tins from the bag he'd placed on the table and opened it. "I've got something purple for you too."

Her eyes widened as she dropped the gloss she'd just dabbed on her lips. "Are those sugarplums?"

"Straight from Gran's kitchen."

She clapped her hands together. "I've never had one."

Me neither. Well, not the kind he'd been dreaming about since they'd met. He plucked a treat from the pile in the tin and held it out. "Taste."

Leaning over, she opened her lips. Her tongue darted out and touched the purple sugar crystals. Kane swallowed, imagining how *his* sugarplum would taste.

His sugarplum?

His stomach plummeted to the couch cushions. Thinking about a future with Beth and recognizing it couldn't happen was one thing. Thoughts popping into his head like an ambush he didn't have time to battle was another. Beth wasn't his. Gran's predictions could not be coming true. He may have gotten himself in deeper with the disarming scientist than he'd intended, but he wasn't sched-uled to meet the woman he'd settle down with until years from now.

Beth leaned closer. The scent of lilacs mingled with the nutty aroma of the sugarplum as she bit into it. He couldn't pull away, even if he'd tried, from her sultry groan and the ravenous look on her face.

The rest of the treat disappeared through her glossy lips. He watched her swallow, his eyes following the column of her neck down to the swell of her breasts peeking from the *V* of her sweater.

"More." She licked her lips. "Please."

Instead of picking another treat from the box, he held up his sugarcoated finger.

She eyed the offering and hesitated. Holding his breath, his pulse pounding with every millisecond that passed, he waited for her to decide how far she would take this moment. He knew how far he shouldn't take it. He should give her the tin, get their bags from the car, and lock himself and his laptop in a room and search for Chavez.

If she backed away, he would.

With a sigh that shot straight to his cock, she flicked out her tongue again. Her slow lick, like she deliberately took her time eating every crystal of sugar off his skin to drive him wild, matched the devilish look in her eyes. She knew what she did to him.

Enjoyed it.

Fuck, she reveled in it.

He leaned farther across the table. Snaking his hand around her neck, he gathered up her curls and tugged her within mere inches of his lips. "Do you have any idea what you are doing to me, sugarplum?"

The security app on his phone beeped an alert. He yanked the device out of his pocket and cursed. "Someone's approaching the rear of the house. Stay here."

Beth whipped her head toward the back door in the kitchen. "How do you know?"

"Superpowers," Kane muttered as he hurried through the rooms like a stealthy predator.

Licking sugar off her lips, she followed in his wake. She wasn't about to stay put. She doubted a trained mercenary like Chavez would openly tromp through her parents' backyard. How had Kane known someone was approaching anyway? She hadn't heard a thing other than his question still sounding in her brain.

""Do you have any idea what you are doing to me, sugarplum?"

He held up his hand. The motion halted her and her contemplation of his question. A heartbeat later, his shoulders relaxed.

"It's your neighbor." He opened the door. "You suck at staying put, you know."

She couldn't argue that, but she had been about to suck the sugar off his finger. Had been thinking about sucking that full lower lip into her…

Rita derailed those thoughts as she entered the kitchen and handed Beth a gold box. "I just wanted to drop these off." She turned her pink-painted smile to Kane. "I hope you two enjoy them."

Beth lifted the lid and sniffed. "Your famous butter cookies. Thank you so much."

Kane slipped past them. "I'll get the bags from the car." He looked back at Beth. "Close the door behind me."

She gave him a salute as she kicked the door closed with the toe of her boot.

Rita pulled her in for a hug. "I just had to come over and say I'm so happy for you."

Beth schooled her features into a bright smile and hugged Rita's plump body. "The relationship is still new. My parents don't even know yet, so please don't tell them." She wasn't prepared to answer questions like, "Where did you go on your first date, and what does Kane do at the Department of Defense?"

Well, our first date was at the hospital because I got caught in the middle of a break-in and hit my head, and then I had a nightmare, and then the date went to hell. And as for work, he's some sort of super soldier with a bionic leg who can take down and disarm two grown men with a simple kick in a matter of seconds.

And what would she say if someone like Evangeline, who was nosy as hell, asked how Kane kissed or if he was good in bed?

Beth's ache to gather data on those scenarios and give a full and accurate report had been building for weeks, but she couldn't allow the pulsing beat between her thighs to guide her decisions. She knew what people said behind her back. Even though their words were hateful and ridiculous, she hadn't figured out how to penetrate the part of her brain that believed the devil's voice.

It's not my fault those men died. I'm not cursed, and I don't deserve to be punished for God only knows what I did or didn't do.

Still, she had to tell Kane about her tragic past before he heard it from someone else.

Rita patted her arm. "Don't you worry. I won't say a word to your parents. Are you and your man going to the party tonight?"

"Yes." Beth bit her lip. "But…"

"Don't worry about that either. Jerry and I won't let any of those busybodies say anything to your man about anything. If one of the coiffed banshees so much as casts a glance his way, I'll drown her in the punch bowl." She rubbed her hands together. "Oh, but I hope I catch Judy

Martin running her mouth. That woman thinks she's better than everyone in this town. Just the other day, she was bragging to the cashier at the supermarket about her daughter, Evangeline. Are you still friends with that girl?"

"We were friends." *Until she blamed me for Danny's death.* "We're more like colleagues now."

"Good. The apple doesn't fall far from the tree." Rita waved her hand. "Anyway, when the cashier mentioned her daughter goes to the community college, Judy, in her most condescending tone…you know the one."

"Oh yeah, I do." Beth seethed inside. "She rolled out that tone at Danny's funeral when she offered to pray for my soul."

"Well, she implied that the cashier's daughter was inferior to Evangeline because she didn't go to an expensive university."

Beth snorted. "Sounds like someone should pray for Judy's soul, but it won't be me."

"And nobody needs to pray for you." Rita put her arm around Beth's waist. "I know you don't care what the people in this town think, but here's my opinion. I may have only seen you and your man together for a short time, but I know what happiness looks like."

If happiness looked like lust, anxiety, and fear rolled into a tight smile, the assessment was spot on.

Rita stood on her toes and kissed Beth's cheek. "I'm proud of you for overcoming your fears."

"Thanks." But Beth didn't deserve praise. She hadn't overcome anything.

* * ⊕ * *

Beth said goodbye to Rita and met Kane at the bottom of the

stairs. He slipped his phone into his pocket and picked up their bags at his feet. "Which way to our room?"

Panic sizzled in her chest at the thought of sharing her intimate space with Kane. "I'll be sleeping in my bed. You get the guest room across the hall."

He motioned for her to go up first. "That's not how this relationship works, sugarplum."

She spun on the first step and faced him. "You are not my boyfriend, and I don't do relationships."

"Neither do I."

Her heart sank. It shouldn't, but it did. Knowing he didn't want her should make it easier to stop thinking about what he looked like naked. Hell, he'd pushed her away the night of their not-quite-date when her desperation for comfort percolated into red-hot lust and she'd kissed him.

But he'd wanted her. She didn't remember much of their encounter, but she'd never forget how he'd kissed her back. For the briefest moment, she'd tasted desire on his full, soft lips. Felt his hard cock against her belly when he'd pulled her close. The memory got fuzzy and embarrassing when he pushed her away and told her to go to sleep. She tried not to think about what she may or may not have said, but she couldn't forget how she'd fought to hold back tears until he'd left the room.

She had her reasons, unfounded or not, for keeping her heart caged in a prison. Apparently, so did he.

Kane pushed open her bedroom door and dropped their bags near her desk adjacent to the window. "This room faces the street, so this is where I'll stay." He pushed the billowy white curtain aside and peeked out.

Beth hooked her thumb over her shoulder. "The couch downstairs faces the street too."

He shrugged off his jacket and draped it over her desk

chair. "I sleep where you sleep, so I'm close if anything happens."

"Fine. Then that's yours." She pointed to the oversized lilac love seat. "It pulls out into a bed."

A grin split his face. "Good thing I look good in purple."

Damn, did he ever. He looked delicious with his arms crossed over his chest. The outline of his corded biceps under his long-sleeve shirt served as a colossal reminder of why he was here. Still, his presence felt right in her pretty purple room, even though the reason was so wrong.

As he pulled off his holster and placed it, along with his gun, on her desk, she couldn't help but wonder what it would be like if she didn't have a bizarre dating hang-up that no self-help book ever discussed.

She stared at the queen-size bed.

Yeah, she could imagine. They'd been alone for five minutes and her plan to not think about temptation was already faltering. But God, there wasn't a woman on the planet who could blame her.

Despite the clouds, light seeped through the curtains and highlighted the curve of his cheek. The cut of his jaw. His fathomless blue eyes that sometimes flashed with sorrow and pain she was only beginning to understand.

Did his past invade his dreams? Scarlett couldn't say much about what haunted Chris, but Beth knew it had to do with the losses he'd suffered and not just the loss of his arm. She shouldn't ask Kane, but she needed to know she wasn't the only one who feared the dark. "Do you have nightmares?"

He raised an eyebrow. A heartbeat later, he sighed. "Yeah. Ever since..." He glanced at his leg. "But lately, they've changed to reflect more recent events."

"Mexico?"

Darkness clouded his gaze.

"Something like that." Looking away, he studied the photos tacked to a bulletin board over her desk. "Homecoming Queen, huh? Of course your gown was purple. Why do you like that color so much?"

She pointed to her high school dance team picture. "It's my school colors."

Desire lit his eyes. Somehow, she knew it wasn't for the seventeen-year-old in the photo in the skintight spandex but for the tortured woman standing before him. She wished she could go back to her teenage self. It wouldn't have been hard to fall for Kane. The only thing that would be hard would be his body.

His leg.

His cock.

She had a feeling it wouldn't just be hard, but impossible not to beg for seconds after experiencing the power, no, the wonder of First Lieutenant Kane Darren. Yet, she couldn't ignore the circumstances that brought him to her bedroom—not just in the one she occupied as an adult, but the one all three boys she needed to visit in the graveyard had kissed her in.

She dipped her chin and closed her eyes. Would falling for Kane be different because he was made of steel?

She glanced at her bed again.

His gaze followed hers. "Don't worry. I'll stay on my side of the room."

"That's not what I'm worried about." She dropped her gaze to the hardwood floor.

He stepped toward her and lifted her chin with his fingertips. "I know you're shaken about what happened at the liquor store, but you're safe here."

"Right, the liquor store."

The stalker.

Chavez.

She'd been so caught up in thinking about getting her maddening lust under control she'd ignored that a freaking drug cartel was after her because she knew the formula to cure opioid addiction. God, that sounded insane.

Kane lifted her chin with his fingertips. "Talk to me."

She pulled in a deep breath, not ready to spill the tragic details about her past, but she owed him honesty, even if his commitment to her safety annoyed her *and* made her feel special.

"When the stalker started bothering me, I felt insignificant. Like I was just another case to the authorities. Like I was blowing things out of proportion because I was afraid of a man I'd never met. Then, after the cops stopped searching for Danny's murderer, I felt even less significant, like I was keeping a dirty little secret nobody believed."

His grip on her chin tightened. "You are the opposite of insignificant. I'm sorry anyone made you feel like you didn't matter." He brushed the hair out of her eyes.

And there he went, making her feel special again.

"When the stalking escalated, Scarlett asked her stepfather if he could hire one of the private detectives he used for corporate espionage. Henry had said he'd be embarrassed to ask his contacts to work on such a frivolous case, and it was my fault I was being stalked because I'd gone looking for sex online."

"That guy is a class *A* asshole."

"No arguments there." She twisted her fingers until her knuckles ached. "I need to tell you something about what gives me nightmares." She stepped away from Kane and moved toward the curtain. "I don't just dream about the stalker. I dream about—"

He pulled her back. "Stay away from the windows. It's not safe." He positioned himself next to the frame and spun her to face him, one eye on the street.

"You're by the window."

"I'm not the target."

"You don't have to look after me in this house. You said it yourself; it's secure."

"I've been looking after you long before I knew you were in danger."

"What's that supposed to mean?"

"Superpowers, remember?" His dimples winked as he pulled his phone out of his pocket and glanced at it.

She grabbed his wrist. "Did Scarlett use her techy magic on that too?" The device tilted enough to see a video feed from her parents' backyard filling half the screen. Leaves blowing around the steps of her house in Alexandria played on the other half.

His explanation from last night about how he'd gotten into her townhome to check for intruders blared in her brain.

"You have your secrets; I have mine."

"You've been watching me?"

With hands shaking from fury and not fear for once, she yanked her phone from her pocket and dialed Nic.

He answered on the first ring. "Everything okay?"

"No. Can you come to my parents' house? Kane needs to leave."

FOURTEEN

Kane cursed his carelessness as he reached to snatch the phone from Beth. She thrust her elbow up. It smacked into the underside of his arm with surprising force as she twisted to evade his countermove.

Breath heaving, curls in her face, she glared at him as she brought the device to her ear. "Listen to me, Nic. You need to relieve your buddy now before I kick him in the balls."

"Stay put," Kane yelled. "We're fine."

He could hear Nic's laughter across the few feet separating him and the pissed-off sugarplum with the surprising moves. She wasn't kidding when she said she had self-defense training. The sharp blow to his arm had taken him by surprise. So had her speed and agility. He held out his hand. "Give me the phone, please."

Nic's chuckle carried through the air again. "Give it to him, Beth, so I can tell him to stop being a dick and be nice to you."

She handed the phone over with a huff.

Kane brought it to his ear. "We're good. I'll call you later."

"Not so fast, *mi hermano*. Haven't you learned anything from me about how to treat a lady?"

Kane hung up on his brother and shoved the phone in his pocket.

Beth pointed to the door. "Get out."

"Not a chance, sugarplum." Even if he were to leave, which he wouldn't, he couldn't until Nic arrived. After the liquor store incident, he wasn't leaving her unprotected.

"Stop calling me that silly nickname."

He shook his head. "Not a chance of that either."

"Fine, then I'll call you stalker-hole." She crossed her arms over her chest. "Get it, stalker and asshole."

"I wasn't stalking you." Well, he wouldn't call it stalking. More like protecting, but he didn't think she'd see the difference right now.

She stepped toward him and lifted her chin. "It was you who upgraded my security system, wasn't it? I didn't win a damn thing. You arranged it so you could have access to my account. My cameras."

He didn't flinch at her accusations. "Yes."

Another step brought them toe to toe. "Have you been watching me?"

He nodded, mesmerized by the fire blazing in her eyes. "But I've only been monitoring the exterior cameras to make sure nobody breaches the property."

Her brow furrowed as she cocked her head. "Why?"

"Because Scarlett's home was broken into. You got caught in the middle, which, by association, put you in danger. And you were so afraid that night. You put on a good show of being tough when we were at the hospital, but I saw through it. And when you fell asleep and screamed for help, in the car on the way home, and then in your bedroom when I watched you sleep, I knew someone had hurt you. I couldn't allow that to happen again."

Long moments went by. She didn't say anything, just stared at him with those beautiful eyes, the gold rims burning like the edges of a bonfire. "You watched me sleep?"

"I've stayed up all night with sick horses so they wouldn't be alone and scared. Of course I didn't leave you." He'd never leave someone he cared about crying alone in a bedroom, or anyplace else, ever again.

Something warm brimmed in her gaze that wasn't anger. She crossed her arms over her chest as if to snuff it out. He chanced a step toward her.

She backed up. "Was Scarlett in on this?"

He glanced out the window and scanned the street. "No. She has no idea. Neither does Chris. I paid Nic's buddy to do the upgrade."

"That's…" she ran her fingers through her hair and pulled at the ends. "That's the definition of stalkerish. God, Kane, did you ever come into my house when I wasn't home?"

"No, I never went inside." He sucked in a deep breath. May as well tell her everything and get yelled at all at once. "And since the break-in, I've been driving by at night to make sure things are secure."

She blinked. "Christ, Kane. You drove by my house every night?"

"Not on the nights I was working." Their teammate Gage drove by since he kept an eye on Scarlett while they were deployed, but Beth didn't need to know that.

"Did you follow me home last Saturday? I thought someone was tailing me for a few miles. I was about to pull into someplace safe when a black pickup turned a corner and didn't appear again."

He cringed to show remorse he didn't feel. "Scarlett mentioned you were at a bar with some guy. I thought you said you didn't do relationships."

"I don't. It was just a drink with a…friend."

He eyed her until she let out a huff and rolled her eyes.

"Fine, Kane. You want to know the sordid details about my dating life? He was a friend with benefits."

White-hot jealousy, like the kind he'd felt when he'd watched the guy kiss her outside the bar, flashed to life. "How much do you know about this dude? Has Scarlett vetted him?"

"Does Scarlett vet the women you hook up with? You said it yourself that you don't do relationships, but Christ, look at you." She raked her gaze up and down his body. "You're prime fling material, and from the way I've heard Nic talk about your nights on the town, you take advantage of it. Do you call Scarlett and ask her to run a background check before you take a random woman to bed?"

"First, I haven't hooked up with a woman since we've met because I've been busy watching over you." He paused as surprise and something he didn't dare try and define flashed in her gaze. "Second. I don't have a stalker after me who might disguise himself as a nice guy at a bar."

The bonfire in her gaze roared brighter. "I'm capable of choosing my own sex partners. I didn't need your protection then and I don't—"

He snaked his arm around her waist and spun her back to his chest. One hand wrapped around her neck. The other yanked her hard against him. Ignoring his body's reaction to her ass pressed against his cock, he grazed her ear with his lips. "Tell me, sugarplum. What would you do if your date had done this?"

"My date was my friend who went home by himself that night, by the way." She executed a maneuver she'd practiced a million times in the gym. As she spun to escape Kane's hold, she smiled. "But if he'd been a threat, I would have done that."

"Impressive. That would probably have worked on a normal guy. But if Chavez and his men..." He shook his head to block the images of what the sick fucks would do to her.

Of what they'd done to Jenna.

Her chest heaved as she backed to the center of the room and faced off with him. "You violated my trust."

"You must trust me some because you were about to tell me about your nightmares."

"I'm not telling you any of my secrets." She twirled her finger around the room. "And you're sleeping anywhere but here."

His phone buzzed in his pocket. He pulled it out and glanced at the number. "I'll take this downstairs. Get ready for the party and stay away from the windows." He pointed to the purple pullout sofa as he strode to the door. "And before I fall asleep on that couch tonight, you can tell me about your nightmares."

Closing the door behind him, he brought the phone to his ear and fought to douse the emotional firestorm blazing through him. "Hey Gran, make it to Atlanta okay?"

"Just landed. Are you with Beth?"

"Yes. We got here about an hour ago." And it had only taken that long for his infatuation with the pretty scientist to bite him in the ass.

"Did you ask that girl to marry you yet?"

"Not going to happen, Gran." By the time he was ready to settle down, Beth would be happily married to a man whose biggest threat to his life was eating too many super-sized meals, not frequent dangerous missions.

Gran let out a long, heavy sigh as he crossed the hall to the guest room. Kane knew that sound and braced himself.

"My dear boy, you can have your career and a family, you know."

"No, I can't." Especially not with Beth. The anguish in her voice when she had nightmares messed with his equilibrium. He'd lied when she said she'd been out cold in the car on the way to the liquor store. She hadn't screamed while she'd been asleep, but she called his name in a muffled plea that had nearly made him swerve off the road.

Gran tsk'd. "What happened to your mother doesn't happen to everyone."

He closed the door behind him and dropped his bag on the bed. "But it happens enough." Learning about a buddy not coming home and his family struggling was one thing. Jenna dying in his arms while whispering her last words to her husband was another. But watching his mom languish in her room, hearing her cry for his father night after night as she drank herself into oblivion, had broken something in him.

Up until now, the plan he'd made to follow his path to serve and put love on hold had been to protect the nameless, faceless woman he'd fall for someday. Now, she didn't just have a name and a face, but a heart he couldn't bear breaking.

"Listen to me, Kane. I only met Beth for a short time, but that's all it takes for me to know when someone is right for another. If she wasn't strong enough to handle the kind of life you lead, the universe wouldn't have put you two together."

A beep sounded in his head. He glanced at the unit in his arm. "Gran, I've got to take this call from Nic. Kiss Livvie for me. I'll talk to you tomorrow."

"What's up?" he asked Nic over the mind comms.

"What's up with you?"

"Beth found out about the security upgrade and that I've been watching, and she's pissed." Kane pulled off his shirt. He'd give her space but only planned to get ready for the party in the guest room, not sleep.

"That must have been one hell of a conversation. Do I need to come out there?"

"Depends. Do we have any new information?"

"Ryan and his team are sifting through Jenna's intel. We should have a report by tomorrow. In the meantime, he's going to send you a file on Chavez and his known associates."

"Good." Kane stepped to a stout Christmas tree on the dresser. His gaze fixed on a silver Christmas ball with "Twenty-Fifth Anniversary" engraved above two intertwined hearts.

Thanks to the enemy sniper who killed his father in combat, his parents never had an ornament like this. Jenna and her husband would never have one either. He couldn't stop himself from wondering if Jenna's husband was trimming a Christmas tree or drowning in a bottle like his mother had when the love of her life didn't come home. If he were to chance a relationship while he was still an active human weapon, would Beth care if he returned to her in a coffin?

Nic snorted on the other end of the connection. *"Dude, you still there, or are you bleeding out cause Beth cut off your balls?"*

"She's getting in the shower, so my balls are safe for now." The sound of water running through the pipes streamed from behind the walls. *"What else is going on at head-quarters?"*

"No sign of Chavez or anyone suspicious in the crowd at the liquor store, but Ryan determined that the store's interior and exterior cameras were hacked. Someone was watching, and someone's been trying to hack into my buddy's security company, specifically Beth and her parents' account."

Kane whipped his gaze to Beth's room. Her parents' security system was configured for the cameras in the bedroom to come online when the house was vacant. But if someone was trying to hack into the system, they could override that and see…

"*Fuck,*" Kane said as he tore across the hall.

FIFTEEN

Beth adjusted the towel wrapped around her naked torso. "Dumbass," she muttered. Her argument with Kane had left her blood pounding so hard she forgot to bring her toiletry bag into the bathroom. She couldn't discern the difference between exasperation and desire right now. Hopefully, a shower would drown the latter so they stopped mingling like reunited lovers and she could think clearly.

Stop thinking about lovers.

He followed me.

Watched me.

Made sure I was safe.

The more she thought about it, the more chivalrous his possessiveness, obsession, or whatever morally gray emotion he thought entitled him to watch her like a stalker sounded, and that was insane. So was the relief she'd felt when he said he hadn't been with another woman since they'd met.

As she grabbed the toiletry bag from her desk, the bedroom door banged open. Kane stalked into the room like it was his. His menacing growl sounded over the running water from the shower as he pulled her into the bathroom.

A half squeak, half moan jumped from her throat as she dropped the bag. It hit the tile floor with a thud. The heat in his protective gaze added to the steam wafting from the shower. Desire roared through her as she zeroed in on his bare chest and the VIPER logo inked over his heart.

She'd heard about the tattoo from Scarlett. All the guys on the team had one, but seeing it in person stole her breath.

Or maybe his washboard abs and the intricate tribal-like ink on his right arm extending from his shoulder to his wrist had something to do with her inability to function.

Her gaze snapped back to the VIPER logo. She reached out to trace the black circular snake with the ominous-looking fangs inlaid over a triangle. The tattoo, designed in shades of gray and black, seemed to writhe with the rise and fall of his chest like it sat coiled and ready to strike at the first hint of danger. Once, twice, she ran the pad of her finger over the inky line. She did it a third time, mesmerized by the contrast of the hard muscle underneath his soft skin.

Her eyes flew to his face. Any concern she had for bad guys watching her swirled down the drain. The only person she wanted to see her naked stood before her in glorious, warrior form. The contrast of tension and excitement—like stopping himself from acting on whatever base instincts pulsed in his mind—took monumental effort, compelling her to take control of the situation. She couldn't go by the window. Couldn't go outside. Couldn't make her own deci-sions about her safety, but she could experience Kane and his fierce beauty.

Just this once.

Flattening her other palm over his tattoo, she pressed against his heart. It sped as fast as hers. She was still mad at him, but her anger at his self-appointed protector, bodyguard, keeper, or whatever status made her want to flip their dynamic. Touching him may be as slippery as the shower floor, but she wouldn't let her heart tumble. Chavez and her curse may have stolen her hard-won independence, but right now, they wouldn't deter her from claiming what she wanted.

He gathered her hands in his. "Beth, stop." He squared his shoulders as if reminding himself of his purpose. The movement tugged her against him. "We have confirmation someone watched you through the city's surveillance cameras at the liquor store. And someone is trying to hack into the cameras in this house."

Steam from the shower fogged the mirror and warmed the windowless room, but she shivered anyway. The information chilled her to the core, but he was here to guard her in all his super soldier glory. While she balked at his overzealous protection sometimes, she couldn't deny he made her feel safe, even with the threat of her stalker, Chavez, or perhaps both watching her. But being watched was an old story that didn't scare her as much as it used to, especially not with Kane standing before her looking as enticing as a new book she hadn't ordered but couldn't help reading a chapter before she returned it.

She pulled away from his grip and skipped to the good part. Sliding her fingers down his torso, she outlined each hard ridge. Delighted in each string of soft, sultry moans and harsh inhales. Relished the ache his reaction ignited in her body until she reached the delectable indent at the waistband of his jeans.

He hissed and grabbed her hand. "Get in the shower. When you come out, get changed in here. I don't want you naked in any rooms where there are windows or cameras."

The protective edge in his gaze and the hint of jealousy darkened to predatory. The brutal intensity of the metamorphosis flamed her need for control.

And him.

He let her go and stepped back. Swallowing, he raked his gaze over her nearly-naked form. "Listen to me, Beth."

Oh, she was listening to every nerve in her body screaming to be touched.

Licked.

Fucked.

That's all she could have with him. No strings, no attachments. And no feelings beyond the white-hot lust coursing through her veins. She could do that. She'd been doing it for two years. Kane was no different than the other men she'd been with. A willing, temporary lover.

He nudged her toward the shower. "Be reasonable and do as I ask. Please."

His gritty, impatient demand, tempered by his plea, skimmed down her belly and settled between her legs. An ache to be *unreasonable*, to push him until he gave her what she craved, streamed through her veins in time with the water pounding the shower floor.

She speared her hands into her scalp and yanked at the frustration she felt from the depths of her core to the tips of her hair. "Don't you understand, Kane? I've been painfully aware of every move I've made for a long time. I don't do anything without thinking about it. Preparing for it. I'm so freaking tired of being *reasonable,* but at least I'm in control. After Danny was killed, I cowered in my house, crying and terrified for weeks, but I forced myself to be a functioning member of society. *I* made decisions as though there wasn't a psycho at large who could return at any time and terrorize me."

He opened his mouth, but she held up her hand.

The towel at her breasts loosened. She didn't make a move to tighten it. "And then my cake was stolen and now you and your super alpha buddies, hell, even Scarlett, keep making decisions about my life without my input."

"Because you are in danger."

The truth rumbled between his gritted teeth, low and frustrated, like she was a child that didn't understand consequences. She understood repercussions all too well, but his rules didn't apply to this room. "Look around, Kane. No windows to spy through. No cameras to hack. Just steam and…" The towel slipped lower. She grazed her knuckles along his steel thigh. "The strongest man I've ever met."

His gaze didn't leave hers. The primal look in his eyes receded as he shook his head. "Not as strong as I should be when it comes to you." He turned to go.

She fingered the knot at her breasts. "Not so fast, cowboy."

As he spun back, she let the towel fall to the floor.

Kane didn't say a word. The charged silence skimmed over her breasts and settled between her legs. An ache to feel his hands, his lips, on her body consumed the reasons she couldn't, shouldn't drop her defenses.

She reached for him. He held up his hand and stared as if contemplating whether to bolt or pounce.

"Beth, we…we can't. You're my responsibility. And I promised Chris and Scarlett I wouldn't touch…" He laced his hands on top of his head. "You should tell me to get the hell out."

She should. All the way out, like out of town and out of her life, yet she couldn't ignore the powerful hum in her veins. "Shut up and touch me, Kane."

Indecision flashed in his eyes. He backed up a step. "You're killing me, sugarplum."

She rubbed a bead of perspiration pooling between her breasts, caught in the most exhilarating moment of her life.

It only took a split second for the predatory glint in his gaze to flare hotter than before.

"Fuck it." He snaked his hand around her waist and yanked her against his chest. His earlier hesitation seeped into the steam as he slammed his mouth on hers, hard and insistent. With just the right amount of pressure to make her lips part on a whisper-soft gasp, he angled her head and melded his mouth with hers. A gasp escalated to a moan as he slipped his tongue between her lips with the cockiness of a cowboy and the determination of a warrior.

As she pressed into his hard chest, sensations from their post-nightmare kiss rushed in with crystal clarity.

How he tasted.

His soft lips.

Now, he tasted like sugarplums, excitement and anticipation. She'd been desperate to lose herself in everything Kane did that night. To get as close to him as possible to counter the nightmare. But this…this kiss bordered on possession. So did the way his hands slid up and down her torso like he was unwrapping a treat he couldn't wait to relish and would unleash hell if anyone tried to take it away.

He felt that desperate.

So did she.

"Perfect." He trailed his teeth along the underside of her jaw as he captured a nipple between his fingers and squeezed.

A low moan skittered from her mouth as she pressed her lips to the base of his throat. Everything she associated with Kane—sunshine, the outdoors, and hardworking male— met her lips. Hungering for more, she arched into his hand.

He groaned low in his throat as he squeezed her nipple harder. His other hand slid down her hip and grazed the dampness between her thighs. "Fuck, Beth."

Fuck was right. She was supposed to be taking back

control, not breathing heavily enough to create more steam than the shower. "Kane, please."

"Please what? More of this?" He tweaked her nipple again.

Tendrils of pleasure and pain intertwined in her belly and spiraled to the spot he'd barely touched. "Yes, that and…"

"This?" He slid his finger down her slit a centimeter at a time as he cupped her breast in his palm. "Is that what you want, sugarplum? Cause this is one of those dirty fantasies I've been thinking about since we met."

"Yes." She grabbed his biceps and squirmed beneath his touch.

More. She needed more of him, especially his steel leg. She'd witnessed how he could use it in a fight. Now she needed to see it. To feel it. To cement in her mind that he was a warrior who could survive the threats he battled on her behalf. To convince herself he could survive her.

It didn't matter any longer who was in control of this steamy encounter as long as her heart stayed out of the show.

She fumbled with the button on his jeans. He picked her up and laughed, the sound devilish, and sat her on the top step of the sunk-in tub and dropped to his knees in front of her.

She tracked the lines of his tattoo again, unable to keep her hands and eyes off the breathtaking ink. "This is beautiful."

"No, you're beautiful. Let me see the rest of you."

She bit her lip. "Show me your leg."

"Me first." He tapped her knees. "Open for me."

"Stalker-hole," she moaned but didn't hesitate.

He stared for a heartbeat, then two. Holding her breath, she spread her thighs wider, laid herself bare. She didn't breathe again until his dimple made an appearance. Grasping her hips, he pulled her to the edge of the wide step. She yelped as her heated skin slid on the cool, smooth tile.

"Hold on to the ledge." He licked his lips. "Don't let go until I say so."

She reached behind her and found the lip of the tub, sure she'd never followed a command so quickly. As he hooked her knees over his wide shoulders, she gasped but held on tight.

"Looks like you can listen when you want to." With a wicked grin, he dove in to gorge on her like a Christmas feast.

Beth held the tub so hard she thought the tile might crack. *She* was about to crack under Kane's greedy tongue that licked her from the crest of her pussy, down to the bottom and back up again. With each swipe, desire built hotter and heavier until her bones liquefied to molten lava.

His gaze never left hers as he speared his tongue between her folds and sucked. She cried out his name under the exquisite pressure. Sobbed it when he sucked harder. With each pull of his lips, the soul-sapping tension she'd been living with seeped from her body and into the ether until the only thing that scared her was never experiencing Kane between her legs again.

Cold air hit her heated core as he lifted his head. "Stay there."

She didn't move save for her muscles clenching with the promise of a spectacular orgasm.

He backed up on his knees and reached into her toiletry bag, where she'd dropped it.

Beth bolted upright. "Kane, no."

"Oh yes." Smiling, he held up her purple bullet-shaped vibrator. "I saw this peeking out of your bag when I searched your house last night."

His salacious grin and the toy in his hand pulled a low moan from her throat.

He scooted on his knees in front of her again. "Tell me, sugarplum, were you planning to use this pretty purple thing all alone in that pretty purple bed of yours?"

"Maybe." Yes. Multiple times.

He dipped his finger into her wet heat. "Do you think about me when you use it here?"

She slid closer, angling her hips and begging for friction he refused to allow.

"Who do you think of when you use this?" He eased his finger out of her and spread her juices on the toy.

God, that was hot. "You. I think of you."

"Every night since we've met?" He hovered the toy near her clit.

"Yes. Every freaking night. Now stop torturing me and turn the damn thing on." She reached for the vibrator.

He grabbed her wrist. "I didn't tell you to let go of the tub."

She grabbed the edge of the tile. The vibrator's buzz filled her head like a siren's song. "Now, Kane, please."

She screamed as the tip touched her sensitive clit. She tried to close her legs against the intense pain-laced pleasure, but his hips braced her knees.

"Damn, sugarplum. Purple looks fucking fantastic on you." He slid the vibrator from her clit to her pussy and tucked it inside of her. "It looks good in you too."

She held on for dear life as his finger followed and curled against her sweet spot. "Kane, please." She'd listen to every one of his demands to stay away from windows and stay put if it meant being treated like this.

"But you know what will look even better on you?" Dipping his head, his gaze still on her, he slid his hands under her ass and lifted her hips. "My mouth."

With a devilish grin, he dropped his head and clamped his teeth on her clit. She detonated, his name on her lips, as man and machine pleasured her in perfect unison, and she soared to a place of wild, glorious wonder. And Kane, her flesh-and-blood, strong-as-steel warrior, milked every contraction until her release ebbed and cathartic tears seeped from her eyes.

Before she could catch a breath, Kane pulled her up and crushed her into his chest. The toy slid from her pussy onto the floor. With aftershocks still sparking in her core, he touched his mouth to hers in a featherlight kiss.

"You okay?"

The question vibrated against her lips as she brushed her knuckles against the bulge straining against denim. "More than okay. Jeans off. Now."

Chest heaving, his gaze on her flushed face, he hissed a breath and stepped back. "Oh no. You're not getting all of me until you finish telling me what gives you nightmares."

His words jerked her head like she'd been slapped in the face. "What? No."

"One secret for another, sugarplum." And with that dimpled smile she couldn't resist, he turned to go.

"Bastard," she yelled as she picked up the still buzzing vibrator and flung it at his back.

He didn't flinch, only laughed as he walked away.

SIXTEEN

Beth stood by the fireplace, well away from the closed blinds, drawn curtains, and the dark night beyond, and rearranged the ornaments on the Christmas tree. After Kane left her panting by the tub, it had taken fifteen minutes before she could hold her hand steady enough to shave in the shower. Another hour to dry her hair and do her makeup. Thankfully, by the time she was done, Kane was in the hall bathroom, and she'd snuck downstairs.

Now, in the living room lit only by the Christmas tree and the sliver of moonlight shining through the slim window panels on either side of the front door, her encounter with Kane played in her mind like a favorite movie on repeat.

Sweet Jesus, she'd never come so hard before. Had she really obeyed when he'd told her to open her legs for him? Tingles danced between her thighs. Strangely, losing control under his bossy, dirty command had given her control, like putting her body, her trust in him recovered a lost piece of herself.

It had been spectacular, but she couldn't enjoy that again. Not just the carnal pleasure. The way he'd made her feel, like she was a queen, and he'd burn a city down to protect her and then worship her on his knees after he rode home in victory, was dangerous.

A girl could get used to that kind of treatment from her man.

No. Kane wasn't, couldn't be her man.

The phone Kane had given her after he'd destroyed the one with the text from her stalker buzzed with a call from Scarlett. Beth reached for it as she fiddled with the lighted garland strung on the fireplace mantle. "You and Chris had no right to tell Kane not to touch me."

"If you're yelling at me for telling him not to touch you, then he must have, which means I won the bet."

Beth dropped the garland like the lights were on fire. "What bet?"

"The one Chris and I made about how long either of you would last before you gave in to your attraction. Even though we did our best friend due diligence to avoid either of you getting hurt, neither one of us thought you two could keep your hands off each other."

"I didn't sleep with Kane. We just…uh kissed."

Which had led to the best orgasm of her life.

She glanced up the stairs. Was Kane in the shower making himself come as he thought about her?

Holy Christmas, why did that sound so deliciously dirty? And why did she have to find Kane so attractive? Nic was pretty in a masculine way that hurt to look at his movie star face. Linc was brutally handsome in a harsh, cold manner, but she didn't pull out her vibrator when she thought about them.

But Kane?

She wanted him on top of her.

Underneath her.

Fucking her against the wall.

God, she'd always wanted to do that but had never been with anyone strong enough to pull it off. But Kane could. The pulsing between her thighs upped its tempo to twelve drummers drumming.

Scarlett's laugh brought the lascivious concert to a halt.

"I can't sleep with Kane." Beth swallowed a sigh.

"Yes, you can, and you should."

Beth chuckled. "Is my shy, sheltered best friend really giving me advice about sex?"

"Well, for once, I have experience that you don't."

"Do tell." Beth picked up the glass of wine she'd set on the end table.

"I've fucked a super soldier."

Beth choked. "Oh my God," she rasped as she fought for breath. She swallowed and cleared her throat. "I'm still not used to your brand-new potty mouth."

"Chris dared me to say it. Now he owes me even more."

"Please don't go into detail about the terms of your bet."

"I won't if you promise to challenge your theory of why you shouldn't be with Kane. You gave me similar advice when I didn't know what to do with my attraction to Chris. Think of it like an experiment."

Beth didn't mention she'd already started testing the subject. "Of all the guys out there to experiment with, Kane is the last person I should choose."

"I've seen the way you two look at each other. Trust your genius best friend. Kane should be the first man on your list."

SEVENTEEN

ane adjusted the belt around his waist as he looked away from the photos pinned to the bulletin board above Beth's desk. Thanks to VIPER's rehab regimen that had made him cry while he gained his strength and learned to walk again, he'd packed on the muscle he'd lost. His dress uniform fit him perfectly once more.

Well, maybe it was a little tight in some places.

He adjusted his hardening cock. After he'd left Beth looking like she couldn't decide if she wanted to devour him, slap him in the face, or run scared, he'd read the files Ryan sent over.

Edgar had been right. Enrique Chavez was a mama's boy. According to intel, Maria Chavez held tight control over her only living child. With her health failing as she reached eighty, rumors floated about her handing over the reins to the next Diablo leader. Rumors also indicated that Enrique wasn't a shoo-in for the job. He had to earn it.

By torturing women and killing people.

Kane would give anything to have his mom back. It

wasn't fair that sick fucks like the Chavez mother and son duo were graced with so much time on this earth together.

After Kane had read about the dysfunctional family dynamic, he'd headed into the hall bathroom to get ready for the party. The cold water helped with the angry, melancholy mood the Chavez report put him in, but it hadn't done a damn thing to erase the smell of Beth on his hands. Her sweet taste from his lips. The memory of pure desire etched on her face. Even though he'd gotten himself off in the shower with visions of her lying naked in the lavender bed, vicious need still thrummed through his veins.

Tonight, he'd done a piss-poor job of keeping his hands to himself, but holy hell. He couldn't have resisted Beth in a towel with her hair curled around her face and her skin flushed from the steam if his entire body had been made of steel. Walking away when she'd demanded he take off his jeans had been more painful than learning to walk again. Maybe it was his need to protect, fix, or do whatever he could to erase the fear from her eyes, but it didn't feel right to share the broken part that made him whole.

Not yet.

Not until she shared what scared her.

She may act like she could take care of herself, and he didn't doubt it. Hell, she'd succeeded in mustering the courage and strength to wrap her wounds in sequins and live her brilliant, best life despite the trauma she'd endured and the lingering threat. He admired the fuck out of her for that, but she needed his protection whether she liked it or not. If only his mother had possessed half of Beth's fortitude after his father was killed, if only he'd known how to help her find it, she still might be alive.

He put on his service cap as he eyed his gun on Beth's dainty white desk. The weapon would stay here tonight, away from curious stares and innocent bystanders. If he needed firepower, he could shoot a V-Strike without anybody being the wiser. He'd only carried the weapon today because Beth's gun seemed to give her comfort and he figured another would make her feel doubly secure.

At the top of the stairs, he paused and looked over the railing.

His breath stalled in his lungs.

Beth stood by the Christmas tree. Her silver sequined gown hugged the curves of her full breasts, the indent of her tiny waist, and flared to encase those soft hips he could still feel under his hands. The shimmery material twinkled with the tree lights, casting her in a glow more brilliant than Christmas, New Year's, and the Fourth of July all rolled into one spectacular package.

As if she sensed his presence, she turned to face him. She froze as their gazes locked. Step by step, his attention on her, he walked down the stairs.

She didn't speak. Just tracked him with those gorgeous eyes like she was his very own Christmas present. Maybe she was. Maybe Jenna had pulled some strings up in heaven with the man in charge and arranged this moment to remind him to embrace "no regrets."

Who was he to ignore an angel? If no regrets meant living for tonight, he'd take that advice. Despite the perils in Beth's future, he burned to make her glow from the inside out. She might not do relationships, might turn to another man to ease her nightmares, but he was all hers until they stopped pretending to confuse a criminal.

But Kane wasn't confused. He wanted Dr. Beth Parker. It was Christmas, after all. Last year, he'd spent it in the hospital, minus a leg. Tonight, he wouldn't regret not dancing with the homecoming queen. Not even the entire Diablo cartel could stop him from completing that mission.

Beth's jaw hit the carpet when she spotted Kane at the top of the stairs. She'd imagined him in his uniform many times, but dear Lord, navy blue looked hot as hell on the man. Even though she'd seen him shirtless, her mouth watered at the expanse of his broad chest, his shoulders, and those biceps encased beneath his jacket.

Dropping her gaze, she followed the line of his torso, tapering in a sinful *V* to his belted waist as he sailed toward her. She jerked her attention back to his face, framed by that sexy-as-hell hat, before she drooled and thought about what Scarlett said.

Challenge your theory.

Was Beth's perception of the past just that? A theory with no proof to back it up? Weren't the three graves in the cemetery proof enough that she shouldn't tempt fate and fall in love again? She wanted to believe the reasons behind those deaths were just bad luck. Maybe it was time to double down on her efforts.

The smile on Kane's face widened as he stopped before her. As he slipped his finger beneath the thin strap of her gown, he flattened his palm to the small of her back. "You look incredible."

She glared at his big hand on her shoulder but stepped into him anyway. "I'm still mad at you for being a stalker-hole."

"I took those measures because I sensed you were afraid of something. I was right."

She snapped her gaze back to his. "But you lied to me."

"I didn't lie." He slid his fingers down her arm and wrapped them around hers. "I just didn't tell you."

"It was dishonest." And even though she considered herself to be a sensible, independent woman, she found his actions oddly endearing and honestly couldn't remember why she shouldn't press her body—and her lips—against his.

"I'm sorry you're upset, but I'd do it again." He raised their hands as if they were dancing and spun her.

She twirled. A giggle slipped from her mouth as she grasped his arms to steady herself. "It's amazing how gracefully you move on your steel leg."

The dark-blue flecks in his eyes pulsed like strobe lights. "I thought you were talking about how gracefully I dropped to my knees in front of you earlier."

Desire flowed between her thighs at the idea of him doing it again. "Is every male at Project VIPER so damn arrogant?"

"We cheated death and came back as super soldiers, so yeah, we're a bunch of cocky pricks sometimes."

She blocked out the *cheated death* part and focused on the *came back*. If he could learn to come back from losing his leg from whatever hell he'd endured, learn to not just walk, but to fight, to live again, then maybe she could accept she wasn't cursed.

But what if you are?

For the first time, she addressed the lies that choked her in cobwebs.

But what if I'm not?

"Kane, I need to tell you something before we go to the party."

Those dark flecks blazed even hotter. "Anything, sugarplum."

Her heart punched against her rib cage as those thick cobwebs wrapped around her belly. "What I'm about to tell you is going to sound far-fetched. Actually, it's going to sound insane."

"According to most of the population, the idea of a real-life super soldier is crazy. I'm only supposed to exist in a comic book."

"Yet here you are." And here she was, for the first time daring to believe he wouldn't laugh at her. As she fought for words, his phone chimed with an alert she recognized. She stiffened. "That's the security company."

His gaze turned icy blue as he pulled out his phone and studied the screen. An agonizing heartbeat later, he held up the device. "Recognize this guy?"

The knot in her gut eased as she watched a familiar figure walk up the pathway to the house. "That's Jerry from next door. Rita's husband."

"Go into the kitchen and stay there."

"But, Kane, it's just Jerry."

"Go."

EIGHTEEN

Kane waited until Beth darted to the kitchen before he opened the door enough to eye the eighty-something-year-old man on the other side. "Can I help you?"

Jerry eyed him up and down through his wire-framed glasses. "Are you Beth's new boyfriend?"

"Yes, sir. Lieutenant Kane Darren."

"Good to meet you, son." Jerry scratched his bald spot. "The wife and I were afraid she'd never date again." He pulled a plain white envelope from his pocket. "I saw my mailbox was open, so I went out to close it and found this." He held out the missive with Beth's name typed on it.

Kane's skin tightened as he opened the door farther and took the delivery. "Did you see who left it?"

"Nope." Jerry reached out his hand. "Thank you for your service. Be good to our Beth."

"Will do, sir. Thank you."

Beth emerged from the kitchen and ran to his side. Her hand shook as she took the envelope from him. Fuck, he hated to see her scared.

"Let me." If he could take every burden from her, he would.

He opened the envelope. The color drained from her face as she stared at the white sheet of paper with the number four typed in a big, bold font in the center.

The names of the three men in the graveyard rattled in Beth's head like a death roll.

Matthew—One

Conner—Two

Danny —Three

Kane—

Oh, hell no, Kane would not be her fourth victim.

She waved at the door with both hands. "You have to go. Call Nic. Or Linc. I don't care if you call Chris and Scarlett to babysit me. Just leave."

In a move as quick as when he'd subdued the liquor store hoodies, he pinned her hands at her sides. "I'm not going anywhere."

"You're number four, Kane." She struggled against his hold, trying to edge him to the door so she could push him out. "Your life is in danger because of me. You need to go."

He pulled her to a recliner tucked next to the fireplace and nudged her to sit. "I survived getting my leg blown off and crawled through the sand to save my life. I can handle a stalker who doesn't have the balls to show himself when he threatens a woman. Now tell me what the number four means."

Panic sizzled in her veins.

Her bones.

Her heart.

An earsplitting alarm pealed in her mind. "It's a threat

that won't remain on paper for very long, and that threat isn't to my life. It's to yours."

He leaned forward and rested an arm on top of the cushion behind her. "Start talking. Now."

"No, I can't tell you." Her whisper held a hysterical pitch that scared her. "I have to show you."

NINETEEN

Beth didn't look at the towering wrought iron gates as Kane parked outside the cemetery. The cloud cover from the impending storm and the streetlights losing a battle with the fog created an ominous enough backdrop for what she needed to tell him.

As he put the truck in park, she sucked in a fortifying breath. "The reason I didn't want you to come home with me is this." She pointed to the gate. "That's where Danny is buried, first grave to the right of the entrance. You know how he died."

She heaved in another breath and pointed down the long driveway weaving through the tree-lined cemetery. "Conner is back there. We knew each other in high school and dated in college. He died in a bar fight when we were home for spring break. One minute, we were hanging out at Mary's Tavern. The next, he was knocked out from a punch that he never woke up from. The fight started because he'd caught a guy from out of town trying to slip something into my drink."

She grasped the medallion hanging in the swell of her

cleavage. "And way back near the woods is Matthew. He was my boyfriend my senior year in high school. One night, a few weeks before graduation, my friend Evangeline convinced me to go to a party in the next town over. When I wanted to leave, Evangeline refused to go because she was hooking up with some guy. I called Matthew to pick me up. He was killed by a drunk driver on the way." She shook her head. "He'd just gone through hell fighting cancer and beat it and then…"

"Is he the reason you volunteer at the hospital?"

She nodded, the slight movement a blunt contrast to the sympathy in Kane's voice. In the microsecond it took him to add up her dead boyfriends, a fourth grave flashed in her vision. She slammed her eyes shut against the waking night-mare, but lighting still struck the headstone her mind conjured one, two, three times. The fourth time, she swayed as a whip of fire etched Kane's name into the black marble and cemented his demise.

Kane caught her arm and steadied her. "And you think the letter in the mailbox is a message that I'm next?"

She opened her eyes and slowly turned toward him. Something dark swirled in his gaze. She couldn't pinpoint the emotion in the dimness, but it ratcheted the tension about to burst the bodice of her gown. "Whoever sent that letter knows about my past." She pointed to the cemetery behind her. "This is the reason Rita was surprised I have a boyfriend. The reason Jerry commented about being afraid I'd never date again."

The reason I can't fall for you.

Kane's brow furrowed. "I'm not following."

Her stomach pitched as the words formed on her tongue. "Every guy I've dated from North Bensen died while we were dating. I'm known in town as the Black Widow." Saying the nasty nickname left an oily taste on her tongue. "Just ask the women in the gossip brigade."

"The gossip brigade?" Kane's lips twisted like he'd eaten something sour. "Why do they think dating you had something to do with those guys dying?"

She shrugged, hiding her cringe at the ludicrous explanation. "According to them, I must have done something to piss off the powers that be. Losing boyfriends is my punishment or curse or whatever."

"You don't believe that bullshit, do you?"

The incredulity in his question, as if he feared she did believe, shrunk her into the seat.

"It doesn't matter if I believe it or not." God, she didn't want to think for a moment that the happenstance of loving her—a woman cursed for reasons unknown but surely deserved, according to some people—had resulted in three deaths. But the time she'd wasted believing in mystical nonsense was as real as the gravestone.

"It *does* matter if you believe in that black widow crap. I'm in charge of your safety and I need all the intel to do my job. So, answer me this. What's worse than someone threatening your life?"

Her teeth clenched as her worst nightmare gutted her heart like a jagged blade. "Threatening the life of someone I love and…" She looked toward the cemetery. Each man in those graves had said they'd loved her, and she'd loved them back. She didn't love Kane, but she couldn't deny their chemistry was like gasoline begging for a match to strike. Once that fire started, there was no telling what path it would blaze or who would get caught in the inferno.

"And what, Beth? What else is worse than someone threatening your life?"

She dropped her voice, afraid if she spoke too loudly, her

fear might come true. "Threatening someone I'm pretending to love."

The same red-hot longing that coursed through her veins flashed in his gaze. So did a terrifying kernel of truth she couldn't acknowledge and dared not ignite.

Kane tapped the number four letter he'd thrown on the dashboard. "Whoever sent this obviously knows you're known as the Black Widow. That knowledge makes you vulnerable. We must have done a convincing job of pretending to be a couple at the liquor store because whoever the hell is watching thinks you love me." He smirked and shrugged. "Which is understandable because I'm awesome."

As she rolled her eyes, she couldn't fight the smile tugging at her lips. Again, she marveled at how he flipped from scaring the hell out of her to making her laugh despite the gravity of the situation. "You think that's a warning?" She glanced at the note. "That if I don't give up the Triple X formula, they'll kill you?"

He shrugged. "Maybe, or it could have come from your stalker. I've looked through the messages he sent you. It wasn't long after his texts and emails escalated that you and Danny were attacked. This latest move is an outright threat from one of them, or both if they are one and the same or working together."

She rubbed her temples. The headache she'd been battling for two years coiled around her brain and squeezed. She didn't know what was worse—two separate lunatics or one rolled into a terrifying package. "I knew this whole pretend relationship thing was a bad idea." She'd kept her distance from Kane these past few weeks so she wouldn't fall for him, but she'd put his life in danger anyway. "No party. We need to go home."

"We're going." He pulled away from the curb and grabbed her hand. "The Dr. Beth Parker I know doesn't hide.

She puts on her sequins despite the fucked-up shit she's been through and dances the night away. You need to be that person tonight."

She eyed the receding cemetery in the passenger-side mirror and swallowed so many emotions she couldn't discern which tasted worse. "I've been pretending to be okay for two years, Kane. I'm tired."

"I'm sure you are, and I admire the hell out of you for fighting, but you can't give up. Not when there's so much at stake."

"Triple X," she whispered. "If the cartel doesn't get to me, they'll find one of my colleagues." She'd questioned why the Diablos weren't after someone who knew more about the drug. While she wished the threat would disappear, she didn't wish it on anyone else.

Kane tapped his leg. "And if the Diablos do target another, they won't have me on their side."

She didn't crack a joke at his arrogance. None of her colleagues had an elite fighting force watching their backs.

Or a super soldier in their bedroom.

"We have to protect the cure." If she hid and Chavez and his men went after one of her unsuspecting colleagues and were successful, all the research and hope of saving millions of lives would be for nothing.

Kane nodded. "Protecting the cure means keeping your sparkly-ass safe until we can eliminate the threat."

She played with a sequin on her dress. The panic receded enough for her to appreciate his humor. "Sparkly ass? Guess I can't argue that."

"And it looks fucking fantastic on you." He tugged at his collar. "And I look dashing."

"Yes, you do." The genuine laugh felt cathartic. "We'll be the talk of the party, though. I wouldn't be surprised if the mayor starts a betting pool about how long you have to live."

Kane shrugged as he turned the corner toward the banquet hall. "Let them talk. I'm not afraid of a bunch of gossipy women."

"You should be. They're brutal."

He winked. "We can take them."

The "we" part of that statement thrilled and terrified her equally. "Between you and Rita and Jerry, I'll be well covered. They're keeping the vultures at bay."

"How many people outside of this area know about this black widow nonsense?"

"Nobody, except maybe Chris. I'm not sure if Scarlett's told him the whole story."

"Then that means Chavez, if the note came from him, is getting his information from someone in this town, and what better way to uncover intel than at a holiday party? Are you up for a mission?"

She squared her shoulders. "As long as you don't become number four, I'm up for anything."

"Good. Here's the plan. We give whoever is watching a show tonight and see if the next taunt gives us a clue about where the message originated."

"And what if the next move isn't a taunt? Or even a threat? What if it's action?" The shot that killed Danny ripped through her mind and shook her shoulders. "What if…"

He laid his hand on her arm. "I'm a super soldier, remember?"

She quirked an eyebrow. "Are you ever going to tell me what makes you so special?"

"I think I proved that upstairs." He glanced at the clock on the dashboard. "I'd be happy to pull over and give you a reminder, but then we'd be late for the party. But if there's a coat closet handy…"

Her shoulders shook again, this time with a snicker. And

again, she appreciated how his sexy brand of charm could yank her out of the darkness, even if falling for that charm might lead him to a dark place he'd never come back from.

As long as you don't become number four.

Kane leaned against the edge of the bar in the festive banquet hall. Despite the thousands of white lights strewn about, the fear in Beth's voice sank deeper into his bones. How a smart woman like her believed in the curse some lady named Judy Martin and her entourage relished telling him about was beyond him.

Black Widow.

If he wasn't a gentleman, he'd spike the punch with something to make Judy and her cronies puke for the rest of the night so no more trash spewed from their collagen-induced lips.

But Beth believed the absurd lie. He'd seen it in her eyes and heard it in her voice. No wonder she had nightmares. She thought she was responsible for every one of those graves in the cemetery.

And he thought he was the lethal one in the relationship.

Beth waved to a group of women her age as she glided across the dance floor to him. His breath caught. Fuck, she was beautiful. She glowed brighter than every decoration in the spacious banquet hall. Looked tastier than the Italian food on the buffet table, and more desirable than anything he could ask Santa for. But her smile when she caught his gaze?

He'd watched every grin she'd offered her friends. Former teachers. The mayor. The catty women who whispered behind her back. The grin hadn't reached her eyes. But when she looked at him and smiled— a real smile relaxing the tension between her brows and around her pretty lips—his stomach did a nosedive.

She trusted him.

Desired him.

Despite her fear, she looked at him like he was the only man in the room. That made him the luckiest bastard in North Benson.

Her hand brushed his as she slid next to him. Winding their fingers together, he squeezed to remind her she wasn't alone. They may not have a future, but she was his tonight. "I met Judy Martin."

"Isn't she a piece of work? Rita and Jerry did a great job of herding her and the brigade away from us, but even the town's biggest soiree of the year won't stop my neighbors from going to bed by nine."

He shrugged. "I handled Judgmental Judy."

"I wouldn't expect less from a super soldier." She eyed a group of her classmates seated at a nearby table with their heads huddled together. Every set of eyes fixed on Kane. "Does that always happen?"

"What?"

"Do women always look at you like you're a piece of decadent chocolate cake?"

He chuckled softly as he brushed his hand along her thigh. Yeah, they usually did, but he hadn't invited one to sample him in weeks.

Smiling, Beth ran her fingers along the row of ribbons on his chest. "Every woman in here is hoping you'll dump me so they can consume you. Must be the uniform."

"First, you liked me fine without the uniform." He gripped her hip and pulled her to him. "Second, sucks to be those other women 'cause I'm taken for tonight."

And if he had any say in it, he'd spend all night convincing her she wasn't a black widow. Contrary to what she believed, it would take more than an alleged curse to kill him. Somehow, over the last twenty-four hours, his life plan had veered course. Instead of avoiding relationships, he'd aimed to make sure Beth didn't blame herself if anything took him from this earth.

Beth leaned into him as a tall blonde in a silky black jumpsuit approached. "That's Judy Martin's daughter, Evangeline."

"Is that the same Evangeline you mentioned at the cemetery who wouldn't leave the party when you two were in high school?"

"Yes. And according to her, you *are* taken."

Kane placed his hand in the center of Beth's back. It was adorable how she offered protection from a skinny female who thought a random hookup was more important than friendship.

"Beth," Evangeline shouted as she extended her arms.

Beth leaned in for a hug and a round of "It's been too long" and "I'm so happy to see you" type of greetings. As the air-kisses ended, Kane wound his arm around Beth's waist and tugged her into his side. Evangeline's gaze, a couple of shades lighter than her tanned complexion, landed on the possessive grip.

"Showtime," he whispered in Beth's ear. "I'm Lieutenant Kane Darren. You must be Evangeline. I met your mother earlier."

"Oh my God, Beth. Is he your boyfriend? I can't believe it." She waved her manicured fingers in front of her face like she'd swoon from the news. "I'm so proud of you considering…" She crossed her hands over her heart. "Well, you know."

Beth tensed. Kane slid his fingers to the middle of her back. Slowly, he kneaded her soft, bare skin under the thin crisscrossing straps instead of telling Evangeline she was just like her mother and that it wasn't a compliment.

Evangeline bounced on her toes. "So, tell me, how did you two meet?"

"Scarlett introduced us." She clasped Kane's arm. "I needed help with something and…" Beth shot Kane a flirty smirk as she laid her head on his shoulder.

"And Scarlett felt I was the right guy for the job." Finishing each other's sentences also felt right.

Evangeline eyed Kane's hands. "Do you work for Project VIPER? You guys all have bionic body parts and work as some sort of security detail, right? I mean, that's what the Department of Defense said in the press release they put out a while back."

"Yes, ma'am. At your service."

"Oh my." Evangeline fanned herself with her hand. "A boyfriend and a bodyguard to boot. He's perfect for you, Beth. Is Scarlett in town too?"

Beth slid her fingers to the base of Kane's neck and toyed with his hair. "No."

He dropped a kiss to the top of her head. He could get used to putting on a show.

Evangeline pressed her painted-red lips into a pout. "That's too bad. I haven't seen her in a while and was hoping to catch up."

A guy Beth introduced him to when they arrived—John or Jake, perhaps—sauntered over with a wave. "Mind if I steal your girl for a nostalgic dance?"

Evangeline nudged him toward Beth. "Of course she doesn't mind; Beth loves to boogie."

Beth shrugged. "You know it." She handed Kane her beaded purse.

Securing it under his arm, he wrapped his hand around

the back of her neck and dropped his head. "Don't make me jealous."

"What are you going to do? Blow the place up with your super leg if he tries to kiss me?"

"If that's what it takes to keep you safe, then yes. I'll burn this whole fucking ballroom down."

He felt more than heard her sharp breath as he nudged her to the dance floor. For a moment, he let himself enjoy the sway of her hips as she shimmied under the red and green strobe lights spiraling around the room. The vision made his cock more than twitch. He turned to Evangeline. The unchecked desire in her calculating eyes calmed his libido down.

Way the fuck down.

Evangeline's gaze landed below his waist. "So, Lieutenant Darren, where's your bionic body part?"

"Under wraps." He plucked two flutes of champagne from a passing waiter and handed one to her. "I heard you just returned from Dubai." Judy Martin had somehow managed to brag about her daughter during her Beth-is-a-black-widow warning. "How did you like the Middle East?"

"It was so rewarding and so challenging. I'd been considering offers for positions all over the world from some of the biggest tech firms. When I got the call saying Henry Richardson, you know, Scarlett's stepfather, suggested me for a high-level project, well…" She took a sip of champagne. "I was on a plane two days later. Have you met Henry? He's such an inspiration. I'm so grateful for all the support he's given me."

"I met him once." *Held him at gunpoint, actually.* "Congratulations on your success."

"Thanks. I worked hard to make a name for myself."

"Hard work does pay off."

"And some of us have to work harder than others."

She glanced at Beth on the dance floor. A sheepish smile overtook the spiteful one from a moment ago as she caught Kane's gaze.

"Forget I said that." She fiddled with the stem of her champagne flute. "I shouldn't have said anything, and I don't really mean it. Must be the booze talking."

Kane remained quiet. Silence was the best tactic when it came to getting someone to talk. And when you added alcohol…

"It's just that…" She sipped her bubbly.

Kane bit back a smile. *Keep talking. And drinking.*

She tipped back her flute and drank half the contents. "Because of Beth's unfortunate, shall we say, luck, she's always had things handed to her without having to work for them. Like every time she kills a boyfriend, she gets a sympathy pass that gives her carte blanche for everything she wants without earning it. She's like the perpetual homecoming queen with all the spoils while the rest of us wait our turn and work our asses off."

Someone has a runner-up complex.

He hadn't known Beth for very long, but from what he could tell, she was one of the hardest-working people he'd ever met. He'd read the glowing reports from her boss. Hell, she wouldn't be involved in a groundbreaking project like Triple X if she wasn't a hard, reliable worker. And she was smart, caring, and dependable. Scarlett wouldn't be best friends with someone she didn't respect.

Evangeline touched his sleeve. "Don't get me wrong. I love Beth like the sister I never had, even though we lost touch for a while. And I'm happy for the success she's achieved. She deserves everything she's gotten." She eyed him from head to toe again. "And she seems to have hit the jackpot with you."

"I'm the lucky one in the relationship." Kane rolled his

statement over in his brain, surprised *relationship* didn't sound so scary.

"I don't know about lucky." Evangeline leaned closer to him and brought her hand to the side of her mouth. "Aren't you afraid you'll be her next victim?"

"Not unless you, or someone else in this town, has a plot to kill me." Kane forced humor into his words and winked. "If that's the case, whoever tries won't be standing for long."

"Wow. Hot, funny, and deadly. Beth is lucky Scarlett introduced you to her. And speaking of Scarlett, can you ask her if she can put me in touch with her stepfather? I've been having trouble getting in touch with him since I got back from Dubai."

That's going to be tough since he's behind bars.

But Evangeline wouldn't know that. The feds were keeping his arrest quiet while they sorted through his network of terrorist connections.

Kane directed his attention back to the sugarplum on the dance floor as if trouble would descend at the mere mention of Scarlett's stepfather. "Why don't you ask Beth to get you in touch with Richardson?"

"I don't want to put her in the middle. Scarlett doesn't like me very much. I think she's jealous because her stepfather took an interest in me."

"I'll see what I can do."

"Thanks. How long are you two lovebirds in town for?"

"Until Christmas Eve."

"I bet Beth wants to be back home in time for mass at our old church."

"That's her plan." He'd been happy to ditch church this Christmas since Gran was out of town, but mass with Beth sounded appealing.

Evangeline tilted her head to his. "We used to play this covert hide-and-seek game in the church that was so much fun. Last time we talked, Beth said she still played it with the kids in her science class. Does she still do that?"

Kane had no idea, but he nodded. It sounded like something a pastor wouldn't approve of, but Beth would do anyway.

"She's always been such a do-gooder." Evangeline toyed with the plunging neckline of her jumpsuit. "Did she tell you about the necklace she's wearing? The hospital fundraising board presented it to her at our last meeting as a thanks for her dedication."

"She didn't mention it." But he remembered the sorrow in her eyes as she'd held the medallion between her fingers and told him about her boyfriend, who beat cancer but wound up in the graveyard anyway.

"Beth had attended the meeting virtually, so I sent her the token of appreciation. If *I'd* been given a gift to recognize my service, I would want it sooner rather than later. I figured Beth would too. Does she wear it all the time?"

"She hasn't taken it off." Not since yesterday anyway. It seemed Evangeline's jealousy started long before that though.

Evangeline smiled as a beep alerted him to an incoming mind comms call.

"Kane, do you copy?" Ryan said.

"Copy."

"We've decoded Jenna's intel. We've confirmed that the Diablos are targeting a research scientist from Beth's agency. The codename they've given the target is Cazampulga. That's Spanish for—"

"Black Widow." His gaze locked with Beth's from across the dance floor. *"Fuck. It's definitely her. I'll explain later."*

"Roger that. Get Beth to a safe location. Now."

TWENTY

Beth's stomach dropped as she watched Kane stiffen. Panic buzzed in her ears. The music faded to a distant hum as she shot a tight smile at her partner and hurried past him.

Kane met her on the edge of the dance floor. "We need to leave." He nodded, then muttered, "Roger that."

"Who are you talking to?"

He didn't answer as he cupped her elbow and guided her to the exit in quick strides.

Beth waved to Evangeline as they sailed past her. "What's going on, Kane? Did something happen? Did I get another message?"

"No, but we need to get out of here." Kane pulled her sugarplum jacket off the coat rack as he walked by. The metal hangar clanging against the wall popped like a gunshot. She stopped and closed her eyes as the sound blasted through her chest.

"Come on," Kane growled.

The cold air sliced into her face as she followed him

outside, but she scarcely felt the snowflakes on her bare shoulders.

He opened the door to his truck. Her heels barely cleared the running board before Kane shut her in. Warmth enveloped her, but she shivered.

Kane jumped into the driver's seat and threw his hat on the dash. "If I say duck, you do it."

She tugged on the seat belt. "Tell me what's going on."

"We decoded intel from an undercover source who used to be embedded within the Diablos." He checked the rearview mirror. "The intel indicates the cartel is targeting an employee from your agency with detailed knowledge of Triple X. The codename for this target is *Cazampulga*, which means—"

The wine she'd drank burned a path up her throat. "I know what it means." She choked on her words. "Black widow in Spanish."

"That's definitive proof that you're the target." He jerked the truck around the next corner. The towering marble angel marking the edge of the cemetery came into view as the black widow taunt played in her mind. Turning to the window, she swallowed the nausea spurting up her throat.

Kane said her name, but she didn't answer. Instead, she stared at the passing graves. Something white waved next to Danny's headstone. Squinting, she pressed her face to the window. "Stop the car."

"What? No."

She ripped off her seat belt and tugged at the door handle.

Kane grabbed her arm. "What are you doing?"

"Stop." She yanked the door open. Kane cursed as he slowed down. As the truck skidded to a halt, she jerked from Kane's grip and jumped out. Her heel landed on a patch of ice and her ankle twisted. Pain lanced up her shin, but she righted herself and ran toward the arched gate. Turning sharply to the right, Kane's harsh voice in her ears and his hands at her waist, she slid to a stop in the snow-covered grass.

Kane yanked her against his chest. "What the hell?"

She stared at the crude wooden cross erected next to Danny's gravestone. A piece of notebook paper blew from a nail in the center. Its edges, wet from the elements, fluttered in the wind. The moisture didn't distort the frightening message written in thick, black marker.

Welcome home, Cazampulga.

Kane tore the paper off the cross and stuffed it in his pocket. A muffled clap cut through the night. He hit the ground with Beth in his arms. A bullet slammed into his steel leg. As he rolled to shield her, he thought the command to activate himself into phase two.

The sting of activation sprinted down his body as he jumped to a crouch and shoved Beth behind him. "Stay down."

Another shot thudded over the wind. Kane dove on top of Beth as a bullet slammed into the center of the cross next to him.

Beth struggled under his heavy weight. "Were those gunshots?"

"From a silencer. Stay."

He scanned the area as he placed himself between Beth and the direction the shots had come from. Nothing moved in the barren trees surrounding the gigantic angel statue.

Even the wind had died down. Holding his breath, he waited for another shot.

"*Status?*" Ryan asked.

"*Gunshots. Both from the east.*"

"*I've got an aerial view of the location. You're in a cemetery?*"

The incredulous note in Ryan's voice wasn't lost over the brainwaves. "*Yes. Hostiles?*"

"*Stand by.*"

"Roger that," Kane said aloud.

Beth tugged at him. "Who are you talking to?"

He silenced her with a harsh "shush," not realizing he'd switched from talking in his head to talking aloud.

Poised to either fire or fight, Kane crouched over Beth, his breaths calm and controlled, torn between guarding her and going after whoever fired those shots. But he couldn't leave her. It wasn't luck that the shot hit his steel leg instead of flesh. Nor was it luck that the second one landed smack in the center of the wooden cross. Whoever made those shots was sending a message.

"Kane."

The fear in Beth's voice ripped through his heart, especially since he knew it wasn't only for her own life but for his. "Hang tight, sugarplum."

"*Area is clear,*" Ryan said. "*Is Beth okay?*"

"*Affirmative.*" Kane didn't need to report his status. If his pulse rate so much as dropped a few beats while he was in phase two, his comms unit would alert headquarters.

"*We've secured a safe house. Nic and Linc are activated and will meet you there. Stand by for details.*"

"*Good.*" And not good. The activation of his teammates meant the threat wasn't just credible but dire enough to mobilize Project VIPER. He tugged Beth up. "Let's go."

Kane hurried her to the truck and deposited her inside.

Rounding the hood, he scanned the street as he climbed in next to her.

She curled into herself as he sped away from the curb. "I've never heard a gunshot with a silencer. It didn't sound like a shot. I mean, when I go to the shooting range with Scarlett, and the night Danny..." An anguished squeak slipped from her throat. "It didn't sound like that."

"Breathe, Beth." He touched her knee. It shook underneath his palm. He stole a glance at her profile as he held the wheel tight with his other hand. "We've got it under control."

"We who?" She glanced back at the cemetery. "Who were you talking to back there?"

"Ryan."

"How? Through mental telepathy?"

"Something like that." He'd been wanting to tell Beth about the enhancements VIPER had built into his body and brain. To share with her how astounded he'd been when he'd woken up in the military hospital and been offered a second chance at his career, and his life. How he'd mourned his brothers who'd lost more than a leg that day and cried for the ones who would grieve for them. How he avoided commitment because he feared leaving someone behind, and how, since meeting her, he'd begun to question that thinking.

He scratched the back of his neck where the chip that networked his body and brain had been implanted. Sometimes, like now, when his adrenaline soared into overdrive, he could swear it sizzled under his skin like a bomb primed to explode. The scratching at his neck turned into clawing as the urge to tell Beth everything grew to a painful itch.

He wanted to explain how it felt to have lethal technology coursing alongside his blood. How going from clinically dead to somewhat inhuman made him feel invincible, yet scared shitless. How the chances of him not coming home from a mission were significantly lower than before he joined VIPER yet astronomically high.

He couldn't share all that, but she deserved to know at least a little bit of the truth. "There's technology built into my body that lets me communicate with headquarters remotely."

"Like when Edgar's voice invaded your truck earlier and scared the crap out of me?"

"Yes, and that was pretty damn funny."

She laughed, the sound off-kilter, but it was genuine, and he drank in every strained beat. "The technology also lets us communicate silently in our heads. We can also share information through this." He held up his wrist. "Chris and Nic have their comms units built into their arms, but Linc and I have to wear them."

"Is that why they teased you about having to wear jewelry the other night when we all met up for dinner?"

"Yeah, 'cause they're dickheads."

Another laugh, this one not as strained, glided from her lips. "You guys take giving each other crap to a whole new level, like when you and Linc argue about whose relatives make the best moonshine."

"My Uncle Pat's is so much better than his cousin's from Alaska. You'll have to try some when we get home."

Her laugh, this time, sounded like it came from the heart. He stared at the road, pleased with himself for making her smile, and prepared himself for her next question. He'd always wondered how much Scarlett had told Beth about VIPER's competencies. Not much, he guessed. Both women respected the integrity of classified information, yet they were family. Just how super did Beth think he was?

One block flew by. Another. A turn out of town and still no sound from Beth. His respect for her upped a notch. She was shot at—twice—for fuck's sake. She had every right to be a hysterical mess, but he was grateful she wasn't.

As a seventeen-year-old boy, he hadn't known how to handle his mother's tears. As a man, he knew exactly how to comfort Beth. His idea of comfort, no matter how innocently intended, would lead to things he wouldn't follow through with until they had a conversation.

He'd told her she wasn't getting all of him until she confessed what gave her nightmares. Well, she had. As much as he wanted the whole damn box of sugarplums, not just a sample, they had to get something else straight before he sank his cock deep inside her sugar and devoured her from the inside out.

Did she really believe pretending to be her boyfriend would get him killed? He shook his head. Who was he kidding? The pretending had stopped almost before it had started. They were good together.

Damn fucking good.

So good that denying his feelings felt like trying to shoot a bullet back into a gun chamber.

Fruitless.

Impossible.

Lethal, because if he died in combat, Beth wouldn't just grieve like his mother had. She'd blame herself.

"Kane?" She didn't look at him. "You were just almost killed."

He noted she hadn't said "we," as if the very real threat of her life being in danger didn't matter. But it did, and he'd do everything he could do to keep her safe from the stalker, Chavez, and from herself. "Those shots weren't intended to kill either of us. One hit my steel and the other hit dead center in the cross. I saw it when I rolled with you."

"Oh my God." Her hand flew to his thigh. Panic rose in her voice. "I didn't realize you were hit. Does it hurt?"

He moved her fingers to where the bullet had gone through his pants. It wasn't the first time he'd had a bullet lodged in his leg. It certainly wouldn't be the last. "It feels like when you go to the dentist and you're numb, but you still feel the pressure from the drill."

He grazed his fingers over her left arm, her skin cold underneath his touch. "Did I hurt you when we hit the ground?"

"No. Just a few scratches, and I twisted my ankle when I ran from the truck, but the throbbing has stopped."

"I'll attend to your injuries when we get where we're going." He reached behind him and pulled her coat from where he'd tossed it in the back seat. "Put this on. You're shivering. And no more jumping from vehicles."

She nodded. "Lesson learned."

"Good." He slowed down as she took her seat belt off and shrugged on the coat. His hands relaxed on the steering wheel as she buckled back in.

"Kane?"

"Yeah?" He tensed at the heaviness in her voice.

"I can't let you be number four."

TWENTY-ONE

A beep sounded from overhead. Beth jumped in her seat. How Kane didn't, even though he was used to it, was beyond her. Then again, everything about Kane was a wonder.

"Status?"

Kane rattled off their location to Ryan. "Are we being followed?"

"No. I've cleared the way for you. You won't be tracked by any surveillance cameras or satellites. The address for the safe house is coming up on your GPS now."

Beth's gaze flew to the video display on Kane's dashboard. A map came up. The little dot representing their vehicle headed them away from her parents' house. "Where are we going?"

"Someplace safe."

"But I have to go back and get my things." Her gun was on her nightstand. Bringing it to the party hadn't been wise because of all the kids running around, and she'd felt safe with Kane, but she craved the cool assurance of the firearm now. Not that having a gun in the cemetery would have helped. There hadn't been a visible target to aim at.

But what about Kane? He hadn't brought a gun to the party, had he? The mind-blowing orgasm in the bathroom had really short-circuited her brain cells because she hadn't even thought about what he'd do if Chavez showed up.

He'd done a good job of protecting her in the cemetery, though. Without hesitation, he'd thrown himself in front of a bullet. It wasn't a cliché. She wasn't being dramatic. The man put her life over his, and that meant he…

Cared.

Her stomach sickened. *Not good. Not good.*

Caring could lead to loving. Hell, she was already falling for him, and they'd only spent one whole day together. What would happen when they were alone again? "We cannot go to a safe house."

"It's the best option for keeping you secure," Ryan said through the speaker.

"No." Any common sense she possessed flew out the window. What if the safe house was a hotel room? Or a tiny efficiency apartment with just a kitchen, a bed, and a bathroom? And she knew what happened in bathrooms when Kane was around. God, there'd be no place private to run from her burgeoning feelings that could get him killed.

I'm not…

Christ, she couldn't even talk herself into believing she wasn't cursed. She dug her hands into her hair and pulled. The prickle in her scalp didn't stop her self-defeating thoughts.

Kane gripped her wrist. "It's going to be okay. Did you hear what Ryan said? Nic is meeting us at the safe house in a few hours. Linc is going to your parents to gather our things." His grip shifted from her wrist to her hand and squeezed. "You know what they say. Three super soldiers are better than one."

"Nobody says that." But at least she didn't have to worry about being alone with Kane. Or Nic or Linc dying. She wasn't falling for either one of them.

"I'm bringing the team online now to catch everyone up," Ryan said. "Stand by."

A second later, Nic, Linc, *and* Chris confirmed their presence.

Beth's head snapped up. "You weren't supposed to bother Chris on his engagement-moon."

"You're a part of something big now." Chris cleared his throat. "Scarlett is here too."

"Of course she is." Feeling more out of control than ever, Beth drew her coat tighter around her shoulders.

Kane reached into the back and pulled out a blanket. "For your legs. They must be cold and wet."

She took the blanket and wrapped it around her. Even though heat blasted through the vents, she couldn't stop shivering.

"Beth, please don't be mad I'm here," Scarlett said. "I made Chris promise to tell me if there were any new developments."

"I'm not mad at you. Just the situation." The whole goddamn situation that started when she'd buried her first boyfriend.

"Good. I took the liberty of explaining to the team the black widow connection."

Beth nodded and glanced at the hard line of Kane's jaw. It had been hard enough to talk to Kane about it. Bless Scarlett for saving her from explaining again.

A gruff cough came over the line. "This is Edgar."

Beth sat up straight. "Admiral."

"Dr. Parker, the intel you've been told about is credible.

You're the only female employee at the National Agency for Health with enough knowledge about Triple X who has reason to be called a black widow." He paused and cleared his throat. "I'm sorry for the losses that you have suffered."

"Thank you." She pulled her hand away from Kane's. Getting close to him was a bad idea, and she craved his comfort way too much. "Who do you think shot at Kane in the cemetery, my stalker or Chavez?"

"Chavez," Ryan said. "Footage video suggests that whoever made those shots was a professional. According to police reports from the night you were attacked, your stalker was sloppy. We can assume he wasn't tonight's gunman. And we can assume Chavez knows about your history with the stalker and knows your alleged black widow curse. That makes you vulnerable."

Beth eyed Kane's gun in the center console. If one more person called her vulnerable, she'd shoot them.

Kane shot her a warning glare as if he sensed her sanity teetering on its precarious edge.

"We have two working theories," Edgar said. "One, Chavez is mimicking the stalker to scare you further, so when he makes his move, you'll give up the information with little persuasion."

A phantom wind whipped through her body. "Persuasion?"

Kane snapped his head to her. "I won't let that happen to you."

She nodded but couldn't stop the montage of "persuasive techniques" from streaming through her mind. "What's the other scenario?"

"Your stalker is working with Chavez. Either way, somebody knew you would be visiting that cemetery. All they had to do was wait. We're working on gathering more intel. Kane is the lead on this job. Your orders are to listen to whatever he says without question."

"Yes, Admiral." She glanced at Kane, the enormity of the situation sinking in like a body being lowered into a grave.

"Good." Edgar yawned. "Report in when you get to your location."

Beth leaned back in her seat and stared out the window.

"We have a couple of hours' drive." Kane touched her knee. "Get some rest. You're safe."

"I know." She stared out the window and kept her fears about *his* safety to herself.

TWENTY-TWO

"*She believes in that curse crap, you know?*"

"*Scarlett?*" Kane bit his tongue against saying her name out loud as he maneuvered the truck into holiday traffic on the Interstate. "*How do you have access to my head?*" Only Chris, Nic, Linc, and whoever was online at headquarters could access the mind comms, but Scarlett wasn't in the office.

"*I'm the one responsible for the voices in your brain, remember? Of course I can talk to you this way from wherever, whenever I want.*"

"*Okay then.*" He was going to call her once he was alone, but now worked too. Beth breathed in through her nose and out through her mouth like she was centering herself and couldn't hear his and Scarlett's conversation anyway. "*What's the deal with Evangeline's interest in your stepfather?*" He relayed her adoration for Richardson and her eagerness to get in touch with him.

"*I'm not surprised. The first words she ever said to me were, 'Hi, I'm Evangeline. I'd love to work for your stepfather someday. Could you introduce us?' She'd been relentless so I caved and*" *invited her to tag along with Beth to a party Henry threw for something or other he felt he deserved attention for. They spent some time talking in a corner. What about, I'm not sure, but Evangeline seemed pleased."*

Kane rubbed the back of his neck. *"I hate to ask this, but is there any way you can meet with Henry and find out what the conversation was about? Anyone who worships a man like that is questionable."*

"You think she has something to do with Chavez?"

Kane's leg buzzed with pent-up aggression. *"I don't think so. She seems too smart to tangle with a cartel, but Evangeline has been there for every death that Beth thinks is her fault, and she comes off as super jealous of Beth's accomplishments. I don't know how all of this is connected. Hell, I'm probably overre-acting 'cause I don't like the woman, but if anything, the connec-tion to Henry is something to investigate."*

"Henry is the last person I want to have a conversation with, but I'll see what I can do." Scarlett sighed. *"I wish Beth would listen better to our conversations about her so-called curse. No matter how many times I remind her that Conner, Matthew, and Danny's deaths are not her fault, she still can't let go of the fear that the next man she falls in love with will die."*

"That gossip brigade really did a number on her."

"Yeah. She doesn't date. Even though she comes off as a party girl, she never goes home with a guy, except for a couple of trusted friends with benefits, as she calls them."

"Not anymore." He wanted to be the only guy she trusted with her body.

"She can't take another loss, Kane."

"I'm not going to die, and neither is she." The promise blasted the serve first, love later conviction he lived by. The force slammed him back into the seat. Sweat formed among the raised hairs on the back of his neck despite the cold air lingering in the cab. Not even an hour ago, he'd been talking

himself out of even thinking about a future with the beautiful, tortured scientist. This morning he'd dismissed Gran's prediction about Beth being the woman for him. Now, he was vowing to keep them both alive so neither one of them would have to live without the other.

Beth wasn't the only one that couldn't take a loss.

"How do I make her realize she's not a black widow? That if I do die, it's the fault of the bad guy who shot me, or blew me up, or ran me through with a sword or whatever, and not hers." He shook his head. *"It makes no sense."*

"But it makes sense to her. Until I met Chris, I thought the only thing that made me special was my brain. And Chris thought he was too dangerous to love. The lies we told ourselves were both wrong, yet we clung to them as irrevocable truth."

Scarlett's words hit him with the force of an eighteen-wheeler. Beth thought she was too lethal to love, which wasn't true. Was his plan to serve first, love later, also a lie? Did it make sense to avoid what was happening between him and Beth because he thought his dangerous existence made *him* too lethal to love? *"How do I make Beth believe that she's not cursed?"*

"Keep fighting."

TWENTY-THREE

Kane guided his pickup truck down a dark rural road. The house they would call home for the next few days sat at the end of a secluded cul-de-sac. The half an acre of open space on both sides and the cornfield behind offered an ideal location to spot someone coming at them from all angles.

The headlights illuminated fat snowflakes falling on the small, modular ranch with faded yellow siding and missing shingles. According to the schematics Ryan sent, it included a garage, kitchen, living room, and bedroom.

One bedroom.

When Nic and Linc got here in a couple of hours, one could take the couch while the other kept watch. And when it was Kane's turn to be on duty, one of them could take the floor. He loved them like brothers, but he would be the only one sharing a bed with Beth. And before she went back to sleep, they'd have a conversation about this black widow bullshit.

And then he'd address the lie his parents' deaths had instilled in his mind and heart.

Beth yawned as the gravel in the driveway crunched under the tires. "Where are we?"

"A few counties outside of DC." He punched in the garage code. "Good nap?"

She nodded, but he knew she hadn't. Watching the spitfire curl into a tight ball, hearing her whimper his name as nightmares clutched her in sleep both fed his fears about falling in love and unraveled them. Somehow, in the space of twenty-four hours, she'd become the person he feared leaving behind.

And the person he feared he didn't want to live without.

Fight for her.

Scarlett's advice made a shit ton of sense, but it was about as vague as the interior of the dark garage he pulled into. He knew how to fight. VIPER had engineered him to destroy. But emotional trauma couldn't be slayed with brute force, bullets, or even V-Strikes. He hadn't been able to help his mother when a love song came on the radio and reduced her to tears. Watching her unbearable agony had left scars so deep he couldn't think about a relationship, let alone a family. If he couldn't fight those demons, how could he fight Beth's?

He turned off the engine. As the garage door closed, darkness enveloped them, save for the interior light in the cab of the truck.

Beth straightened in her seat. "Are Nic and Linc here yet?"

"No. They'll be here soon."

She sighed. "Looks like I'm stuck in this dress until then."

He wasn't complaining. "Stay here while I make sure the place is secure."

As he turned to open the car door, she touched his shoulder. "Be careful."

He nodded, his brain scrambling to find a way to ease her fears and coming up short.

A quick but thorough sweep of the house that smelled as dank as the garage revealed the place hadn't seen a remodel in several decades. Wood paneling throughout gave the place a gloomy aura like it had been built as a set for a slasher movie. The faded olive-green kitchen appliances and the threadbare shit-brown carpet added to the murder-waiting-to-happen vibe. And there wasn't a Christmas tree or decoration in sight.

Beth was going to hate it.

At least it was warm. He undid his belt, jacket, and dress shirt and draped them over the back of a chair. Tugging at the collar of his T-shirt, he strode into the garage. As he flipped on the overhead light, he spotted Beth exiting the truck. He motioned for her to stay put as he rounded the hood.

"What is it?" She swiveled her head looking for threats in the barren space.

"Nothing. All clear." He retrieved a spare gun from the glove box. Beth didn't have hers and might appreciate the added security. Tucking it into his waistband, he held out his hand. As she took it and climbed out, the sight of her bare legs triggered his cock to twitch like a dog wagging its tail at the sight of a bone. And those heels? God, he even found her feet sexy. Wrapping his other hand around her waist, he lifted her from the running board and set her on the concrete floor. "No matter where we are, you wait for me to open the door."

"Even in an empty garage?"

"Yes."

"Don't you think you're taking this 'listen to Kane' thing too far?"

"No." He guided her around the truck and into the kitchen.

Her heel snagged on something, and she stumbled.

He caught the arm of her fluffy coat and stopped her from face-planting into the orange Formica table. "See, you do need my protection." He followed her gaze to a bubble in the yellowed linoleum floor. "That land mine could have blown you through the roof."

She stared at the bullet hole in his pants. "It still amazes me how you can switch from warrior to cocky cowboy mode in a heartbeat."

"VIPER's therapist says humor is a common coping mechanism. I'm assuming you have a therapist too?"

"How could I not?"

She drew her lips into a tight line. Instead of pushing her to talk more, he slid his hands inside her coat and tucked them under her collar. When she glanced away, he commanded her gaze back to his with a low growl of her name.

She jerked her attention back to him. The gold flecks in her eyes burned as she decided if she would answer his question. Instead of pushing her to talk, he pressed his thumbs into her tense neck muscles. She melted under his hands. A deep rasp purred from her throat as she dropped her gaze.

He cupped her chin and raised it. "Don't look away from me, Beth. Especially when I make you moan."

Before she could answer, he found another knot and applied pressure. This time, she purred. Louder. Deeper.

"That's it, sugarplum. Eyes on me."

"Kane."

The way she said his name, half plea, half reprimand, almost dropped him to his knees. She thought he had two sides? Well, he'd uncovered two sides of her too. The vulnerable side of her needed to feel protected. The frightened side that hid deep beneath her brighter-than-the-North-Star persona yearned for the connection she'd scared herself into believing she couldn't have.

The need to bend her over the kitchen table and fuck her until the only thing she feared was never coming under his touch again didn't just ache; it hurt. And now that he'd sampled the sweetest, hottest treat to ever grace his tongue, there was only one remedy to appease his bone-deep craving.

A tremulous breath shook the coat from her shoulders. "We shouldn't."

He slipped the fur from her arms and skimmed his hands down her bare back, down lower to where her dress wrapped around her waist and dipped his fingers under the material. "Tell me why." He still wasn't fully reconciled with the reasons he'd denied the chemistry between them, but incinerating the lie she told herself took precedence.

"You…" She fisted his T-shirt. "You know why."

"I want to hear you say it." He wanted the woman who opened herself up for him earlier. The one who let him spin her under the Christmas tree. He wanted every part of her she held back. And wise or not, he wanted to give her all of him. Now.

"Kane, please."

She squirmed against him as if unsure if she wanted to dive in or flee, but he held her tight. "Say it, Beth."

"We shouldn't do this because I don't want you to be number four." Tears veiled her eyes. "I won't let you be next."

"You've said that already. Say the other thing."

Tears clung to her eyelashes. "I can't because I can't help believing it's true."

He gripped her chin hard enough to leave fingerprints. "Say it out loud. Say it so your scientific brain can hear how ridiculous it sounds."

She didn't whimper or even flinch. She just stared at him as a battle between fact and fiction waged across her beautiful face. He hated making her realize that she alone held the power to break her so-called curse. But his Marine Corps training taught him if you wanted to build someone up, every reservation they had about themselves had to be broken down. Every vulnerability and fear admitted. Every lie exposed.

It wasn't until one was stripped to a raw, truthful state that they could be reborn into the strongest version of who they strove to be.

"Come on." He brushed a finger over her lips, his voice low but leaving no room for argument. "Say it, Beth."

"I'm…" She swallowed. Another tear skittered from her eye. "I'm a black widow. Falling in love with me is a death sentence."

TWENTY-FOUR

Beth tried to look away from Kane. She judged herself enough for believing in the foolish curse. She didn't need to see disappointment or pity in his eyes, or worse, watch him walk away from her again.

"Why did you push me away that night in my bedroom when I was having a nightmare?" She dragged her gaze back to his, desperate for answers she wasn't sure she wanted to hear. "I needed you and then you left me alone when I was scared. Why aren't you pushing me away after I just admitted my darkest, stupidest secret?"

He backed her to the wall next to the garage door. "Because this time, when you're begging me to fuck you, you're awake and coherent."

Her eyes widened so far they pooled with fresh tears. "I never begged you to fuck me."

She hadn't, had she?

"Yeah, you did." He braced his arms against the wall and caged her in. "And it turned me on as much as it broke my heart because you were so scared."

"I was scared, and maybe I did beg you, but going to the

hospital brought back so many memories I'd worked so damn hard to suppress." She lashed her hands onto his hips. Her fingers skimmed the line where steel warrior met soft flesh-and-bone, hard cowboy. "I needed this body you call super. I needed you to tell me it was going to be okay because when I was with you, before and after the nightmare, I believed that I was all right." The passion in her voice deflated. "And then you left when I wasn't."

"Is that why you called Nic instead of me when you were scared at the bakery? Because you were mad I left you alone?" He gently stroked her cheek with his knuckles. "Walking away was the hardest thing I've ever had to do, but I didn't leave. I went to my truck to get my phone charger. By the time I came back, you were passed out. I slept in your chair and watched you. Talked you through another dream and held your hand. You never woke up, but you calmed down enough to fall back into a restful sleep."

"I think I remember that." Her words came out low and sultry, her heart beating in rhythm with his labored breaths and her mind reeling in disbelief. A snippet she'd forgotten teetered on the edge of her memory. "Did you call me sugarplum?"

He stroked the iridescent collar of her coat. "You wore this when I took you to the hospital and you looked as sweet as my favorite candy. I spent all night wondering if you tasted sweeter. And then you kissed me, and I knew it was true and I wanted more. So much fucking more, but even if I had let myself take what you offered, I was afraid I couldn't give you what you needed."

"What did you think I needed?" She held her breath, praying the cocky cowboy answered instead of the serious protector.

"Not for me to fulfill every dirty fantasy I've had about you."

"I wish you would have." She pressed her palm against the bulge in his pants.

A pleading moan skated from his throat as she slid her palms up his chest and over abs so defined she could feel every glorious indent under his shirt. Venturing outward, she followed the fascinating V of his torso to his hips and back down to his thighs.

He cursed under his breath. "My leg is made of steel, not the rest of me. I didn't trust myself not to touch you. You're too fucking hot and I care about you too much."

She jerked her hand away from his erection like it might stab her. Caring for her could lead to a graveyard with his name etched on a tombstone.

"Come back to me, sugarplum." He slipped his fingers into her hair and manacled the base of her neck to stop her from pulling away. "Tell me where your mind went just now."

She shook her head.

"Beth."

That commanding tone renewed the pounding desire in her veins. God, she wanted, needed every side of Kane so much she ached, but she wasn't made of steel either, especially her heart.

As she tried to push past him, he spun her to face the wall. "Remember what I said I'd do at your parents' house if you didn't listen?"

She not only remembered the conversation. She replayed it on a regular basis.

Pressing his chest into her back, he nestled his hard cock between her ass cheeks as he gathered her wrists and pinned them above her head. "I'll give you a reminder. It had to do with making your ass as red as the front door." Dipping his head, he nipped at the sensitive skin below her ear. "Trust me, sugarplum, the effects from a sharp bite of pain and the ensuing pleasure can be a wonder drug."

White-hot heat blazed between her legs. Apparently, fear hadn't completely overtaken her senses. "Jesus, Kane, I thought you were a country gentleman."

"Not in the bedroom, sweetheart. Tell me what upset you so we can get to the part where I make you scream my name again."

"I didn't scream…"

He spun her to him. "Oh yes, you did, darlin', loud enough for Rita and Jerry next door to—"

A pop louder than any gunshot she'd ever heard rocked the small house. She spun her head to the garage door as it imploded inward. The force pushed her backward. Her head smacked into the refrigerator. Bright spots flashed in her vision as Kane shoved her. Like at the cemetery, he rolled a second before they hit the floor and took the brunt of the impact. Less than a heartbeat later, breath whooshed from her lungs in a painful rush as her shoulders slammed into a cabinet.

Heat poured in from the garage and scorched her face. As she pulled in her next breath, she coughed. Clamping a hand over her mouth, she tried to stop the smoke inhalation, but her throat burned like it was on fire.

Kane rolled off her and nudged her toward the back door. "Stay down," he yelled over the crackle of flames.

Eyes tearing, she crawled behind him across the linoleum. The hem of her dress caught on the leg of the metal kitchen table. The material ripped as something sharp cut up her thigh. She cursed but kept moving. A wall of smoke greeted her as she emerged just feet from the back door, but the distance to fresh air seemed like miles.

Kane stood, his steady hands guiding her up as they reached their escape route. Flames consumed the wallpaper and licked precariously close to his back, but he shielded her from the destruction. As he yanked the door open, his pants leg caught fire.

"Kane." The words scraped up her throat like sandpaper, but she kept yelling. Was his super leg fireproof? The rest of him sure as hell wasn't.

He roared something unintelligible as he yanked her out the back door. Cool air hit her face as he pulled her into the vast, fenceless yard. They tumbled onto the snowy grass. Air trapped in her lungs as Kane sprang back up and pulled her with him. The tattered remains of her dress tangled around her waist. Blood dripped from a long cut on her thigh, and she'd lost a shoe.

He tore off his T-shirt and handed it to her. "Tie this around your leg."

She kicked off the other heel, barely feeling the cold, wet grass under her feet or the pain in her thigh, and quickly tied the shirt around the wound. As she straightened, he pressed a gun into her hand. Adrenaline pumping, she wrapped her fingers around the warm metal and cocked it.

Kane would not be number four if she had anything to say about it.

Kane screamed the command in his brain to activate himself into phase two. As the sting dashed from his neck down his leg, he squeezed Beth's hand and pulled her to the side of the house that wasn't consumed by fire yet.

"*Kane, do you copy?*"

Ryan's voice roared in Kane's ears. "*Copy.*"

"*Incoming hostiles from the east and west.*"

"*How many?*"

"*One in a vehicle in the front. Six approaching the house.*

Three from each side. They arrived in a van seconds after the explosion."

"Copy." The police and fire department would be here any minute. The hostiles' best strategy would be to draw them out and grab Beth before the authorities arrived, which meant they were coming in full force with the intent to kill.

You can't be number four.

He tuned out the memory of Beth's desperate voice and surveyed the surroundings. There was nowhere to take cover in the barren backyard except for a shed on the edge of the cornfield. Sprinting to that was too risky.

That only left one choice.

Engage.

"Three hostiles approaching from each side of the house." He pointed to the gun in Beth's hand as he yelled over the flames. "Stay behind me and shoot at the first one you see, but don't move from your position."

"Where's your gun? Why do we only have *one* gun?"

"Trust me and listen like your life depends on it because it does." He pushed her into a crouch and leveled her with a look that said, "Stay here."

She nodded at the silent command. The fear in her eyes stamped itself into his mind. Her trust branded his heart.

"They're rounding the house through the flames on the east side," Ryan said.

Kane channeled enough intensity to blow up another truck into his silent command.

Fire. Fire. Fire.

V-Strikes meant to kill speared through the flames. One hostile came into sight on the outskirts of the inferno. Kane hit him with a strike to the heart. The hostile's gun went off and the shot went wide.

"Hostiles rounding the corner on the west."

Another shot sounded behind him. He whirled to Beth

to shove her to the ground. Instead, he whispered her name in awe and fear as he watched her raise the gun and hit a burly figure square in the chest.

Shoving her toward the house, he stepped into the open. He ignored her shout to get back as he envisioned the destruction he aimed to rain down. With a growl, he fired a V-Strike toward a hostile on the east side. The target fell to his knees. A bullet from Beth had him crumpling face-first into the grass.

"Hostiles on your six," Ryan said.

Without turning around, Kane fired V-Strikes from the back of his thighs. Beth's bullets punctuated his efforts as more V-Strikes streamed from the front of his calves toward another hostile in his sight line. A moment later, a quick scan assured all reported threats were neutralized, at least for the time being.

"All clear," Ryan said.

Adrenaline galloped through him as he pulled Beth from where she'd taken cover behind a rusty garbage bin. Sirens wailed in the distance.

"SUV is fleeing. Nic is minutes out. He'll meet you at the road on the far side of the cornfield."

Kane acknowledged Ryan as he grabbed Beth's hand and took off. As he pulled her into the barren field, snow poured down in a sheet of white. She cried out as she stumbled on the prickly ground. He scooped her into his arms and took off in a run.

As he crunched through cornstalk remnants, one thought kept running through his mind.

He couldn't be number four any more than Beth could be the next Jenna.

TWENTY-FIVE

Beth awoke to so many aches in her body she couldn't pinpoint which one hurt the worst. With a groan, she opened her eyes and searched for the clock on her nightstand. The familiar red lights didn't meet her gaze. She blinked. Still no red numbers. No photo of Danny next to her lamp. Nothing except darkness.

Bolting upright, she groaned as the night played out before her open eyes like a first-person shooter video game.

Laughter rattled from behind the faint outline of a closed door in front of her.

Kane?

She strained her ears. The beautiful sound sluiced through her body like a healing potion. A moment later, Nic cursed in Spanish. Linc called him a pussy. Kane's delighted howl drowned out the rest of the conversation.

She looked up to the ceiling and thanked the heavens. Tears sprang to her eyes. Kane lived, but she'd shot, likely killed, a man last night. Maybe two. All she clearly remembered was Kane, weapon drawn like a gunslinger from the

Wild West, walking into the middle of the only road in town and facing his enemy like a man.

But Kane wasn't just any ordinary man. He hadn't even needed a gun to take down armed cartel enforcers sent by the devil himself.

She pressed her fingers to her aching temple. What had she witnessed? Kane had stood under the clouds in the frigid night like he'd been the one sent by the devil. The pure concentration and menace that hardened his features and the beautiful, stalwart lines of his corded body terrified and mesmerized her at the same time. And then the hostiles in front and behind him had fallen one by one as if a look from him could actually kill.

Could it?

Kane had scooped her up and carried her into the night without checking to see if any of the mercenaries had gotten up. At least two—yes, definitely two—she recalled as details sharpened in her mind, had reason to be unconscious. She'd shot them, for Christ's sake, but how had the others fallen?

She sat up and kicked off the covers. A white bandage covered her thigh where she'd cut it on the ugly kitchen table. An ache sprung in the wound as if her acknowledgment triggered the pain to kick in. Had she hit her head too? It hurt like a bitch. Maybe she'd banged it hard enough to distort her recollection of the night's catastrophe. Maybe Kane had had a gun and she didn't recall him using it.

Or maybe he really was a superhero.

Holy hell, he'd looked like one. Last night may have been a blur, but she vividly recalled every vibrating muscle in his chiseled stomach as he stood as still as a wolf poised for attack. Remembered every rise and fall of his broad, solid chest that made his VIPER tattoo writhe like a beast salivating for prey. Through every graceful move that either scared the bad guys enough to back off or scared them to death, he stared at her with a promise to protect.

And she'd believed him. Believed he would throw himself in front of a bullet again or run through fire to save her. And more than that, despite the terror of the explosion and the ambush and the men with guns who emerged from the smoke, she believed Kane would come out of it alive.

Now, in the light of day, the fear she'd buried under adrenaline and sheer will to survive slithered through her overstimulated mind.

Swinging her legs over the bed, she winced as an ache spiraled up her leg. The outline of a lamp came into view. Reaching, she flicked it on. Soft light illuminated the white walls and ceiling. A quick glance confirmed the room contained nothing but the big bed she'd woken up in and the nightstand.

"Nice," she hissed. Maybe in her spare time, she'd contract with VIPER as an interior decorator for their safe houses. Hiding from danger was bad enough. Doing it in a colorless room with no Christmas bling in sight except her dirty gown in a ball under the window covered in heavy black curtains qualified as torture.

Just how had her gown wound up over there? She dropped her gaze to the red Marine Corps logo emblazoned across her breasts. Fisting the gray T-shirt, she yanked it up to her nose. Kane's scent clung to the material like she'd clung to him as he'd carried her away from the burning house and fallen bad guys.

She didn't remember much after that except Kane talking to someone, probably through that cyborg voodoo magic. But the magic wasn't just confined to his head. Based on how fast he'd torn through that cornfield with her cradled in his arms, super speed had been engineered into his leg too. A man didn't get that fast from running track in high school.

After that, everything went dark. She didn't recall the rendezvous point. Not the drive here, wherever here was. Nor did she remember being put to bed, much less Kane removing her dress and slipping his shirt over her head.

Heat flooded her cheeks. She shouldn't be embarrassed Kane had seen her body. Hell, he'd licked her pussy from the inside out last night and it had been…

She slid her hand down her belly to the juncture of her thighs covered in the silky lilac thong she'd worn under her gown. Kane's mouth had been heaven. Yet knowing he'd attended to her injury, got her into his soft T-shirt, and tucked her into the comfortable bed seemed more intimate. It was about time he was intimately honest with her about what she'd witnessed last night.

TWENTY-SIX

Kane snapped his head to the bedroom door as Beth walked out, a bit wobbly on legs that looked incredible below the hem of his T-shirt.

He crossed the small living room and reached her in three strides. Grasping her shoulders, he shielded her body with his. Nic and Linc didn't need to gawk at the beautiful, hot mess in his clothes.

She glanced toward the windows. A sliver of sunlight peeked through a gap in the drapes. A car honked from the front of the house, followed by the grinding of a garbage truck. "Where are we?"

"Just outside of DC at another safe house. Tell me how you feel."

"Like you have some explaining to do."

Dark circles marred the skin under her eyes. She smelled like the fire from last night, but her snark hadn't taken a hit. And thank God she wasn't hiding under the covers in a dark bedroom like his mother had after her trauma. Beth was tougher than that, but if last night had broken her, he'd be here to help put her back together.

Linc cleared his throat behind them. "I'm headed out to do a perimeter sweep."

"And I'm on guard duty," Nic said.

Kane hooked his thumbs in the front pocket of his jeans as he watched them leave. He'd been sick with worry since he'd gotten Beth into bed a few hours ago. His own slumber had come in short bursts as he lay next to her, only leaving to check in with Nic and Linc who took turns sleeping on the couch and keeping watch from the SUV parked in the driveway.

If there was ever any doubt she was a target, there was none now.

"Tell me how you're feeling." He used the tone he'd employed last night when he'd told her to stay put.

"I'm fine."

So much for listening to him today. "That's a bullshit answer and you know it."

"I'll give you real answers after you give me some." She shifted, switching her weight from one foot to the other and winced.

"Shit, Beth. You shouldn't be standing with your feet all cut up like that."

She slapped him on the shoulder as he lifted her in his arms. "I can walk, Kane. Put me down."

He set her on the couch. "You're hurt."

"But you're not." She fisted his long-sleeve black T-shirt in her hand. "How are you not hurt? Or dead?"

Kane's adrenaline kicked in as she pressed him for details. She was riled up and he was burning to expel pent-up energy. They both could use a good fight. Hopefully, at the end, she'd realize she wasn't a black widow.

He knelt in front of her and grabbed her ankle. "I thought you didn't want me dead?"

"I don't." Her leg jerked as he ran his finger along the bottom of her foot. "How bad does it look?"

"Better. I cleaned up the cuts and put antibiotic ointment on them."

"Thanks. What happened last night?"

"All six hostiles who engaged with us are connected to the Diablo cartel. No sign of Chavez though."

"Do you think their goal was to take me?"

"Yes, whoever is messing with you, whether it be the stalker or Chavez, is done playing."

Determination shot through her eyes. "Tell me everything."

"Ryan saw a van pull into the cul-de-sac at the same time of the explosion, which was my truck blowing up. I really liked that truck. My favorite shotgun was in there."

"Thank God you left your cowboy hat at my parents' house. Its demise would be a tragedy."

"Cause I'm sexy in it, right?" He grinned, remembering her comment about how she admired how he could go from hardened warrior to charming country boy in less than a second. If acting like a bigheaded cowboy made her laugh, he'd boast about himself all day.

"Too sexy for your own damn good and arrogant as hell." She sighed as his hands slid up her ankle and massaged the bottom of her calf. "Keep talking about what happened, and don't stop what you're doing to my leg."

"Yes, ma'am." He'd do anything to coax that soft sigh from her again. "All six hostiles are dead, a couple of them by your gun. How do you feel about that?"

"I've been training to defend myself for two years. I've always wondered if it was enough to save myself in a real situation. Now I know, and it's oddly comforting, yet I'm horrified. Does that make sense?"

"Perfect sense."

She bit her lip. "What does it say about me?"

And there it was. The doubt. "I'm no therapist, but I think it says you're a survivor. If you didn't doubt what defending your life in exchange for another's did to you, then you wouldn't be human."

She pulled her leg from his hands and tucked it underneath her. Leaning back into the cushions of the oversized couch, she studied him. "Are you human? Because what I witnessed last night was not of this world." She shifted her knees and sat up straighter. "Christ, Kane, you didn't have a gun. Those cartel guys fell and didn't get back up. And you did nothing but stand there…but you didn't just stand there. You looked surreal, like some sort of godlike warrior blessed by the heavens and created in hell."

"So you think I'm a god?"

"Nice try to distract me with humor, but it won't work this time."

No, it wouldn't, but he couldn't share the full extent of what he was capable of. If she got captured by Chavez and they questioned what her Project VIPER boyfriend could do…

He squeezed his fingers into fists. "The less you know, the better. Trust me."

"I do trust you. You put your life before mine last night —twice—and didn't die. That's a first."

"So you trust me to keep you alive, but you don't trust me not to die?"

She waved a finger. "Oh no you don't. This isn't about me. We're talking about the superpowers you joke about. But are you really joking? Did Scarlett really make you into a cyborg or something?" She shook her head. "God, that sounds as crazy as me being a black widow, but I know what I saw. How is it possible to kill a man without moving an inch?"

And he regretted killing all of them. He should have left one of the bastards alive to interrogate. But mercy, even for the benefit of the greater good, hadn't been on his mind. Pure anger, fueled by what he'd seen them do to Jenna and what he knew they would do to Beth, fueled the intensity of his V-Strikes.

Beth stared at him, her breath puffing in short pants. "And I know those men didn't drop dead because their heart stopped beating at the sight of you looking so beautifully deadly."

His mind stuck on the beautiful part. Only somebody as beautiful as Beth would see that in his lethal body. Right now, he'd die if he didn't show her how heavenly things could be between them.

No regrets.

He didn't want not taking a chance to be the biggest, beautiful regret of his life. Now he knew what Scarlett meant when she'd said fight for her. Fighting for Beth's life had been easy. Fighting for her to believe she wasn't cursed was the real battle.

"I wish I could tell you about what I did last night and at the liquor store, but—"

Realization lit her eyes. "You used your cyborg voodoo magic to take down the hoodie guys too? I knew something was off."

If she was being sarcastic, he'd laugh his ass off at "cyborg voodoo magic," but she was serious. Short of seeing the V-Strikes stream from his leg, she'd witnessed him at his deadliest. His need to tell her the truth burned his insides. Maybe if she knew how much power flowed through his body, she wouldn't be afraid he would die. Then again, maybe if she knew the perilous situations he faced because he'd been created to have that power, she'd be even more scared.

He opened his mouth to say that if he told her the truth,

he'd have to kill her, but shut it. She didn't need flippant. She needed honesty, and he wouldn't lie to her. "I killed those men with my, uh, technology."

"But you didn't kill the ones in the liquor store."

"No, they weren't trained mercenaries like Chavez's men." He sat back on his heels. "They were stupid kids."

"How did you kill the mercenaries?"

"It's classified."

She leaned forward. "Well, declassify it."

"I don't have that authority." His leg jittered, egging him to appease her curiosity.

"I bet Edgar does. He has the clout to make things happen fast 'cause he's the admiral."

"It's not that easy. I don't even know if he can authorize that."

She grabbed his wrist. "Use this fancy watch and call him. Or phone home to headquarters or whatever the hell lingo you use. Or maybe write a letter to Santa. It's Christmas Eve, for Christ's sake. I deserve a present after all I've been through. You told me back at my townhome that I'm part of the VIPER family since Scarlett is my bestie, but I'm not. I'm treated like the weird out-of-town cousin who's staying for a week and has to follow everyone else's schedule." She looked around the sparse living space. "And would it kill VIPER to at least put a Christmas tree somewhere? There is nothing festive about white walls and worn furniture."

Desire spread in his core. God, she was gorgeous when she was worked up. "You're right. You do deserve a present, but I can't give you that." He'd be asking Edgar for permission to reveal not just his secrets but the team's as well.

She crossed her arms over her chest. "It's only fair that you tell me your secrets since I told you mine."

He'd gladly share if he could, but his superpowers weren't the only secret he was keeping. Sometime during this conversation, everything he'd been questioning about his relationship beliefs boiled down to one truth. If Beth knew they both feared his demise, but for different reasons, she'd never let go of her black widow belief.

He touched her leg and rubbed a slow circle above the cut he'd bandaged last night. "I can't share that one. Pick something else you want to know."

TWENTY-SEVEN

Beth blurted the most logical response she could think of. "Take your pants off."

Kane's eyes grew three sizes too big. "What?"

"Take them off. If you can't tell me what that super leg does, you can at least show it to me." She licked her lips, her mouth salivating as she reached for his belt.

He brushed her hands away. "Not so fast, darlin'. I'm all for show-and-tell, but we have a little something to discuss first. You never told me what gives you nightmares."

She pouted and reached for his belt again. "I not only told you what gives me nightmares. I showed you."

He gathered her hands in his and sat next to her. With a tug, he forced her to angle her body toward his. "Yes, and I appreciate how hard that must have been for you, but there's new information I've uncovered that you're holding back. I need specifics."

"Oh, I'll be specific." She dropped her gaze to the zipper of his jeans and zeroed in on the other sizable reason she needed him to take off his pants. "Get naked. Now."

His nostrils flared. The unabashed desire in his eyes made her belly flip.

"You have two seconds to tell me, sugarplum, or else."

She remembered his threat about what he'd do if she didn't tell him about her dreams. As she opened her mouth to protest, he wrapped his arms around her waist and threw her over his shoulder. Standing as if she weighed nothing, he strode into the bedroom with one hand on her backside and the other wrapped around her kicking legs.

She pounded his back. "Put me down, you big brute."

"Not a chance, sugarplum."

In another swift motion she had no time to counter, he sat at the foot of the bed and pulled her across his lap. Her T-shirt rode up to her waist. "Kane," she shrieked as his hand landed on her bare ass. The blow wasn't hard, but the sting and the razor-sharp desire between her legs stunned her. "You cocky bastard of a cowboy. I'm going to—."

Pleasure zapped through her core as his hand covered the area he'd struck and massaged the sensitive flesh. Sweet Christmas, even when he spanked a woman, he had two sides. Holy Christ, did she crave both.

He lowered his mouth to her ear, his broad chest covering her back and held her in place. She should have felt vulnerable, and she did, but in the most delicious way. Her fantasies of being in this position with Kane didn't come close to the thrilling reality of being at his mercy.

Every nerve in her already charged body heightened as he slipped his finger under the strap of her thong and pulled the material against her clit. A guttural moan grated from her throat as she ground her pussy against his leg and sought more delicious friction.

"Keep moaning like that for me, sugarplum." He delivered another smack to her ass cheek.

Desire soaked her panties as she obeyed.

Wrapping his hand in her hair, he guided her gaze to his. "You look at me when I make you moan, remember?"

"Stop acting like a Neanderthal and maybe I will." She arched her back, her hair still in his hand, delicious prickles in her scalp. Her ass stung from his blows as the ache between her legs escalated to maddening heights.

"Answer my question, and I'll give you plenty more reasons to moan my name."

"I didn't moan your name, you egotistical…" He grazed her clit with his finger. "Kane."

"I don't know, sugarplum. That sweet sound you made sounded familiar."

He landed another smack to her heated backside. His other hand slipped between her legs. "God, you're wet, Beth. Tell me what I need to know so I can fuck you already." He shifted her to straddle his thighs and face him. "Is that what you want? For me to take you, because right or wrong, smart or stupid, God knows that's what we both need."

Falling for him was the last thing either of them needed, but the past and the future didn't exist. Only Kane, the damning, delicious ache in her core and his long hard cock straining against his jeans, mattered in the moment. Death could bust through the window and demand number four, but he'd have to wait until she was done experiencing every-thing the super soldier underneath her could offer.

She tried to grind against his cock, to seek what she'd spit in the devil's face for, but Kane held her firmly around the waist.

"I hate you," she groaned.

"No, you don't, and that's the problem. Tell me what you dreamed about last night. And in the car yesterday. My new intel is based on what you said while I watched you sleep, and I need to know if it's accurate."

"You watched me sleep again?" That should creep her

out. Instead, it turned her on. What was wrong with her? "If I tell you about my bad dreams, will you take your pants off and show me your leg?"

"I'll show you anything you want. Better yet, I'll let you touch." He ran his finger under the hem of her shirt and grazed the underside of her breasts. "And taste," he said as he pulled her to him and pressed a kiss to the hollow of her throat. "I'll stand in the middle of the room like the god you think I am and let you worship every part of my body all fucking day."

Helpless in the most frightening, thrilling way possible, she took his face in her hands and met his gaze. "I dreamed about a headstone in the graveyard." She panted. "With your name on it."

She tried to look away, tried to hide the catastrophic glint burning her eyes, but he cradled her chin in his hand.

"Jesus, Beth. Do I mean that much to you?"

Nodding because she feared speaking her affirmation, she bit her lip. The incredulity, not the judgment in his voice, spurred her to continue. "When I dream, I can't fight seeing the others, and now you, six feet under."

He shifted her hips so her pussy ground against his hard cock. "Feel that? I'm very much alive."

Damn, was he ever. She moved against him as a groan, half laced with trepidation about voicing her fears but brimming with the anticipation of claiming her reward, mewled from her mouth. Her gaze locked with his. In its warm blue depths stirred life and fire, desire and determination, and so much spark she melted. Those three headstones in that graveyard were the embodiment of everything that had been taken away from her by the curse. Or fate. Or plain bad luck. But Kane hadn't just thwarted the doomed destiny she'd been afraid to sentence him to. He'd kicked it to hell with his steel.

He was here, hot and hard and oh so beautiful.

Scarlett's advice yelled in her mind like a cheerleader. *Challenge the theory.*

She pressed her hand to her chest to squash her anxiety. She could do this. Could put her scientific brain into action and analyze the hardest quandary she'd ever faced, but to challenge the theory, she needed data. She slid off Kane's lap and stood at the foot of the bed.

He held on to her. "Don't hide from me."

"I'm not. I'm collecting information." She crossed her arms over her chest. Her feet ached, but the questions bursting inside her heart stole the attention. "Do you love me?"

Kane's head jerked as if she'd slapped him. "What?"

"Do you love me? I don't love you." With each breath, she ignored the voice in her head calling out her lie. Instead, she savored the molten desire flowing through her body like feral electricity. "I like you a hell of a lot and care about your well-being. And it's no secret I want you." She sucked in a deep breath and released it slowly. "I can't believe how much I want you. How do you feel about me?"

She held her breath as a myriad of emotions whizzed across his face so quickly she couldn't discern them.

He stood and mirrored her pose. "I feel the same."

"Good." She ignored her heart that begged for a different answer and noted the way he hadn't looked her in the eye when he'd given it, but he said what she'd needed to hear. "Then we've established we don't love each other." She walked a few steps, but pacing hurt too much, so she sat down on the side of the bed.

A vein throbbed in his corded throat. "Where are you going with this?"

As close as she could get to the glorious soldier if she could challenge the theory successfully. "Just listen. It's your job to protect me. You're not doing it because we're in love or because we're in a committed relationship. You were ordered by Edgar to accompany me home and act like my boyfriend because of a threat to a groundbreaking drug I've been working on, correct?"

"Yes, but I would have helped you even if Edgar didn't order me to. You're Scarlett's friend. *We're* friends and where I come from, friends help each other out."

Oh, she wanted to be very friendly with him right now on a biblical level, but she wasn't done with her research. "Yes, but you wouldn't be here if Chavez wasn't thrown into the mix. So let's look at the facts."

He eyed her bare legs. "Why am I looking at facts when there're plenty of other things I'd like to be looking at about now?"

"Because Scarlett told me I should challenge my theory about why the men I date wind up in the cemetery. That's what I'm doing. Collecting data before I draw a conclusion and then act on it."

Kane grinned. "Scarlett is one of the smartest people I know. You should listen to her." He rose and stood before Beth. "And you're equally smart, so take your friend's advice and listen to facts, not gossip."

She nodded. "Fact number one. I was in love with the others, and they said they loved me, but we …" She waved her finger in a circle between them as if she held magic to make what she was about to say true. "We aren't in love."

Well, at least he wasn't in love. Now wasn't the time to address her feelings she needed to deny.

"Nope." A mischievous smile tilted his lips. "No love here. Just simple lust. In fact…" He tapped his chin with his finger. "Sometimes you're more stubborn than my mule back home."

His dimpled grin strained her urge to bypass her haphazard scientific method and jump right to the conclusion. "Fact number two. The others were all from my hometown. You're from West Virginia."

He tipped an imaginary cowboy hat. "I'm an honest-to-goodness hillbilly."

A bona fide hottie was more accurate. "Fact number three. The others died trying to protect me, but it wasn't their job."

"I've been meaning to talk to Edgar about bonus pay for having to work during Christmas."

"Fact number four. The others were ordinary guys who weren't trained to defend themselves in a fight. You're a super soldier."

"All good arguments, Dr. Parker. I think there's only one conclusion we can draw based on the information at hand."

She pulled in a deep breath and silenced doubt and the truth she couldn't admit. "I think we can say with relative confidence the data suggests that you're safe from my curse. Let's do this before I analyze it with a clear mind and change my conclusion."

"Are you saying I drive you to distraction?" He snuck his hand under her T-shirt.

"You know you do. I think…" She sucked in a breath as his fingers grazed the top of her panties. "I'm clearly not thinking straight, but I believe you're safe for now. Fuck me before something changes."

TWENTY-EIGHT

or now?

Did that mean before her arguments fell apart? There were only two that could unravel. That he was doing this because she was a job, which was most certainly not the case, but he wasn't about to tell her that, and that they didn't love each other. Did she plan on falling in love with him? That idea didn't work with his serve first, love later life strategy, but since they'd met, that plan had been sliding like an avalanche, stone by stone.

Her hungry gaze zeroed in on his waist. "Take your jeans off so I can see what makes you so super."

Stepping back, he pulled off his T-shirt and tossed it behind him. Her salacious grin, devoid of the soul-deep trepidation he'd seen earlier, curled his lips up so high they hurt. "I've never shown my leg to any woman."

She slowly shook her head. "I don't believe for a minute that you've been celibate for over a year."

"I didn't say that. Since I've gotten this…" He brushed his hand down his thigh. She wasn't the first who wanted to see his steel, but she was the first he wanted to share his scars and his enhancement with. Until he'd met Beth, he'd never wanted to impart what he'd tragically lost and miraculously gained. Didn't want to answer painful questions, and he'd never wanted to scare anyone. He thought his deadly super leg was cool as all hell but feared everyone might not have the same opinion. "Well, let's just say I've gotten the job done in the dark with my pants down but not off."

The gold flecks in her eyes blazed like the fire burning deep in his core.

"The lights are still on, cowboy. Are you okay with performing in these conditions?"

He flicked open the snap on his jeans. His cock cheered at the imminent action. His mind balked at the lies he told to finally commence it. "It's my mission to make sure any service I provide you is satisfactory." He edged the zipper down tooth by tooth. "And I mean in every, every way."

She licked her lips. "I appreciate a man who can get a job done thoroughly."

"You have no idea how thoroughly." He hooked his fingers into the waistband of his pants and smirked. The muscles in his abs coiled in anticipation. "But I'm about to show you."

"Please."

"Nervous, sugarplum?"

"No."

Her husky denial skated across his skin and bit into his eager cock. "Impatient? Excited, perhaps?"

With a hard yank on her hair, she dragged her palms down her breasts, her belly to her thighs, her thumbs pressing inward to the sweet bundle of nerves he couldn't wait to play with again.

"For the love of God, Kane, just give me all of you."

Slowly, he pushed his jeans past his hips, ready to give her everything. "I'm all yours, sugarplum. Come and get me."

"Dear Lord." Air, words, and any and all sounds paused in Beth's lungs. Kane, in all his super glory, was that beautiful. That breathtaking.

The sleek, black prostheses with an inlaid hexagonal pattern melded to his hip in an oddly foreign yet perfectly natural union of science and nature. The curves, the lean muscle size, even the perfect human shape right down to his toes that contracted into the carpet were an anatomical carbon copy of his flesh-and-bone leg.

Holding her breath, as if he might vanish if she touched him, she reached out and touched the spot where man met machine.

He hissed her name.

She smiled but didn't look up, too mesmerized by the feel of the corded skin under her fingertips. A hexagonal pattern-shaped tattoo camouflaged the scarring. The beautiful artwork seemed to bleed from the unyielding steel and into his sensitive flesh.

Slowly, she traced the ink. With each hard ridge under her fingers, her heart broke from what he'd been through. As he pursed his full lips as if granting her time to explore the gift of his body took a monumental effort, she marveled at what Project VIPER had created. Kane wasn't just a super soldier. He wasn't just a scientific and technological miracle. He'd been transformed into a glorious creature with unnatural, deadly secrets only a select few knew about.

And he'd trusted her, chosen her, to share the part he kept under wraps.

He sucked air through his teeth as she pressed her lips to the thickest of the scarring.

"Does this thing come with a user's manual?" The scientist in her wanted to know how it worked. The woman in her wanted to feel it pressed against her body, pinning her in place while he used his voodoo magic to fuck the curse out of her mind and into a dark abyss.

"I'm an experiment in progress."

Thank God VIPER had chosen him to be a subject. No, not a subject. A survivor. A real-life action hero brought back to life.

My hero.

She pulled her hands away. The warrior who stood before her was so mesmerizing, so surreal, she feared losing herself in his wondrous immensity. Like whatever powers he'd used last night to take down the bad guys would burn her if she got too close, leaving a mark, changing her forever.

But knowing him had already changed her. "You're incredible."

He didn't answer, but a proud, not arrogant look, like he was still in awe of himself, crossed his features. Her gaze fixed on his erect cock. She licked her lips as she stared at his hot-blooded appendage that looked as super as his leg. "Did VIPER enhance that too?"

His dimples framed his cocky-as-hell smile.

"That's one-hundred-percent me, darlin'. And yes, I know how to use it. No manual needed, but hands-on exploration is encouraged." He grabbed her wrist and placed her palm against his leg where skin met steel. "You can start here and work your way to the center."

Scooting off the bed, she fell to her knees in front of him. "It's so smooth." She glided her hand from his hip to his thigh in a slow, hard stroke, surprised she couldn't feel the hexagonal pattern under her fingers. "Can you feel that?"

"Yes. Not like I can feel you on the rest of my body, but yes."

She continued her exploration lower and lightly pressed her fingers into the back of his knee. His joint flexed in response. "That's amazing. Does it hurt? Not when I touch you. I mean, does it still hurt from the trauma and the surgeries? I know you said the aches come and go, but does it hurt after diving to the ground with me in your arms?"

And not even the reminder that she needed protecting—and that he could die doing it—could stop her from discovering the wonders of this magnificent man. She rose on her knees and explored her way back up his leg.

"No, it doesn't hurt." He shifted his hip slightly. "But something in that vicinity aches."

She ignored his not-so-subtle hint and her own body's response to kneeling before this godlike man and thoroughly explored the inked seam where metal met flesh. "The work on this tattoo is incredible."

His body jerked under her touch. "We all have them to cover the scarring."

She pressed her fingers deeper into the pattern. "It's beautiful, tragic, and scary all at the same time. How can that be?"

"Like you, sugarplum. Beautiful and tragic."

She looked up at him. "And scary?"

He brushed hair out of her eyes. "When you order me around? That's scary sexy."

She blinked away sudden tears. "This puts you at an even greater risk of dying."

"Ain't going to happen anytime soon." He wiped her worry away with his thumb. "I gave the Grim Reaper the finger last time and he's too afraid to come back for more. If anything, it makes me more likely to survive. Some black widow curse made up by a bunch of gossips is no match for me. I'm not going anywhere but deep inside your tight, sweet body, understand?"

He didn't give her time to answer. Grabbing her shoulders, he pulled her flush against him and slammed his mouth to hers.

She stroked his steel thigh with one hand and palmed his thick length that felt just as hard with the other. "I'm so thankful God spared this."

"So fucking thankful," he murmured into her mouth as he wrapped his hand around the nape of her neck and deepened the kiss.

In a clash of teeth and tongues amid a litany of pleas and moans, he kissed her as if she were the key to his survival. With one hand on his leg, the other on his cock, she reveled in the contrast of smooth steel and silky skin, both with a core of unyielding strength.

Shifting her hand to the base of his erection, she squeezed. His animalistic hiss snaked through her veins. The intense hunger in that incoherent sound rocketed excitement through her blood and fear in her heart. She wanted his cock so deep inside her they'd become merged like his steel and flesh, but falling for him had the potential to destroy her.

Without breaking the kiss, he yanked her panties down. "Are you on birth control?"

"Yes. And I had a physical last month. I'm clean. And I haven't been with anyone since I met you."

"Same here." He shifted his hand between their bodies and slid his fingers against her wet clit. "Is the reason you haven't been with anyone else because you've been thinking about me?"

She didn't answer. Instead, she pulled his lip between her teeth and wiggled her hips closer to his hand.

He bit the shell of her ear. "Answer me."

"Yes." As he slipped a finger in her tight pussy and crooked it against her slick walls, all thoughts other than the pleasure Kane could incite fled. "Do it. Now, please."

"The sound of you begging might be my favorite Christmas carol, sugarplum." He added a second digit and danced them inside of her.

"I wasn't begging." She panted. "That was an order."

"There's that scary, sexy side I was talking about. Wrap your legs around my waist."

Hooking his hands under her knees, he picked her up and carried her to the bed. "Ready for your Christmas present?"

He laid her down and eased inside her before she could respond. Stars rioted in her head as he stretched her to the point of pain. She panted as her body adjusted to the welcome intrusion that quickly spiraled into hot pleasure. Grasping his shoulder, she dug her fingers into his skin. Her other hand clasped warm, smooth steel at his hip.

He pulled his hips back, his cock still teasing, his arms securely around her.

She held him tighter. "Kane."

"I've got you, sugarplum."

"I know." She'd never felt more secure in her life, but she was falling anyway and powerless to stop the plunge. "More, Kane. Give me all of you." There was still space between their bodies. She wanted nothing between them.

No curse.

No secrets.

Not even air.

He pressed his mouth to hers, the tip of his cock hovering just inside her pussy. "Ready for me?"

She pressed her heels into his hard ass. Biting his lower

lip, she groaned into his mouth. "Show me those superpowers, soldier."

The bed shook as he slammed into her. Her savage scream and his primordial grunt echoed in her brain as he covered her with his body and filled her completely.

He stilled. "You okay?"

"Yeah." She shifted her hands to his ass cheeks and squeezed.

He took the blatant hint. The slap of flesh on flesh on one side and flesh on steel on the other filled the small room as he set a punishing rhythm. He never pulled out completely, as if he couldn't bear to lose this intimate, erotic contact as he played her pussy like it was a fiddle and his cock was the bow.

And damn, did they make wild, beautiful music together.

Helpless, she clung to him and savored each stroke, each curse from his lips. As he raised his head, she relished the vicious need in his eyes.

For two years, she'd felt out of control. But pinned under his unyielding body, unable to move except to hold on tight and whimper his name as her orgasm built and built, she'd never felt more in charge of her life.

Her choices.

Her heart.

In this moment, there were no doubts. No curses. Just her and her super soldier, and damn if he didn't live up to her lofty expectations.

He snuck his hand between them and squeezed her clit. "Come for me, sugarplum."

At his command, her orgasm spiraled into a twister. She whimpered his name. Another squeeze, another reminder he controlled her pleasure, and she burst into a million glowing pieces. His name ripped from her lips. A desperate plea for him to come with her followed so they could experience the supernatural together.

She rode out her orgasm and held on like he'd disappear if she let go. As he reached the pinnacle with an unearthly roar, she couldn't stop the words strangling her heart from leaving her lips.

"Don't you dare die on me, Kane."

TWENTY-NINE

Kane listened for Beth's breaths to settle into a steady rhythm before he left the room. He wasn't in the habit of lying, but he'd lied to the woman who trusted him with her body, with her deepest secret. He couldn't address the untruths now. Stirring up that cluster-fuck of emotions was as volatile as the threats against her life.

She'd said she didn't love him. He'd lied his ass off when he said he didn't love her. Hell, he wasn't even sure if this terrifying, free-falling feeling qualified as love, but it was damn scary. He'd spent time on a Navy ship, but all that time at sea didn't teach him to navigate the uncharted waters he'd lost himself in since he'd met Dr. Beth Parker.

He checked his comms unit as he pulled himself out of bed and away from the temptation to bury his face between her legs and wake her up with another orgasm, and then fall asleep again with her tucked safely in his arms. Nic was still outside watching the front of the house and Linc was moni-toring the perimeter in the back. He checked in with both. Assured all was secure, he quickly dressed and quietly made his way into the living room. His phone flashed next to his laptop with an incoming call from Gran. "Merry almost Christmas Eve. Having fun?"

"Yes. Did you and Beth set a wedding date yet?"

So much for not thinking about his feelings for the sugarplum in the bedroom.

"Gran, I barely know her." But he knew she loved Christmas. Supported her hometown, shared her love of science with kids, and was committed to saving lives. Enjoyed living in DC. Liked to be in charge because it made her feel in control. Believed she was a black widow but didn't want to. That she was afraid to fall for him.

"I knew your grandfather for only a few days before we got married. And your mother and your father got hitched after a few weeks. I could tell your mother was the one for my son the first moment I met her, just like I know Beth is the one for you. Stop being a pussy and make that girl your wife."

"Gran, we really need to have a conversation about your word choices."

"Oh, please. You should hear the gals at bingo when their number isn't called. And never mind when the announcer says '*O* sixty-nine.'"

He put his hand over his ear. "Jeez, Gran. I don't want to hear that. Do you even know what it means?" Thinking about Gran and her friends talking about oral sex certainly did the trick of halting his libido to a grinding stop.

Gran giggled. "Of course. Do you need me to explain it to you?"

Fuck no. "I'm good. How's Livvie?"

"You know how your sister is. She rushes in without thinking, but she'll figure out soon this guy isn't the one for her."

And then she'll be devastated and swear to never fall in

love again. *Until the next time.* He hoped the next guy Livvie brought home had Gran's stamp of approval.

Wait, was he buying into Gran's sixth sense nonsense? It had to be nonsense. Right? But what he felt for Beth, what he swore he wouldn't feel until years from now when he retired and death wasn't a constant shadow, felt…divine.

"Gran, how do you know two people are meant for each other?" He couldn't believe he was asking, especially since his mission was to make Beth understand that curses from a higher power didn't exist. But did a sixth sense come from a higher power, or was it really something inherent in Gran? He didn't think *his* instincts were nonsense. Trusting his hunches about danger kept him alive. Who was he to say Gran's didn't hold value?

"I don't really know. I just do. It's a feeling. Like I can sense a strong magnet pulling two people together."

Kane nodded. Even before he'd witnessed Beth's nightmare on their not-quite date, he'd sensed she was afraid of something. "Tell me more, Gran."

"Well, the best example is when I met your mother for the first time. The charge I felt stole my breath when she walked into my house holding your father's hand."

Kane asked the questions he'd been avoiding for years. "But if they were so in love, why did she…"

"Give up? She didn't give up. She fought as hard as she could."

Fighting didn't entail missing his and Livvie's graduation ceremony because she was too drunk to drive or sleeping so much she couldn't stay awake to tell them good night. "But she checked out, Gran. Dad died and she couldn't live without him."

"She checked out and I allowed it because she needed to for a while. My way of dealing with my son's death was to lose myself in you and Livvie. Everyone deals with loss differently. Your mom needed time to sit with it, to feel and absorb and process while I pushed through. It wasn't until you and Livvie went to college that I allowed myself to fully grieve."

A thick lump clogged his throat. He'd dove headfirst into campus life to combat his grief and never realized how much he'd missed at home. "I'm so sorry you went through that by yourself."

"Don't be. It's what I had to do. What I'd already been through when your grandfather died. You were deployed and didn't see how hard I took his death. It was months before I could bring myself to get behind the wheel of the Buick."

"Gran, I…"

"It's okay. I'm proud of you for following your dreams, but you need to know this. After you and Livvie left for college, your mom started making progress with her grief. She'd gone to a support group and met a few friends. Had talked to me about going to AA. The night she was killed, she'd met her new girlfriends at a bar for someone's birthday. I was so proud of her for going out. And yes, she had been drinking, but she hadn't been driving."

"I remember her mentioning grief counseling, but I didn't know she was thinking about going to AA." That took strength and courage he admired. He kicked himself for not recognizing it. "I just thought she hung around the house all day in Dad's old sweatshirts."

He pictured Beth in his T-shirt. Would she wear it when he was away, waiting for him to come home alive? The belief he'd held on to for so long—serve first, love later—crept back in at the bittersweet idea.

"Kane, honey, I know your mom wasn't fully present after your dad was killed, but she tried her best, and she would have gotten there. When we talked about AA, she was so excited for you and Livvie to come home from college during Christmas break to their old mom."

Thinking about coming home for the holidays to the mom he remembered before she lost herself to grief stung Kane's eyes with hot tears. Instead, he'd come home during Halloween for her funeral. "I don't know if I can do that to Beth, Gran. How can I let her fall in love with me and leave her behind if I die? What if she winds up like Mom?"

"It's not up to you who she falls in love with." Gran's tone hardened to the one she used to reprimand him as a kid for not minding his manners. "I know the kind of life you choose to live. Your mother and I both knew the risks when we fell in love with military men. Beth is a smart woman. She knows the risks too. But if you ignore what's happening between the two of you, there's a risk of regretting not living every moment you've been granted on this earth together. Understand?"

"Yeah." He understood that Beth, Scarlett, and now Gran were the three smartest people he knew. "Beth has this irrational idea that she's cursed, and I don't know what to do about it." He didn't wait for Gran to ask why. Instead, he spilled the whole story in one breath.

"Sounds like her fears are as irrational as yours."

A call from Scarlett stopped him from agreeing. With a quick goodbye and a promise to send Beth's number to Gran so she could wish her a Merry Christmas, he switched to Scarlett. "What's up?"

"How's Beth? Is she alright? I figured you two might be sleeping after the night you had and didn't want to call, but I've been so worried even though I was assured you were both okay."

"Your bestie is fine. She was awake earlier, but she fell back to sleep." *After I fucked her into sweet oblivion.* "You did a great job of teaching her to shoot, by the way. She did well with the gun last night."

"She's a natural."

"That she is. Did you have a conversation with Henry yet about his connection to Evangeline?"

"I was about to call you. Henry is meeting with his lawyer in a few minutes. Edgar is about to send me a link so I can have a video chat with him about Evangeline. I thought you might like to join."

"Hell yeah." He also wanted to wring Henry's fat neck, but glaring at him would have to do.

"Hold on. I'll send you the link. We have five minutes with him."

Scarlett came on the line, looking professional as always in a red blouse and her blonde hair pulled back in a sleek ponytail. A radiant bride-to-be smile lit her face. Her happiness would piss Henry off.

After a few minutes of going through security channels, Henry appeared on the screen. The polished man who'd graced covers of business magazines for decades looked like hell in a cheap gray jumpsuit that matched his thinning hair.

Henry smiled. "Scarlett, I knew you'd call to wish me a Merry Christmas. And you brought one of your VIPER pets. How nice."

Kane gave Scarlett credit for not telling him to fuck off. He, however, didn't have such restraint. "Hope you're enjoying the first of many incarcerated holidays."

Henry's cheeks turned as crimson as Scarlett's blouse.

Kane savored the reaction. "Do you remember Scarlett's friend, Evangeline Martin?"

"Hmm, let me think." Henry tapped his finger on his cheek. "Oh yes, I met her at the party I threw when I was named Washington, DC's Businessman of the Year." He turned to his lawyer sitting next to him. "Did you hear what

I just said? Businessman of the year and they have me locked up. Can you believe that?"

The lawyer didn't answer.

Scarlett smiled into the camera. "Please answer Kane's question, Henry."

Henry smirked back. "Look at you, thinking you can order me around now. Nothing's changed, girl. I'm still your family."

Scarlett just smiled wider. "No, you're not."

Kane bit back his own grin. No wonder Beth and Scarlett were best friends. They both had backbones of steel. "Answer the question."

Henry sat up straighter in his seat and puffed out his chest. "Evangeline was looking for my expertise on a cybersecurity project she needed help with. She seemed like a good kid who respected her elders, not loud and obnoxious like Beth or ungrateful for my assistance, like some people I know." He shot Scarlett a glare. "So I decided to grant her my advice."

Grant? Damn, the guy thought he was still the king, even behind bars. Kane slid to the edge of the chair. "What kind of advice?"

He steepled his hands under his chin. "All I remember is that she needed an advantage. I put her in touch with someone who could help her."

Kane muffled a curse. "Who?" The last thing they needed was more players in this game.

"You expect me to remember insignificant details like that? She must have appreciated what I did, though, because a few months later, she asked for my assistance again."

"And you got her a job in the Middle East." Kane leaned closer to the screen. "She's back in town and has been trying to reach you. Do you know why?"

Henry sat back in his chair and laughed. "She probably

wants my help again. Even though I'm locked up, I still have connections with important people."

A loud beep sounded from inside the interview room. "Time's up, Miss Kerrigan." A second later, the screen went dark.

"Fucking dead end," Kane muttered as he shot Scarlett an email asking her to find out who Henry had referred Evangeline to. As he shut the laptop and rose from the table, a mind comms alert sounded in his brain. Hurrying to the window, he pushed the shade aside and scanned the street for a threat much bigger than the vapid blonde who treated Beth like a pariah.

"Someone's driving around the block too many times," Nic said. *"Video feed is coming to your comms now."*

Kane looked at his wrist. A black sedan passed the house too slowly for his comfort. *"If it comes around again, stop it."*

"That's the plan."

The bedroom door opened behind Kane. He didn't turn to Beth. "Get back in there."

"Has something happened?"

He ignored the alarm in her voice as he activated himself into phase two. "Someone's circling the house. It's probably nothing." But the hair on the back of his neck rose, and it wasn't from the sting of activation. "Grab my gun from the table, then stick by the bedroom doorway. Be ready to run on my order. Got it?"

Kane heard her startled agreement as she scurried to heed his instructions. Long seconds ticked by as he watched Linc casually cross the street and take cover behind an RV parked at the curb.

Beth poked her head out of the bedroom. "What's happening?"

He held up his hand to silence her as the sedan turned the corner.

"If the car slows again, we take out the tires on my command," Nic said from the SUV parked in the driveway.

"Roger that," Linc said.

As the sedan approached the house, the driver's side window rolled down. Before the dark glass lowered an inch more, all four tires blew in rapid succession. The car spun a hundred and eighty degrees. As it careened onto the lawn and into the lamppost, the screech of metal crashing into metal reverberated in the house.

Beth screamed.

"Stay here and lock the door behind you." Kane didn't wait for an answer as he slipped out the front and schooled his mind in mission mode. "Cover her," he said as he rushed past Nic and inhaled the stench of melting rubber.

Slowly, he made his way to the driver's side of the sedan. As he approached, a glint of something metallic at the top of the window flashed in the sunlight. *"Gun."*

He fired a V-Strike. The shot shattered the window into thousands of dark crystals. The glass on the passenger side suffered the same fate from Linc's barrage. Tiny shards crunched under Kane's boots as he carefully approached, his gaze trained on a figure with black hair slumped over the steering wheel.

Linc reached through the window and yanked the driver upright. Blood gushed from the busted nose of the familiar face. "Chavez?"

"Looks like him." Even though the unconscious man appeared thinner and much less menacing than in the intel files, Kane had no doubt he stared at the Diablo enforcer.

A hiss gurgled from Chavez's throat as he opened his eyes and glared at Kane. "You're a dead man. *Mi hermano* will…"

Kane didn't doubt that Chavez had plenty of mercenaries he counted as brothers who would be gunning for them.

Linc released his grip as the enforcer lost consciousness again and slumped back onto the steering wheel.

"Is that Chavez?"

Kane twisted his head. Beth stood on the stoop, his gun aimed at the sedan. Rooting his boots to the ground, he fought the urge to tackle her back into the house. "Get inside."

She stepped onto the grass, weapon still drawn as if protecting him. "Is that him? Is this over?"

"Back. In. The. House."

Nic's curse broke the silence over the mind comms. *That was too easy.*

"Agreed," Linc said.

God, Kane hoped they were fucking wrong.

THIRTY

Beth rose from her seat at the massive conference room table in VIPER headquarters and stared at the screen taking up an entire wall. Two years' worth of messages from her stalker scrolled like the closing credits of a horror flick. She looked away as the final slide showed a photo of Chavez, but not before she caught the sinister look in his dark, menacing eyes.

She wiped her hands on the black knee-length skirt Scarlett brought along with a plum-colored sweater and her tall black leather boots. A shower and her favorite clothes had settled her adrenaline after the chaos back at the safe house. Now, anxiety ran rampant through her body, threatening to stop her heart.

She looked at Ryan, who sat behind a technology console embedded in a long, sleek silver table. The setup looked as high tech as Kane's leg. "Please take that man's photo off the screen."

"Sorry." Ryan tapped his computer. The display went blank for a second before the VIPER logo appeared. "I wanted to show you the history we found on the phone inside Chavez's car. We also found a stack of photos of you inside the glove box."

She nodded as she wrapped her arms across her chest. Relief that her stalker had been finally apprehended and anger that he'd done it at all thrummed a volatile current through her body. She should be celebrating Chavez's capture, or experiencing the catharsis of closure-induced tears, but neither happened. Something she couldn't identify, more like didn't want to acknowledge, paralyzed her body and brain.

After she'd watched Chavez's car careen onto the lawn, Linc herded her to the SUV and brought her to headquarters. Once inside, she'd been escorted to a room to wait to be debriefed by Admiral Edgar. Neither Linc on the drive nor Edgar during the debriefing would explain how the tires on Chavez's car had simultaneously blown. Edgar reminded her that everything she'd witnessed was classified and assured her Chavez was in FBI custody at the hospital with a concussion.

That had been hours ago. She wasn't even sure what time it was. Midnight maybe? Was it Christmas Eve yet? Lord, she hoped not. Watching her nightmare unfold in sharp literary clarity did not make her wish list.

Neither did spending it in a sterile government facility. But Kane was in the building somewhere. Edgar assured her that Scarlett and Chris were home from their engagement-moon and at headquarters, safe and sound.

"Beth."

She whipped her head to the door. Kane stood under the VIPER logo painted above the frame dressed all in black and looking every inch a super soldier, from his long-sleeve shirt to his tactical pants to his boots. He crossed the few feet and cupped her cheeks in his large hands, his gaze assessing every nuance of her face.

The concern in his gaze, his steady, powerful touch and

his earthy smell righted her tilted world enough to take a full breath. "Please tell me it's over. Tell me Chavez's associates are being rounded up and that I'm not a target any longer." But even as the plea left her mouth, she knew the answer. She'd only known Kane a short while, but she could already read the truth in his eyes.

He wrapped his arm around her waist. Without letting her go, he pulled a chair from the conference table. "We just got word Chavez's been drifting in and out of consciousness. The FBI hasn't been able to get any information out of him yet."

"Dammit." Her stomach pitched in time with the pounding in her head. She collapsed into the chair. She'd been praying to God, Santa, and any other deity or mythical creature who might be listening for Chavez to wake up and spill the Diablos' secrets so Triple X would be safe and she could enjoy Christmas with Kane.

Without the threat of him dying trying to protect me.

She pinched her nose to suffocate the thought.

I'm not a black widow.

The name still tasted like poison on her tongue, but it didn't sicken her as much as it used to. Even though Kane had helped exorcise the curse, she didn't have the strength to fight the stubborn tendrils that lingered.

Edgar strode into the room. He stopped at the head of the table next to Ryan. "We're working under the assumption Chavez was your stalker but not the force behind snatching you to get the Triple X formula."

Beth nodded, drowning in a weird state of relief and dread, and clinging to unsubstantiated hope. "But he could be both, right?"

Kane sat next to her. "I know you want this to end, but it's not likely Chavez is behind everything. He was too easy to apprehend. We suspect he was doing a drive-by, trying to get a glance of you for his own sick perversion, and got sloppy. If he'd been acting under orders from his higher-ups to snatch you, there would have been a trained team like the one that ambushed us at the first safe house."

She jabbed her fingers into her temples. Kane made sense, but she scrambled for a better explanation. "I get it, but maybe I'm not the cartel's target. Maybe Chavez mobilized his buddies to come after me at the safe house because he's obsessed. The history on his phone proves that. Maybe this was all about me and nothing about the drug."

Edgar tugged at his mustache. "You're the only one known as the Black Widow working on the project."

"No, she isn't." Ryan shot up from his computer console so fast his chair spun. "We just got word that her colleague, Dr. Estelle Sable, has been reported missing since."

Beth jumped from her chair. "Sable is a blackish color. And Estelle is a…" The pizza she'd eaten during her debrief threatened to come back up. "She's a widow. A black widow." The panic she'd kept at bay stormed through her like a nor'easter. "You have to find her. She's in her seventies." She swallowed bile. If the Diablo cartel's tactics were half as torturous as Kane led her to believe, not only was Dr. Sable's life in danger, but so were the millions of people who could benefit from Triple X.

"Fuck." Kane looked at Ryan. "How did we miss this?" He shot his gaze back to Edgar. "And it doesn't make sense. If Sable was their target all along, why did they come after Beth?"

Beth grabbed Kane's shoulder and spun him to her. "Figure that out after you find Dr. Sable. She can't withstand torture. She's tough as nails, but…"

Edgar held his hand up. "There's a team working on it. Once we confirm a location, we'll extract her if necessary. I'll keep you posted. In the meantime, don't go anywhere by yourself until we get more information and are certain you aren't a target."

Beth knotted her fingers in front of her mouth and squeezed, but they still shook.

Kane drew her to the side of the room. "I'm sorry about your colleague. I promise I'll do everything in my power to bring her home alive."

"I know you will. That's what I'm afraid of." She kicked his bionic shin. She preferred the painful reverberation in her toes to the fear-spiked panic in her heart. "Your leg may be made of bulletproof steel, but the rest of you isn't."

THIRTY-ONE

"Come on." Kane tugged Beth out of the conference room and down a long hallway lined with paintings of military battle scenes. She had to jog beside him to keep up with his long, determined strides, but he didn't care. The only thing on his mind was making Beth believe he'd come home alive.

"Where are we going?"

He stopped at a scanner by a door at the end of the hall and peered into it. "I need to show you something." The seconds it took for the device to verify his retinal signature seemed like hours. As soon as the door opened, he tugged Beth inside and pinned her to the wall. "You want to know about the voodoo magic Scarlett and the rest of the brainiacs here at VIPER put in my body?"

"Did Edgar give you permission to tell me?"

The perk of excitement in her voice assured him that sharing his secrets wasn't just right; it was essential. Edgar had instructed him to only use his weaponry if it was a matter of life or death. Telling Beth what VIPER engineered him to be, why his chances of surviving the bloodiest, harshest, deadliest situations imaginable *were* life or death. It killed him to know she feared she'd be the cause of his demise. She needed to know that coming back to her gave him more reasons to live.

"No, I don't have permission, but I'm telling you anyway." He wasn't waiting for Edgar to sort through red tape. The worry needed to be wiped from her psyche now. He trusted her to not tell a soul about what she was about to witness. She'd kept Triple X to herself for years. He had no doubts she'd keep VIPER's secrets and no doubt his brothers would understand why he disclosed classified information. Beth wasn't just Scarlett's bestie any longer. She was part of the VIPER family because she was…

Mine.

He wasn't about to tell her that yet though. Hell, he wasn't ready to say it aloud either, but between Jenna's last words, Gran's insight into his mother and her warning about regretting not living every moment on this earth with the snarky scientist he hadn't meant to fall for, his thought didn't seem so scary.

Beth took in the four bays with paper targets at the end in the shape of bodies. "This is a shooting range."

"Yeah, it is." He picked up a pair of thick, red-tinted glasses and handed them to her. "Put these on and watch."

"Watch what?"

"You can't see what I'm about to show you unless you put the glasses on."

She opened her mouth, presumably to ask more questions, but he silenced her with a quick kiss. Against her lips, he murmured, "Just do it and watch."

Slipping into bay number two, he stared down the long stretch and focused on the target. He'd never been in the range without his brothers, but it didn't feel weird. Being here with Beth, sharing what he'd become, felt almost as intimate as making love to her.

He froze as his thoughts echoed in his brain like a gunshot.

Shit, is this what it felt like to be in love? What Chris had felt like when he'd fallen for Scarlett? Like he'd tear down any enemy that threatened the woman who had infiltrated his mind and heart so quickly, so easily, he'd been powerless to stop it. Chris had put his job on the line to protect Scarlett. Kane was about to do the same thing for Beth. If Edgar found out—no, when Edgar found out because that man knew everything that happened at headquarters—Kane would be in big trouble.

He grabbed glasses from a hook by the door and shoved them onto his face. He didn't care about the consequences. The only thing that mattered was proving his point.

And the way to do that was to blow shit up.

On that thought, he activated his weaponry and welcomed the deadly current. The pain-laced pleasure reminded him that he was alive. That being a super soldier didn't sentence him to the same fate as his father. That he hadn't lost everything that day in the desert. That he'd been granted a second chance at life—at love—and he'd been too afraid to take it.

He glanced back at Beth as he adjusted the safety glasses that allowed him to track his V-Strikes as they streamed down the corridor and found the target. Witnessing his weaponry in action always gave him a thrill, but he spun to face Beth as he thought the command to fire.

The wonder on her face, like she'd unlocked a scientific secret that could change the world, made him feel ten feet tall. Her work with Triple X *would* change the world, and he was the lucky devil who had a shot at witnessing it with her.

No regrets.

Serve first, love later.

The two camps battled in his mind as V-Strikes streamed from his leg in rapid succession, each one fueled by his drive to obliterate everyone who hurt the smart, beautiful reason a war waged in his mind. As his V-Strikes hit the target, he locked his gaze with that reason and ticked off the degenerates who had hurt her.

Chavez.

The men in black who'd infiltrated the safe house.

Judy Martin and her big-mouthed entourage.

A few seconds and a dozen V-Strikes later, he powered down his weaponry. His breath puffed in short pants, not from exertion but from what the amazement etched on Beth's pretty face did to his heart.

Catching his breath, he motioned to the speaker on the wall next to the door.

She yanked off her glasses and hit the button. "Holy shit, Kane. Are those lasers?"

He smiled at the astonishment in her voice as he pulled off his own glasses and exited the bay. "We call them V-Strikes, but they are a kind of a laser."

She stood on her toes and kissed his cheek. Her other hand covered his heart. "Based on what I just saw, you truly are a superhero."

He felt the reverence in her words deep down in his core. "Yes. I am, but I didn't bring you in here to show off." Although hearing her say it inflated his ego and his heart tenfold.

"You seem kind of excited by that display, and who could blame you? That was out-of-this-world." She pressed her palm against his chest. "No wonder your heart is racing so fast."

He gently nudged her away as excitement pounded in other places besides his heart. "As you pointed out, the only bulletproof part of me is my leg, but I need to prove to you I'm well-protected when I go into battle. A bulletproof helmet covers my head and face. Body armor covers my arms, my other leg, and torso. My neck is even protected by it. I have the fastest reaction time of any soldier out there because I don't have to pull a trigger. Scarlett engineered us to control our weaponry with our minds. I think, and a chip implanted in the back of my neck works its cyborg voodoo magic, as you call it, and the V-Strike lands where I want it to."

"Holy shit. My friend really is the biggest genius on the planet." She brushed her hand along his thigh. "I can't fathom how this is all possible. I have so many questions."

"The science behind it isn't what matters right now." He snagged her hand and pressed her palm against his steel. "This makes me a human weapon, but it's more than that. As you know, I can communicate with the team in my head. The technicians at headquarters can see me in the field and give me real-time data as an operation goes down. They monitor my vitals and if I'm incapacitated, they can shoot V-Strikes remotely from my body to keep hostiles away until help can come."

Blood slowly drained the awe from her face. "That all sounds amazing, but really, really dangerous."

"My job *is* dangerous, but VIPER has more advantages than any other fighting force out there. The chances of me surviving a mission are much higher than not."

When she didn't respond, he cupped her face between his hands. "Do you get it now? Do you understand that I'm safer than most people walking around on this planet? That if I die, it's because someone—that has nothing to do with you—went through a lot of trouble to make it happen."

"I get it. You're a marvel of modern science." She glanced toward the decimated target. "No, make that modern warfare. You're nearly invincible." She bit her lip. "And incredible."

With a tug, he pulled her flush against him. He smiled at her surprised gasp when his erection pressed into her belly. "Repeat the part about me being a marvelously incredible superhero."

"No, your ego is already too big." She grew silent as she traced the muscle of his flesh-and-bone leg through his jeans. "But then again, I'd be damn confident if I could shoot deadly lasers out of my body."

He hissed as her knuckles grazed his hard cock. "Um, there's only one thing I can shoot out of that, and if you don't stop touching it, I'm damn confident my target will be your pretty mouth."

Instead of using her tongue for a comeback, she licked her glossy lips.

The blood in his cock thrummed at the sexy as fuck sight. "Does that mean you're about to send me off on a dangerous mission with a huge smile on my face?"

Gloomy shadows veiled her bright eyes. Her gaze fell to the floor as her shoulders slumped.

Shit. Dangerous mission was the wrong thing to say.

He could see an intimate battle between facts and fear raging in her eyes. Could feel it in his soul as deeply as his own clash between *no regrets* and *serve first, love later,* raged in his head. He'd brought her here to prove he was strong and nearly invincible, and she'd believed him. Her understanding, her admiration for what VIPER had made him into hadn't only inflated his ego, they'd given an advantage to the side of the battle he wanted, no needed with every breath he took, with every beat of his heart, to be the victor.

No regrets.

The winning mantra pounded in his brain along with his

determination. "Beth, tell me that you get me. You are not a black widow."

"I know," she whispered.

The slouch of her body said she didn't. He raised her chin with his fingers. "What can I do to help you make you understand that you're not?"

"There's nothing you can do. It's me that's screwed up. I'm a woman of science who believes in a foolish curse. Or used to believe. Maybe." She pulled her lower lip between her teeth. "God, Kane, I've held on to this for so long. I can't let it go overnight."

He cupped her elbows and raised her defeated body. "Yes, you can. I let my demons go in the space of a few days."

"What demons?"

Memories rushed through his mind in bittersweet lucidity. His mom and dad slow dancing in the living room. The sobs she hid behind her bedroom door when his dad shipped out for months. Her joyous, tear-filled smile when he returned. Leave. Cry. Repeat. He'd grown up watching the cycle until it didn't repeat any longer and his mom got stuck on cry.

But Beth hadn't got stuck on cry. She hadn't gotten stuck at all except on that stupid black widow crap. If anyone was tough enough to handle the risks of being in a relationship with him, it was Beth.

Sighing, he scrubbed the stubble on his chin. "The demons I'm talking about are the ones that told me I couldn't get close to a woman until I was out of the military because I was afraid of leaving her behind." He sighed into his hand and blew out his fears like an extinguisher to a five-alarm blaze. "Afraid of abandoning my family. Thanks to grief so bad, so strong, Livvie and I lost my mom before she died." He laced his hands behind his neck and squeezed the gut-wrenching words out for good. "And then she did die, and I blamed myself for not realizing that she was alone and scared and maybe just needed someone to be strong when she couldn't."

Beth touched his cheek. "That's why you felt the need to help me, wasn't it? Because you didn't want me to go through it all alone."

He nodded as he leaned into her palm. The softness of her skin absorbed the last of his worries. "I knew the risks my father took each time he deployed, and I was proud of him for it. But the only risk my mom took was loving a man who chose a lethal career. But now I know that she understood the risks too, and even though the worst scenario broke her, it didn't break her completely. Gran set me straight about how hard she fought to build herself back up after Livvie and I left for college." He moved her hand from his cheek and laced their fingers together as the broken parts of him mended at their touch. "Now I'm fighting for you, Beth. Fight for me."

She placed their joined hands over her heart. "I'm so sorry. For you and your mom."

"I don't want your sympathy." He squeezed her hand to accept her understanding and support though. "What I want is for you to realize you deserve happiness." His voice rose along with his desperation. He couldn't admit his love until she accepted that the three gravestones in the cemetery weren't her fault. "You are not cursed." He gently shook her shoulders to drive home his point. "Not. Cursed. Understand?"

"I'm trying, but you can't be the next boyfriend I mourn, Kane." She shrugged him off and backed away. "And I get what you are saying. You are less likely to die than any other soldier out there, but my heart can't take it." She placed her hand over the beating organ. "It never pounded like this for the others. It won't just break if something happens to you. It will explode and leave me in a billion jagged pieces."

His heart sped up. "What are you saying, Beth?"

Tears welled in her eyes. "I'm saying I think I'm falling for you, but I'm scared and…"

He yanked her against him. Cupping both cheeks in his hand, he silenced her protests with a kiss. When he came up for air, two words that scared him more than any mission he'd faced but felt right burst from his lips against hers. "Marry me."

THIRTY-TWO

Beth jerked her head back. Her heart stuttered as she stared at Kane. "What?" Had she heard him right? She waited another erratic heartbeat, then another, but his lips didn't twitch into a smirk. Was he serious? "Did you just ask me to—"

The ludicrous question disintegrated on her tongue as his lips crashed to hers. The kiss, no, the onslaught, shocked her heart into overdrive.

"You heard me right, sugarplum."

His words hummed across her skin in a desperate yet firm confirmation as he kissed her so hard, so deep she didn't doubt his sincerity, but she doubted her sanity because her first instinct had been to say yes.

"Marry me, Beth. You said that you can't lose another boyfriend. Marry me and I won't be your boyfriend. I'll be your husband."

"Kane." Her breath hitched on his name. "We can't." The idea was absurd. Certifiably ridiculous, yet…

A vision of him in uniform, waiting for her at the end of

the aisle in her favorite church by the Washington Monument flashed in her mind.

She shook her head. "No. You're not making any sense."

"You know what doesn't make sense? The fact that my cock isn't between your gorgeous lips yet."

Her jaw fell open. Watching him go from hardened warrior to joking cowboy still awed her. But his one-eighty from *marry me* to *suck my cock* triggered a riot of need in the place that burned for him again.

He smirked as he caught her bottom lip between his fingers. "See what being married to me will be like? Constant one-liners."

And a constant ache to taste.

To suck.

To indulge in every part of his gloriously flawed and magnificently rebuilt body.

She reached for the button on his black pants and yanked it open, powerless to stop herself, even if she wanted to. "And what about the marriage thing? Was your proposal a one-liner too?"

"What do you think?" He pushed her hand to his erection.

She smiled at his sharp inhale. "I think you're insane." But God help her, she was just as insane as him because she dropped to her knees in the middle of the wildest conversation she'd ever had.

A low growl grated from his throat. "My proposal should make perfect sense in your mind."

The only thing that made sense was finally tasting him. Cupping the bottom of his shaft with one hand, she drew the tip into her mouth. His cock felt like his body. Satin over steel. So did his groan. Like pure, silky pleasure rasping from a rough warrior. His eyelids drooped as he wound his hand through her hair. She sucked him in a bit deeper, swirling her tongue around his rigid length and hummed against him.

"Was that an agreement, sugarplum?"

She tried to pull her mouth away to tell him no, that she couldn't marry a man she'd only known a few weeks, and for such a bizarre reason to boot, but he tightened his grip on her hair.

"Oh no, darlin'. You started this. Don't you dare stop."

Humming louder, she sucked him in deeper. Harder. Relished his taste. The blatant, desperate need in his voice. The firm grip on her hair that roused just the right amount of pain and felt like he'd never let her go. Like he'd use that fantastic body to shield her from anyone who barged through the door. Had he locked it? She didn't recall and didn't care. The whole VIPER team could shoot V-Strikes around them and she wouldn't stop digging her fingers into his muscled thigh and even harder steel.

"Fuck, Beth. Your mouth feels like…"

She raked her fingers around to his magnificent ass and squeezed. He jerked his hips. His cock hit the back of her throat. Tears danced in her eyes. She welcomed them and looked up at the breathtaking catalyst.

Brutal need smoldered in his gaze as he braced a hand on the wall behind her. "If you keep sucking me like that, I'll haul you to the closest church right now and marry you if it means I'm the lucky bastard who gets the privilege of this every night."

Every night. For the rest of their lives. Could they really be together? Could he survive her curse?

"Look at me, Beth."

She raised her gaze. The tense set of his jaw as he fought for control nearly toppled her over the blissful edge. Was that one of his superpowers? Almost making her come without even touching her? Or maybe it was making her believe they had a future and he wouldn't be number four.

He yanked her up to him. "I fit perfectly in you." Gathering the moisture on her lower lip with his thumb, he bunched up her skirt with his other hand and grazed his fingers along her wet pussy. "Perfectly. In every fucking place."

"Yes. Perfect." She ground her hips against his as she wrapped a leg around him, needing to get closer but knowing she'd never get close enough.

"This is going to be fast and hard, but I promise you when I get back from extracting Dr. Sable, I'm going to lay you out on my bed and take my slow, sweet time tasting every inch of your body."

"Promise you won't die?" She knew he couldn't promise immortality, but based on the show he'd put on, he could promise to use every advantage VIPER had enhanced him with so he'd come home alive and fulfill his decadent vow.

"I won't die." He fisted the sides of her thin lace thong. "Not even the devil is cruel enough to deny the plans I have for you." With a sharp tug, he tore her panties.

Beth gasped as the material ripped against her aroused skin. "More, Kane. Fast and hard. Now."

Hooking both hands under her ass, he raised her off the floor. "Wrap your legs around me."

She clung to his shoulders and anchored herself around his waist. "Against the wall. That's how I want you."

"Been thinking about this moment, sugarplum?"

"Yes." Her desperate admission matched the salacious grin on his face. "Have you?"

"I've been training for it my whole life." He shifted her hips with ease as if she weighed nothing and lined up his cock with her eager pussy. Staring at the impending union, leg jittering, he groaned. "Damn, Beth. See how good we are together? Tell me you feel it too."

"I do." She felt everything. His tight grip on her ass. The wall against her back, his unyielding body at her front, but instead of feeling trapped, she finally felt free in the arms of the most lethal man she'd ever met. "I do, Kane. I trust you, now fuck me."

He held still, denying her more of him. All of him. "I knew you were my kind of girl the moment I met you. Fire and snark all wrapped up in a sweet package for me to enjoy. Only me, Beth."

"Only you, Kane." She clung to the biceps she couldn't get enough of as she rocked her hips against him.

As he slid inside her, she dropped her head to his shoulder. Another rock of his hips had him fully seated within. Her head snapped up and she met his gaze. She thought he'd filled her completely at the safe house, but this angle let him hit a place so deep she knew she'd be marked forever with a new kind of curse as beautiful and unbreakable as the man claiming her.

"Only us, sugarplum." He pulled his hips back until his cock hovered at the entrance to her pussy. "No regrets, no matter what the future holds. You're mine and I'm yours. Got it?"

Hooking his hands around her knees in a grip so strong she'd have marks in the morning, he drove into her with the force of a tsunami. Her body slammed into the wall, but she didn't feel any discomfort. All she felt was the power in his promise, the strength in his conviction, and the truth in his tone.

"No regrets, Kane."

He froze, his gaze fastened to hers as if processing her words. She caught the exquisite moment the vow cemented in his heart. Those flecks in his eyes blazed like sapphires for a heartbeat before they seemed to burst into hundreds of fiery stars. She held her breath, committing the moment she made him lose control to memory as he unleashed himself like a soldier fighting for his life and rammed into her without mercy.

She lost herself in the cadence of their hips slamming into each other, her release building along with her pleas for him to fuck her harder, faster, to never stop. Every scrape of his teeth against her jawline, every guttural sound from his lips obliterated the cobwebs smothering her hope and crippling her happiness. As he splintered the last cursed bond caging her in a dark hell, her orgasm crested.

She shuddered from the internal explosion that abolished her fears and fallacies and cracked open her guarded heart. The shroud she'd been hiding behind for so long lifted to reveal Kane. Glowing like the warrior he was, willing and eager to battle the devil himself to protect not just her but their future, he roared her name on a promise she'd take to the grave.

As she rode out the ecstatic storm against his unfaltering strength, everything clicked into place. She finally understood what she'd been afraid of all along, and it hadn't been a stupid curse.

THIRTY-THREE

Flames lapped at the altar in the old church. Kane stood behind black, heavy smoke twisting around him like cobwebs. Beth called to him. Arms outstretched, fire licking the cuff of his uniform jacket, he reached for her but couldn't penetrate the thick veil.

"No." Beth shot to a sitting position and swallowed, her throat aching from roaring Kane's name in her sleep.

A gentle touch grazed her fingers. Scarlett smiled from her perch next to Beth. "Hey, it's just me."

Beth rubbed her eyes and scanned the break room Kane had carried her to last night, where she'd fallen asleep in his arms. Not a trace of the super soldier remained visible. No T-shirt tossed over the chair by the door. No boots by the bed. But she could still smell him, feel him in the depths of her body and her soul, and remember him marking her as his own.

Scarlett grasped her hand. "What were you dreaming about?"

"Nothing." Beth pulled in a gulp of air, this one not hurting as much because it tasted like the soldier who made promises last night that she believed with all her heart. Apparently, her subconscious wasn't on board yet.

Shaking off the nightmare, Beth pictured Kane illuminated in an ethereal light as he waited for her at the altar. She wasn't entirely free of the curse yet, but she'd fight it. That fantasy was a good start.

She sighed and shifted. Her muscles protested in delicious pain as she pulled her sweater over her belly. What happened to her skirt? She swung her gaze and spotted it at the bottom of the cot. "Where's Kane?"

"He's with the team planning Dr. Sable's extraction. They got intel a few minutes ago."

Beth thanked the powers that be. "Where is she?"

"I can't tell you. I shouldn't have told you that much."

"That's okay. I understand." Kane told her all she'd needed to know last night. Oh, she had plenty of questions for Scarlett about the fascinating science behind everything, but they could wait. "Thank God they found her. What if the intel isn't good? Dr. Sable had a knee replacement a few months ago. She's still walking with a cane. What if—"

Scarlett held up a hand. "Alright. I'll tell you a few more things. One, the intel about Dr. Sable's location is extremely credible. She's one whip-smart lady and I can't wait to ask her a million questions about her work. Two, she is being held locally, not in Mexico like they feared. Three, our boys will absolutely bring her home alive." She squeezed Beth's hand. "And they'll come home alive too."

"They will." Beth closed her eyes. Dr. Sable would be okay. Triple X would be safe. Kane would come back soon and...

Rapturous tingles rioted in her core as scenes from last night played in her mind. Kane pinning her against the wall. His powerful body crashing into hers as naturally as if she was an extension of him. The way the universe paused as he slammed into her. The exhilarating peace of blocking out the noise in her head so she could savor every single thrilling sensation.

Scarlett raised her eyebrows. "Did you two do that last night?"

"What?" Beth followed her friend's gaze to a hole in the wall lining up perfectly with the edge of the cot. Kane promised he'd lay her out on his bed and take his slow, sweet time with her when he got home from rescuing Dr. Sable. Their time on this cot had been anything but slow. It had been sweet on an elemental level, infused with hot, demanding hunger that left her so sated the space between floating back to sleep and her orgasm blurred. She also didn't remember the bed cracking the plaster.

She remembered the gaping crack Kane had made in her belief in her curse though.

Scarlett patted her knee. "Get up. We have a mass to get ready for. The boys didn't want us to go, but Kane begrudgingly switched to your side. He said he knew how important it was for you to go to your favorite church on Christmas Eve."

Emotion welled in Beth's throat. Yesterday she'd loathed that Edgar and Scarlett, and Kane and the VIPER boys were making decisions about her life. But yesterday she hadn't felt like part of their family. Now that she knew some of their secrets and was falling in love with the hottest of their members, she didn't mind the excessive caution.

Scarlett rose from the bed. "But there are stipulations of course, considering the situation. Gage, who is always on my tail when Chris is deployed on a mission, and Dr. Hudson Langley are coming as our protection detail. You met them both at my engagement party. There will also be a VIPER support team who will secure the building beforehand. Once we're in the church, we don't leave until the service is over, and only with Gage and Hudson."

Beth nodded. "Okay, but I feel bad that I'm making people work on Christmas Eve."

Scarlett waved her hand. "No worries. Gage's daughter has a cold and will be asleep at his sister's house by that time, Hudson's wife, Tessa, is volunteering at a soup kitchen, and the others are all single and don't have any family in town. I hear they have big plans for some party afterward."

"Good. What time is it now?"

"Almost noon. We need to eat lunch and get home so we can get ready. I know you like to get there early."

"Yup." If you didn't get a seat up front, you couldn't see the dozens of poinsettias arranged on the altar steps. And she didn't want to be stuck staring at the back of some guy's head. Some of the kids who took her science class were in the choir and she wouldn't be able to wave to them.

Something twinkling caught her eye. She craned her neck around Scarlett. A small Christmas tree sat on the table next to the door. It hadn't been there last night. She knew because that's where Kane's pants landed when she'd tossed them across the small room. "Where did that tree come from?"

Scarlett sighed and placed her hand over her heart. "Kane stole it from my office before he left. He wanted you to wake up to sparkle on Christmas Eve morning."

Beth placed her hand over her heart too. Tears stung her eyes. "That was…"

"Sweet. Did you challenge the theory?"

Beth bit her lip. "Yes."

"What was the outcome?"

"He asked me to marry him."

Scarlett's eyes bulged out of her head. "Well, I never factored in that variable."

"Me neither." *Not in a million years.*

"What did you say?" Scarlett clapped her hands together. "Please say I'm going to be a maid of honor."

"No. I told him he was ridiculous. He thinks getting married is a loophole."

Scarlett tapped her chin with her finger. "It is a damn good argument."

"No, it's not." Beth grabbed her skirt and tugged it on. "It's insane."

"No more insane than you thinking a curse is responsible for three deaths."

Beth sighed as she retrieved her boots from under the cot. "I know. I'm working on letting that go."

"Are you making progress?"

"Still gathering data." Beth glanced at the tree. "But the outcome is looking favorable."

"If there's one thing I've learned since I fell for my super soldier, it's that science and logic hold no weight when it comes to love. Maybe you'll find some divine intervention at church."

Beth huffed out "maybe" as she tugged on her boots. Neither she nor Kane had said they'd loved each other. The thought of saying those three words scared and exhilarated her, but excitement had an edge. "Any idea when the boys are expected back?"

"Hopefully in time to meet us at mass."

No, Beth wouldn't hope. She wasn't cursed. The million dazzling pieces she'd shattered into when he'd made her come last night created a mosaic of truth. She hadn't been afraid to fall in love again because she feared killing another boyfriend. She feared another loss killing *her*.

Kane will come back.

Still, she crossed her fingers for good measure.

THIRTY-FOUR

Kane's leg jittered in the passenger seat as he adjusted his bulletproof vest. "So glad we're not headed to Mexico."

"Five minutes out," Linc said from the driver's seat of a VIPER-issued SUV.

Five minutes out was good, and they were only fifteen minutes from where Beth would attend the evening Christmas mass. He'd blocked the everlasting high of last night's life-changing experience while they'd examined the intel and devised a plan to extract Dr. Sable. That had taken several hours. Now, they were underway. If they did their job quickly, and Edgar kept the debrief even quicker, he could have his sugarplum naked under her Christmas tree before midnight. And then he'd spend all Christmas Day convincing her the curse wasn't real, but his love was.

How he'd fallen so hard for Dr. Beth Parker in such a short time wasn't even a mystery. He didn't believe in curses any more than he believed in flying reindeer, but he finally believed in Gran's sixth sense. Dr. Beth Parker was the woman for him. The whole time he'd been denying his attraction, he hadn't been fighting her or even himself. He'd been fighting against fate, and he certainly had no control over that.

That fight ended today.

While he couldn't control Beth, nor did he ever want to, he'd do his damn hardest to convince her they should be together. He wouldn't allow curses and fears to keep him from spending every night wrapped around her sweet body, but he couldn't shake the uneasiness in his gut. Apprehending Chavez had been too simple, and they still didn't have any clues as to why.

Kane glanced at his comms unit. The little red dot representing Dr. Sable's location was exactly where it had been since they'd begun tracking her via a minuscule device under the skin of her wrist.

Chris shook his head from the back seat. "I can't believe a grandma implanted an untraceable tracker in her body."

"Me neither." But her daughter, who thought her mother's suspicions about nefarious people stopping at nothing to obtain the information inside her head was over-the-top radical, was plenty grateful for the extreme caution.

"I can't wait to implant a device like that in Scarlett."

"You plan on chipping your woman?"

"Damn straight I am. If she'll let me. This rash of terrorists kidnapping beautiful scientists is going to send me to an early grave."

"Sounds like a good plan." He'd like to put one in Beth too. Oh, she'd put up a fight, but he'd welcome her fiery resistance.

"I'd say you're both *loco*." Nic opened his eyes from where he'd sat quietly next to Chris. "Crazy, like in the batshit kind. But I see Scarlett agreeing to that, if only for research purposes." He looked at Kane. "Not sure about your woman, though."

"Me neither." First, he had to get her to agree to officially be his.

Beth paused on the stone stairs of the old church and inhaled the crisp scent of impending snow. Sure enough, fat flakes fell from the clouds, blanketing the night sky. Looking over her shoulder, she smiled at the Washington Monument and wished upon the tall, graceful monolith that Kane would return to her soon.

She turned her gaze back to the entrance. Welcoming organ music filtered through the doors flanked by two-story high pine trees. Smiling, she linked her arm through Scarlett's. Gage and Hudson lingered closely behind, their heads on a swivel. She didn't see any of the other security detail Scarlett mentioned but didn't doubt their presence.

As she and Scarlett entered the vestibule, a precocious eight-year-old from her science class bounded toward them.

"Hi Miss Beth. I like your shirt. I wish my mom would have let me wear something comfy instead of this stupid thing." She tugged at the sleeve of her deep-red velvet dress.

"You look beautiful, Madalynn." Beth smoothed her hands over her black pants and bent down to look the child in the eye. "But I get not wanting to be uncomfortable. My favorite coat got dirty last night." *Burned to a crisp probably.* "I'm so bummed I couldn't bring myself to wear another one."

"Oh no. Not the purple sparkly thing." She touched Beth's shoulder. "But this shirt is so pretty, and it's the same color as my outfit. We can be pretty and uncomfortable together." Madalynn leaned close to Beth's ear. "Bummer we can't play hide-and-seek in the basement, though. Mom says

I'll get dirty and it's not appropriate on Christmas Eve anyway."

"She's right." Madalynn would ruin her dress playing in the dusty basement. Worse, she'd hurt herself trying to bust the boarded-up entrance to the underground tunnel that led to the pastor's old residence across the street. The kid had a betting pool about who would be the first to break through.

Madalynn rolled her eyes. "Okay. Mom and Dad saved seats for you and your friends up front."

"Thanks, sweetie. Be there in a—" Her secure phone buzzed in her purse. She pulled it out and frowned at the unknown number. She sucked in a hopeful breath. Maybe it was Kane. "Hello."

"Beth, this is Gran. I hope you don't mind me calling you."

Beth's shoulder slumped. "No, not at all."

"Kane gave me your number. I wanted to wish you a Merry Christmas."

"Thanks. Merry Christmas to you too. Please hold on a minute." She turned to Scarlett as she put the call on mute and pointed to a door off the vestibule. "I'm going to go in the office and talk to Kane's grandmother, where it's quiet. Go find Madalynn and her parents and I'll meet you up there."

Scarlett nodded. Gage followed her down the aisle.

Hudson entered the office and scanned the area. Crossing the small space, he checked to make sure the door that led to the basement was locked. "We secured down there earlier, but don't leave this room. I'll wait for you outside."

"Thanks." Beth ducked into the tiny office that housed a rickety desk, a rack of white choir robes, and a bookshelf with coloring books and crayons to occupy the younger kids during the service. "I'm back, Mrs. Darren."

"No worries, dear, and call me Gran."

"Okay, Gran. Are you looking for Kane?"

"No. I know he's working. How are you holding up with him gone?"

Beth opened her mouth to say she had no right to worry about him, but he'd been inside of her just a few hours ago. She had every right, and she had a feeling that Gran would see through her facade. "I'm worried sick."

"I'd like to tell you it gets easier, but it doesn't. Do you love my grandson?"

"Yes." The answer rolled off Beth's tongue before she had time to think about it. "But—"

Gran huffed. "I know you think you're cursed. Kane has his ungrounded fears as well, but the two of you are so worried about death that you aren't living. Do you regret loving those boys?"

"No. They were wonderful human beings, but Gran…" Calling her Gran felt natural as if she'd known and trusted the woman her whole life. "I don't understand why they were taken from me. I didn't do anything wrong to deserve it."

"Did those nasty women in your town say you did? Kane told me all about them. They sound like a bunch of unhappy hags who have nothing better to do with their lives but make up malarkey about others. Am I right?"

"Yes, and yes."

"Well, there's two ways you can think of it. First, curses aren't real and it's just coincidence those three boys died, but it doesn't seem like you believe that."

"I'm getting there, but there's more to my madness than being afraid my next boyfriend will die."

"You're afraid to lose someone again, and it's hard to separate your fears."

"Yes," Beth whispered. The truth she'd realized last night burned in her mind like gospel instead of a fluttering hope.

"Why can't I just accept that curses aren't real, bad things happen for no good reason, and life moves on?"

"Because you have deep, powerful emotions, and you know how I know that? Because I saw the way you looked at my grandson and I hear the worry in your voice now."

The truth squeezed at her heart. "What's the second way to think of my bad luck?"

"Maybe the universe sent those boys to you because you're special. Maybe they were angels sent down for a reason, on a mission, and you gave them what they needed to complete their work here on earth. Maybe you were their blessing."

A shiver ran through Beth that had nothing to do with God or the Holy Ghost but the realization of what dwelled within her heart. "I never thought of it that way. There's always been a piece of me, the emotional, or maybe the spiritual side or whatever, that thinks I'm part of something I can't explain. And I never thought to look for a positive explanation." A sense of peace hummed like a choir within her. "Who knows. Maybe there is one."

"I knew you were a smart girl."

"Smart enough to know it's about damn time the universe rewarded me for putting up with its bullshit." She slapped her hand over her mouth. "Sorry, Gran."

"If you're going to be hanging around with my grandson and his VIPER buddies, you'd better up your profanity game. God knows I have. And I do think the universe is repaying you for being part of something bigger than yourself. That is, if you're ready to take a leap of faith and claim your reward."

"And Kane is my reward." Her heart swelled to the size of the gigantic wreath on the church door.

"Yes. You know how I know that? 'Cause my Kane is special, and fate wouldn't just match him with anyone ordinary. And Beth, I don't think you have to worry about Kane being an angel called back to heaven and leaving you alone here on earth. Trust me, that boy ain't no saint."

No, he wasn't, and that's what she liked about him.

A noise, like metal scraping metal, sounded from the basement. As she spun toward the sound, the first notes of a Christmas carol permeated the walls of the room. The door seemed to shake with the vibrations from the powerful organ on the balcony above her as her phone vibrated with an incoming call.

Kane?

Hope rose in her chest.

"Gran, I have to go. Merry Christmas."

As she lowered the phone, the door to the basement opened. Beth gasped as a familiar face appeared in the shadows.

THIRTY-FIVE

"*Go time*," Ryan said in Kane's head as he and his brothers neared the vacant building where Dr. Sable was being held in an office on the first floor. With efficiency and stealth, they flanked to their positions. Adrenaline hummed through him as he switched to warrior mode. Beth was safe, but Dr. Sable wasn't, and he'd promised his woman he'd bring her friend home.

His woman.

The thought was caveman-like, but fuck, he liked the sound of it. He tamped down the thought of how he'd satisfied her twice last night and took out two of the guards stationed at the warehouse with successive V-Strikes. A minute later, he received confirmation all the hostiles outside the building were down.

Silently, like the well-trained team they were, they entered the building and fanned out to their predetermined paths. Kane hurled twin V-Strikes at the Diablos outside a door. They fell as Nic and Linc entered the room.

Metal glinted in Kane's periphery. Spinning, he landed a

roundhouse kick with his steel to a thick chest. The Diablo flew into the wall and crashed to the ground.

"On your six."

Kane ducked and spun at Chris's warning. The barrel of a rifle came into view. Firing a V-Strike from his thigh, he visualized it hitting his target's gut. It found its mark.

"All clear," Chris said, emerging from the stairwell.

Kane scanned the hallway. *"All Clear."*

"Sable is secure," Nic said as Kane slowly entered the room.

A plump, gray-haired woman sat in an office chair in front of a desk. Two unconscious Diablos lay on the floor on either side of her. Other than the furniture and a laptop, the dimly lit postage-stamp-sized room was empty.

Dr. Sable ran a hand over her spiky hair. "You guys must be the rest of the cavalry."

Kane removed his helmet. "Are you okay, ma'am?"

Chris helped her rise from the folding chair.

She oscillated on her feet but didn't crumble. "Yes. I knew they wouldn't hurt me until they got the information. They think I'm old and weak and would drop from a heart attack if they tortured me, and then they'd have nothing." She kicked one of the hostiles with the toe of a worn cowboy boot. "This one doesn't know how to talk properly to his elders. I know Spanish and understood every one of his insults. Asshole."

Kane bit back a snicker. Dr. Sable and Gran would get along great. "Did they get any data from you?"

"God, no." She kicked the other fallen Diablo as Kane and Chris escorted her out of the building. "I'm a professional. I've been preparing for something like this my whole life. Kind of bummed that it's over so quickly. It was a rush, although I was glad the one who kept flipping his knife and threatening to cut me left. He scared the crap out of me."

She sighed and stretched her neck. "Although, according to some of the gals in my book club, that blood kink thing is kind of hot."

Wishing he could unhear that tidbit, Kane led her outside. Nic and Linc would stay at the scene and work with the FBI to secure the Diablos while he and Chris brought Dr. Sable back to headquarters.

As he helped her into the back of the SUV, she sighed and rested her head against the seat. How could the woman relax after being kidnapped by a drug cartel? He waited for some sense of closure, peace, or even the high he loved from reaching a goal to quell the uneasiness churning with the adrenaline in his veins, but the maddening edge wouldn't abate. "We're missing something."

"We're missing a lot," Chris said. "It's been making Scarlett crazy that she can't figure out how Chavez tracked you and Beth to the safe house. There wasn't a tracking app on his phone, but it doesn't mean someone wasn't feeding him the information from a source we haven't uncovered yet."

"We need to find that fucking source."

Dr. Sable snapped up her head. "Back up, boys. Did you say Chavez? That's the jerk's name who kept flipping his knife like a show-off and ordering the others around."

Kane snapped his head to the back seat. "Are you sure his name was Chavez?"

"Yes. Seems his little brother was arrested, and he wasn't too happy about it."

"Brother?" Dread licked up Kane's spine. "Chavez doesn't have a…" He slammed his hand onto the dashboard. "Fuck. When Chavez insinuated his brother would kill me, he hadn't meant someone from his cartel family; he'd meant a biological brother."

"Chavez's siblings are supposed to be dead."

Kane pulled up a photo on his phone of the man they'd

apprehended from the second safe house and showed it to Dr. Sable. "Is this the knife-flipper?"

"Almost, but not quite. The idiot looked nearly identical to him, but his face was fuller. And this guy's creepy black eyes appear the same, but not nearly as scary as the man who held a knife to my throat."

The piece Kane had been missing slid into place with a sickening click. "Did he say anything else?"

"He told the others to handle me while he went to get his brother out of the hospital so they could get the other *cazampulga* together."

THIRTY-SIX

Beth choked on words that wouldn't form.

Evangeline's form vacillated in the doorway like an apparition, her face as white as the choir robes hanging on the rack. Blood as red as holly berries dripped from her bottom lip.

"What happened to—?"

The question crystallized in Beth's throat as Evangeline fell face-first into the room. Beth lunged to catch her. Her phone and purse slipped from her hands as she caught Evangeline by the shoulders and crumpled with her to the hardwood.

Organ music pounded in her head as she dragged Evangeline up. "What are you doing here? What happened to your face?"

Evangeline touched a fresh bruise on her cheek as she tugged Beth to the basement door. "You need to come with me."

"Tell me what's going on." Beth pulled herself from Evangeline's grip and bent to pick up her phone and purse. "You're scaring me."

Tears ran down Evangeline's cheek as she kicked Beth's belongings under the choir robes. "You need to come. Please."

"Why?" Beth burrowed her thin heels into the floor so hard they'd surely leave a mark. She opened her mouth to scream for Hudson.

Evangeline slapped a hand over Beth's lips. "If you don't come with me, the Diablos will kill me."

The cartel name and the fear in Evangeline's voice blasted a shiver down Beth's spine. The basement door pushed open the rest of the way. A short man with a beard as thick as his body and biceps three times the size of Kane's filled the frame.

"Both of you. Move."

Cold sweat erupted on Beth's forehead as she trained her gaze on the gun with the silencer attached to the barrel. If he shot it in here, nobody would hear it over the organ. "What is he talking about, Evangeline?"

"Please don't hate me. I didn't mean for it to go this far." She eyed the medallion hanging around Beth's neck. "They said they'd kill me if I didn't help snatch you, so I put a tracker in your necklace."

Beth yanked the medallion that burned like the devil away from her skin.

Biceps cocked his gun. "Move."

A knock sounded on the door from the vestibule as the organ quieted. Biceps wrapped his beefy arm around Evangeline's neck and ducked them into the basement shadows. "I can hear you through this door. Say a word and I shoot your friend and whoever walks in. And then I give the word to have your boss shot."

No. She fought for air as the basement door closed and hope for Dr. Sable's successful rescue sank to the basement. If she was still in the cartel's clutches, where did that leave Kane?

"Miss Beth, the pastor said we need more crayons and—"

Beth spun to Madalynn. "Go back to your seat, sweetie."

Hudson poked his head in. "All good?"

"Yes." She forced the word out along with her smile. "I'll help Madalynn and be out in a minute." The first notes of a Christmas hymn chimed through the vestibule as Madalynn rushed to her side. "Close the door so we can hear each other over the organ. It's about to get louder."

As Hudson shut them in, the basement door squeaked open. Beth shoved Madalynn behind her.

The child tugged at her sweater. "You said no hide-and-seek, but someone's down there."

The door didn't open farther, but Beth caught the barrel of Biceps's gun peeking through the slim gap. She grabbed a box of crayons from the shelf. "Take these out. I'll meet you at the pew." She bit her lip hard against the urge to scream for Hudson, but she couldn't risk Madalynn, Dr. Sable's, or even Evangeline's life.

Madalynn stomped her foot. "I know you're playing without me. Let me have fun too, or I'll tell the pastor that you said the *f*-word when you lost last week."

"Madalynn, please just listen for once." This kid's sass was going to be the death of them all. Literally, if she didn't get out of here.

Or maybe not.

Beth reached behind her neck and undid the clasp on her necklace. The smooth metal felt like barbed wire as it slid through her fingers. She bent to Madalynn's height. "You're right. I am playing. Adults only." She handed Madalynn the necklace and prayed that counting on an eight-year-old who always did the opposite of what she was instructed was a good plan. "I need you to hold on to that until I get back. It's so sparkly that it could lead someone to me, even in the dark. And don't tell anyone about this." She lowered her voice. "It's a top secret initiation for new members."

Madalynn's eyes widened. "Cool. More people to play. I promise I won't tell."

"Please tell the man outside that my parents called, and I'll be another few minutes."

As soon as the vestibule door shut behind Madalynn, the basement door opened. Biceps stepped into the light with Evangeline clutched in front of him.

Evangeline winced as he jammed the pistol into her temple. "Please, Beth. Just come."

The rising notes of the organ muffled her last words. Beth took a deep breath and dragged herself to the threshold. Biceps yanked her through. As her boots dragged along the stone floor, he secured a heavy metal bar across the door.

Kane cursed as he jammed his finger into the end call button on the dashboard of Chris's SUV. "Why the hell isn't Beth picking up?"

Chris reached forward and hit Scarlett's name on the display. She answered on the first ring.

"Where's Beth?" Sweat poured from Kane's brow as he tightened his fists.

"On the phone with Gran in the church office. Hudson just went to check on her."

Relief inundated his system as the sound of an organ played in the background. "Put Gage on the phone."

Muffled voices filtered over the line for a painful heartbeat.

"This is Gage. What's wrong?"

Kane relayed what he'd learned from Dr. Sable. "Find Beth."

"I'm heading to the office now."

Kane's heart hammered his rib cage. Dammit, he was the one who was supposed to be in danger of dying, not her. He knew apprehending Chavez had been too easy. He should have locked her down at headquarters, but he wanted to make his sugarplum happy on Christmas Eve. Instead, he'd gotten her...

"Fuck." Failure tasted like blood on his tongue as he thought about the unacceptable possibilities.

Gage cursed over the line agonizing seconds later. "She's not there."

Hudson clicked into the call. "There's a door to the basement in the office. It was locked from the office side when she went in there. I checked. Now it's barred from the basement side. We found her purse and phone on the floor. And blood."

Kane slammed his palm onto his steel leg. He felt the impact in every fiber of his flesh-and-bone being. A lot of good his superpowers did Beth if she was missing. He connected with Nic and Linc through his mind comms. *"Beth's been taken."*

Linc cursed. *"So has the Chavez we captured. Minutes after he woke up, a team of mercenaries busted him out of the hospital before he could be questioned. Nic is pulling up satellite feeds but isn't having any luck. We're fifteen minutes out from the church."*

"We're one minute out," Chris said.

Hang on, sugarplum. I'm coming for you. And when he found her, he wasn't letting her go. Ever.

THIRTY-SEVEN

The cold muzzle of a gun jammed into Beth's temple. Biceps nudged her with his free hand down the wide stone stairs lit by a single dim bulb. "You know the way."

Evangeline stumbled next to Beth and sobbed. "I'm sorry."

Beth's dislike for Evangeline grew to hatred as dark as the basement. "For what? For putting a tracker on me or helping a cartel plan my kidnapping through a secret passage?"

The tunnel had been built before it was mandatory to submit building plans to city hall. Most of the parish members didn't even know it existed. Evangeline must have told the Diablos to break into the old residence across the street and bust through the boarded-up passageway. Last time she'd been down here, all looked secure, but nothing was impenetrable.

Not like Kane. He was impenetrable. She needed his strength, his speed, everything extraordinary about him, but she couldn't wait for her super soldier to ride in and save her.

Biceps might not be threatening to kill her, but they wouldn't let her live once she'd served her purpose.

She paused midstep and teetered in heels. If she got herself out of this alive, she'd strangle the last of her irrational fears and start living.

And tell Kane she loved him.

Focus, Beth. She didn't have her gun, but she'd learned to defend herself in other ways. To do that, she needed to stay calm and alert so she could attack when the opportunity arose.

Biceps growled behind her. "Move it, or I'll shove you down."

Evangeline's sobs grew louder.

"Shut up." Beth hissed as she counted the steps to keep her panic contained.

Nine.

Ten.

The counting didn't help. The dank smell that never bothered her before clogged her nostrils. How long would Hudson wait for her to chat with her parents? The service didn't start for another few minutes. And what if Madalynn kept a secret for once and didn't tell anyone about the necklace? Beth's impromptu plan hinged on it getting back to Scarlett so it could be reverse tracked.

"Hurry up." Biceps jammed the gun into her lower back.

She bit her tongue to keep from crying out and stepped down again.

Eleven.

She needed to take a chance. If Biceps got them through the tunnel and into a vehicle it would be so much harder to find her.

Twelve

She bit back a squeak and paused as another plan, this one reckless, took shape. "Careful. The thirteenth step is uneven. The kids trip on it all the time." As she stepped down, she ducked and pushed Evangeline into the stone wall. She ignored her scream as she crouched lower and heaved all her weight back into Biceps's legs. He cursed in Spanish over the muted organ music as his stout body sailed clear over her head and tumbled down the unforgiving stone.

Beth yanked Evangeline up. "Hurry."

"Stop."

She ignored the command and ran to the top of the stairs. The music grew louder the closer they got to the landing. A muffled shot—like the one she heard in the cemetery—reverberated off the walls. Evangeline screamed and pulled Beth down with her. They toppled down the stairs in a tangle.

Beth's chin hit the stone. Her tooth sliced into her lower lip. Blood coated her mouth as the impact reverberated in her bones. Fear spiked her adrenaline as a tall figure emerged from the shadows.

"Stand up, *Cazampulga,* or the next shot hits your *amiga* instead of the wall."

The cruel nickname burned her from the inside like thousands of spiders pricked at her skin and burrowed underneath. She spat out the nastiness along with blood. "She's clearly not my friend if she led me here." And this guy clearly wasn't Biceps. His accent was too smooth. His shadowed frame too tall, and his features too sharp. As he stepped into the dim light, her stomach dropped to the stone.

Chavez.

"You're…" She blinked. He still stood there, all six foot something, tall, dark, and even more menacing than his photos. A terrified squeak chirped from her throat. "You're supposed to be in the hospital."

"That's my baby brother. You'll meet him soon."

She cradled her aching jaw with her hand as the

enforcer's face blurred in her vision. "You don't have a brother." Not one that was alive.

He waved the gun in his hand toward the tunnel entrance. "Move."

"Come on." Evangeline's voice shook as she held out her hand. "They mean business."

Beth ignored her and pressed her palm to the cold stone. Clammy sweat dripped down her face as she rose and sneered at Evangeline. "I'm not going a step farther until you tell me what you've done."

Chavez wouldn't kill her yet. She had something he wanted. She didn't care what they did to Evangeline. She prayed Dr. Sable had been rescued and they were bluffing about killing her. But what if they weren't? She could already be dead. So could Kane.

No. She clutched her stomach and spit up bile. Voices echoed around her, but the fear-forged buzz in her ears muffled the words.

Biceps grabbed her arm. The violence in his face that was already bruising from his roll down the stairs snapped her panic to rage. Moaning like an injured animal, she raised her knee and shot a kick to his groin. He grunted as he swung his pistol at her face. She raised her forearm to block it. Pain lanced through her wrist as bone struck metal. Heaving, she twisted and ducked to avoid his next blow. As she tried to scoot away, Chavez roughly grabbed her by the hair and jerked her head back. Too afraid to even pant, she stared into the eyes of the devil.

"I'd love to play more, *Cazampulga,* but I promised my brother you'd be unharmed when I handed you over to him. After I get the formula for Triple X, of course, but he'll forgive a few bumps and bruises in the name of making you cooperate."

Pain ripped through her scalp. She fought for breath. "Go to hell."

He cursed and yanked her against him. "I like the fight in you." He slid his hand from her hair to her throat and squeezed. "That soldier who will become number four when he tries to rescue you doesn't deserve your fire. Then again, my brother doesn't deserve you either, but he spent all that time stalking you, and he did see you first."

She clawed at the hand choking her airway. Wheezing, she fought for breath as a gravestone with Kane's name on it burned behind her eyes.

Kane wouldn't die. He couldn't.

She wasn't a black widow. Everyone had been wrong. *She'd* been wrong. She was Kane's and he was hers until death do them part, which wouldn't be today.

As she blacked out, she vowed to kick this Chavez's ass when she awoke, right after she kicked her stalker's.

THIRTY-EIGHT

The last thing Kane expected to find when he and Chris burst through the church doors with Dr. Sable in tow was Scarlett and Gage talking to a little girl.

Scarlett patted the child's hand. "This is Madalynn, who happens to have Beth's necklace and won't tell me where she got it."

The woman standing behind Beth glared at the kid. "Madalynn. I know we talked about keeping what others say to ourselves, but it's okay this time to share your secret."

"But Mom, Miss Beth said—"

Kane dropped to his knees in front of the child. "You can tell me. I'm Beth's boyfriend." From the corner of his eye, he caught Hudson swinging an axe at a door inside the vestibule office. Kane could blow that in a second with a V-Strike, but the kid who might know something took precedent.

Madalynn bounced on her toes. "Are you guys getting married? Can I be your flower girl?

The sound of splintering wood revved his impatience. "You can be my best man if you tell me where Beth is."

"No. I want to throw rose petals and walk down the aisle and wear a tiara. Are you here to play the game with Miss Beth?"

"Yes." *Forever. After I kill whoever took her.*

"I'm in," Hudson yelled.

Kane ran into the office and sprang to the shattered door. Leaping over the remnants, he started down a dimly lit stairwell.

"Wait for intel, Kane."

He spun to Chris. Fuck, he was right. He looked at Scarlett. "Where does this lead?"

Madalynn bounded into the room. "That's the basement where we play hide-and-seek. Miss Beth is down there playing with some new friends and wouldn't let me join this time, but she let me hold her necklace. She said it's so sparkly that it could lead someone to her in the dark." Madalynn slapped a hand over her mouth. "Don't tell her I told you all that. It's a secret."

Pride and hope skittered along his bunched muscles. Damn, his sugarplum was smart. She'd known he'd need help to find her and left a clue with a pint-sized blabbermouth.

He ran down the stairs with Chris on his heels. Behind him, Scarlett yelled to Gage to get her laptop out of the car so she could find the other Chavez. The flashlight built into Kane's comms unit illuminated streaks of blood on the stairs. It had to be Beth's. The mass had just started when he'd arrived. She'd fight anyone who made her miss it.

Kane's own blood boiled. When he found Chavez, he'd strangle him with his bare hands for snatching Beth out from under everyone's, including God's nose, and ruining her holiday.

Chris laid a hand on his shoulder as they hit the landing. "We'll get her."

They'd fucking better. He'd survived losing a leg. He

didn't want to find out if he'd survive losing Beth. Finally, he understood a fraction of the anguish his mother must have felt when his father died.

His steel leg hummed along with the fear-fueled energy coursing through his flesh and bones as he rushed into the basement. No, he'd never fully understand because Beth wasn't dying tonight.

"Status?" Scarlett asked over the mind comms.

"Clear except for blood on the stairs."

Scarlett cursed under her breath. *"The main church and the perimeter are secure. Local and satellite surveillance have been scrambled by a hacker. According to Madalynn, there's a boarded-up tunnel, but I can't find anything about it in the city's plans."*

Kane ran faster through several dark rooms. Sure enough, the flashlight illuminated a doorway at the rear of the last one. A pile of boards and crumbled sheetrock lay over the threshold. *"Found the tunnel. Where does it lead?"*

"To an old house across the street, according to Madalynn."

Ryan joined the conversation and rattled off the address.

"We're two minutes out," Linc said.

Kane tore through the dark, musty-smelling passageway. The distance felt like a mile instead of the width of a two-lane street. At the end, he found another smashed door. Forcing himself to slow down, he breathed through his wrath and nodded to Chris.

Silently, their movements as coordinated as the last time they tangled with the Diablos, they entered the basement. The scent of lilacs lingered in the air as if calling to him like a siren's song.

"The house has been abandoned for a couple of decades, according to city records," Ryan said.

"Roger that." Kane prayed he'd find Beth unharmed but knew in his churning gut she wasn't there. He'd find her.

Somehow, he'd always find her. Protect her, just like he'd been doing for weeks.

He nodded to Chris again as they entered the kitchen at the top of the stairs. A sweep of the gloomy, dusty space revealed nothing. Kane's leg jittered so violently it rattled the worn floorboards as they entered the living room. Where was she? He hadn't been kidding when he said he should put a tracking chip in her.

Tonight was Christmas Eve, for fuck's sake. The brightest night of the year with all the lights and candles, and the star of Bethlehem, and all that other festive crap. Why couldn't a heavenly beacon help him find Beth? Or why couldn't she still be wearing her necklace that was so sparkly it could lead someone to her in the dark? He could use an advantage, divine or not, to counter whatever method Chavez used to track Beth like a covert hide-and-seek game.

He froze. *Covert hide-and-seek game.* He concentrated on slowing his breathing and recalling where he'd heard that phrase. A few breaths later, last night's conversation with Evangeline about Christmas Eve mass pushed to the front of his brain.

"We used to play a covert hide-and-seek game in the church that was so much fun."

The part of the exchange about Beth's necklace jockeyed for attention.

"I sent Beth the token of appreciation. Does she wear it all the time?"

"Fuck." He'd never had the urge to hurt a woman before, but he did now. *"Scarlett. Check the medallion and see if there's a tracker in it. And find that bitch Evangeline."*

THIRTY-NINE

Beth's head pounded as she peered at the two Chavezes sitting across from her on bench seats spanning the length of a windowless van. Evangeline sat between them, hands bound in front of her with zip ties, like the blubbering filling of a Diablo sandwich. Biceps and another thug flanked Beth. Both smelled like a boy's gym locker.

She tested the tight bonds at her own wrists. Pain rocketed up her arm. At least she didn't have duct tape over her mouth like Evangeline.

As the haze from being choked until she'd blacked out cleared, she studied the brothers dressed in black jeans and black leather jackets. If they weren't cold killers, their nearly identical mellow-brown skin, shoulder-length black hair, and hawkish facial features might make them attractive. To her, they looked like poisonous snakes, especially the thicker one, whose picture had been enough to scare her.

Enrique Chavez.

The enforcer, who'd appeared leaner in his wanted photo, had about ten pounds of muscle and two inches of height on his brother. His stalker sibling leered at her with an unfocused gaze rimmed by purple bruises above a bandaged nose.

Good. He deserved a brain bleed from his concussion. If she could buy the lamppost he'd crashed into a drink, she would. While his gaze was softer, the intent in their murky brown depths was no less sinister and much creepier than his sibling. He was the only one in the van without a gun in his hand, though.

She swallowed. Saliva burned a path down her abused throat. "Are you twins?"

Her stalker glanced at his brother. "He's not my twin, although I do have one."

She struggled to grasp information she knew was stored in her brain but couldn't find it through the chaos.

"I can see the gears working in your pretty head, *querida*. You're wondering if I'm one of the twins who died." Her stalker held out his hand. "It's nice to meet you after all this time. I'm Santiago Chavez, the brother who is dead to the world but not to those who love me. Welcome to my family."

"You're my stalker." She shrank into the cold van wall as she addressed him for the first time. If her hands were free, she'd cover her ears to stop his accent from pealing in her head like a death knell. She'd always wondered how she'd feel when she met her stalker face to face. Revulsion at hearing the voice that haunted her dreams hadn't made the top of her list, but it did now.

"I'm your *admirer*. I wish we could have met two years ago, but after your abduction didn't go as planned, I was relegated to watching you from afar because you were identified as a person of interest regarding Triple X. You needed to concentrate on your work and I respected that. I was so pleased when I got the go-ahead to interact with you again."

The enforcer waved his gun at his brother. "Two years ago, the job that you took without mother's approval was to scare her via cyberspace, but you screwed up by making contact. And your job this time was to track her, not send her messages, not steal her cake and watch, and not pay two juvenile delinquents to rob a store and watch again." He looked at Beth. "Those incidents weren't part of the Triple X mission, but the obsessed fool enjoys scaring and then watching you for some reason."

She leaned forward as far as she could without falling off the seat. She'd lost weeks of her life hiding inside her house because of one sibling and the last few days because of the other. Now that she was face to face with the devil brothers who seemed to have some tension between them, she wouldn't spend another minute cowering. "Why?"

Her voice hitched as she strangled a fear-induced sob. Courage had been so much easier to rally when she fantasized about kicking her stalker's ass, but she refused to look away from the man who had stolen so much from her. "Why have you made my life a living hell?" She snapped her gaze to the enforcer. "And why are you coming after me? You already have Dr. Sable. She knows much more than I do about Triple X."

"I'll let your friend answer that first question." He ripped the tape off Evangeline's mouth.

She covered her lips with her bound hands and screamed.

Beth didn't have the bandwidth to muster sympathy.

"She hired me to meet you online." Her stalker raised his voice over Evangeline's sobs. "The plan was to pursue and scare you."

"What?" Beth's gaze snapped to her so-called friend. "And why on earth do you know someone in a drug cartel?"

Evangeline shook her head so hard it bounced against Santiago's shoulder. "I didn't know who I was hiring. I asked Henry Richardson if he could put me in touch with a talented hacker. Henry said he never liked you anyway, so..."

Beth shot toward Evangeline. The thugs yanked her back. Good thing because she would have killed her before she spilled her sordid story. "Are you stupid?" She already detested Richardson for what he'd done to Scarlett. Full-blown hatred consumed her now. "That man is just as evil as these devil brothers."

The enforcer pointed his gun at her. "Watch what you say, *Cazampulga.*"

Beth doubled over. Fighting nausea, she hung her head. She heard her stalker reprimand his brother for yelling at her, but she blocked him and his ominous accent out and concentrated on Evangeline's gurgled words.

"I'm so, so sorry. I had no idea what I was getting myself into. I thought I was hiring some techy nerd, not one of the world's best hackers. I contracted with him to cyberstalk you for a few weeks, not months. I made it clear that there wasn't supposed to be any physical contact. And I didn't hire him to kill Danny, I swear."

Beth lifted her chin. The world tilted for a second before she caught her breath. "And that makes what you did better? Danny's dead because of you, and you have the nerve to call me a black widow?"

Evangeline sniffed back a gob of snot dangling from her nose. "Nobody was supposed to get hurt. I just hired him to make your life difficult for a while. You always had it so easy."

The van hit a bump. Anger exploded with the impact of Beth's body against the wall. "What the hell does that mean?"

Evangeline's lips twisted. "You always got off without having to work hard like the rest of us, all because someone died."

Rage and disbelief seeped from Beth's pores like the snot mixing with Evangeline's tears. "You think I benefited every time I buried a boyfriend?"

"Let's count the ways. Exempt from senior year finals. Carte blanche to miss school. Prom queen, even though your date was dead. Isn't sympathy the reason you got that sweet college internship? Because your boyfriend, who beat cancer and then died in a car accident helping you, had a father at the National Health Agency who pulled strings."

"No." Tears assaulted Beth's eyes. "It wasn't like that." But clearly the gossips thought she relished the attention. For years, she'd been trying to figure out why the universe chose to punish her. Rolling her shoulders, she shrugged off the nagging uncertainty for good. She hadn't done a damn thing except endure abuse from hateful, jealous women. All because she'd been the recipient of well-intentioned sympathy from people who cared.

Evangeline wiped her nose on her sleeve. "The whole town saw exactly what you were—a sympathy whore. You didn't deserve the advantages you stole from me."

"Advantages? Like a stupid homecoming crown?" The absurdity wrenched a strangled laugh from Beth's throat. "You think I basked in the spoils of death?"

"You must have because as soon as I made things tough, you finally struggled. How did it feel not having everything handed to you?"

"You crazy fucking…" The thugs held Beth back again from hurling herself at Evangeline. "You told me Danny's murder was my fault because I'd broken up with him and went on that dating site."

Mascara mixed with Evangeline's tears. "It was your fault. Danny should have never taken you back after the horrible argument you guys had. You didn't deserve a second chance. *I* deserved a chance with him. You stole what I wanted. Again."

The tears Beth couldn't fight any longer boiled over into stark disbelief. "Christ, Evangeline, I always knew you were the jealous type, but I never thought you'd purposefully hurt me."

"Didn't you hear what I said? I didn't plan for him to take things so far." She tilted her head to the stalker. "He was supposed to give you the kind of attention you wouldn't benefit from. The kind that upended your perfect, merry life. It scared the shit out of me when he shot Danny. I had to ask Henry to help me find a job in another country, so I'd be far away in case I was connected to the murder."

A hysterical laugh seared Beth's throat. "You should have stayed there."

"That was my plan, but he…" she gestured to the enforcer as the van turned a corner. "He came to Dubai. In a meeting with the CEO of my company and Henry Richardson, I was told that if I didn't come home and give them information about you, they'd kill me."

The enforcer smiled. "I don't just like to grab and go when I'm snatching someone. I like to find their vulnerability and drive it home so when we meet face to face, they understand what the stakes are. Our intel alerted us to your budding relationship with Kane Darren. Your friend told us about your curse. And then she gave us the perfect way not just to scare you but to track your whereabouts." He nodded at Evangeline. "I appreciate your cooperation. Do understand that it pains me to have to kill you."

Beth ignored Evangeline's cries. "Not if I do it first, and then I'll kill Henry Richardson." She curled her fingers into her palm. White-hot pain shot through her injured wrist, but it had nothing on what she'd inflict on Richardson if she ever saw him again.

Her stalker leaned forward and reached out his hand. "I'll take care of Richardson for you, *querida.*"

The enforcer slapped it back. "Remember what happened last time you acted on your own? I told you to be patient and wait for me to come to the States to claim her the right way, but you went off half-cocked in an alley with a gun you didn't know how to use and botched it up."

Snippets from that alley flashed through her mind. The paralyzing fear the moment before she and Danny were attacked. The vicious, agonizing crack of her bone. The distant, desperate sound of Danny calling her name. The gunshot. Her scream. All because he wanted to… "Claim me."

There was only one man she'd let claim her.

The stalker swayed as he stared at her breasts. "I couldn't wait to make you mine."

Beth cringed at his sick, unfocused eyes. "And kidnapping is how you chose to woo me?"

His body rocked to the side as the van veered to the right. "You'll come to love me eventually. I'm incredibly wealthy. I have a beautiful home in Mexico fit for a queen with everything you could ever want."

Beth snorted. She already had everything she desired. "Ain't I lucky that a well-off psycho fell for me."

The enforcer shot across the van and slapped her across the face. "Enough insults."

Beth's head snapped to the side. Pain rioted up her nose and down her jaw.

The stalker grabbed his brother's arm. "Did you forget your promise to use *mild* coercion to get her to talk?"

"Mild?" Beth lifted her bound hands to her cheek. "I'm pretty sure my wrist is broken." She was also pretty sure the devil brothers didn't feel any brotherly love for one another.

Her stalker bowed his head. "I'm sorry, *mi querida*. My brother tends to get carried away. Once you give him the information about Triple X, you'll be all mine, and he won't touch you again."

The enforcer reached across Evangeline and fisted his

brother's shirt. "Your drive-by yesterday screwed up my operation to snatch her. Instead, we had to resort to taking the backup plan. Now that the old bat has been rescued, your woman is our only source of intel. I'll get that information however I choose."

Sweat beaded the stalker's forehead. "It's not my fault her boyfriend rescued Dr. Sable. I mean her ex-boyfriend. Kane Darren will die for touching what's mine."

A sinister smile crossed the enforcer's face. "Not so fast, little brother. Her cooperation, not your jealous revenge, determines if her soldier becomes number four."

FORTY

Warped floorboards creaked under Kane's boots as he followed Chris out of the old house. The wind blew snow under the small awning and whisked away the lilac scent trailing him through the rooms. He didn't feel the icy flakes hit his skin as he followed Chris down the steps and met Linc and Nic at the curb.

"Perimeter is clear." Linc eyed a group of teenagers on the porch across the street. "Those kids said they saw a group of people hurry into a van parked in the driveway and take off a few minutes ago."

"Fuck." Although their intel indicated the Diablos hadn't taken Dr. Sable to Mexico to extract what she knew about Triple X, that didn't mean they weren't planning on taking Beth there. *"Scarlett, did you find a tracker in the medallion?"*

"Yes. Ryan is working on reverse tracking it. He just got a report from his analyst who did a deep dive into Evangeline and the company Henry Richardson referred her to in Dubai. There's speculation that the organization bankrolls the Diablo cartel. Intel suggests that Henry and the CEO have been communicating recently."

"We need to question Evangeline."

"We're working on contacting her."

"Work fast." Images of what could happen to Beth assaulted his mind like a flash bomb. The need to shoot something sizzled through his leg. What was the point of being a super soldier if he didn't have an enemy to obliterate on his way to get his girl? *"Any word on Chavez's brother?"*

"We've got a team working on it," Scarlett said. *"Wait— Ryan got a location. Beth is being held in a warehouse near... son of a bitch. She's near the same private airstrip my stepfather kept his jet at."*

Chris clapped him on the shoulder. "At least we know the area. Let's go find your woman."

As Kane ran toward the SUV parked in front of the church, wedding bells rang in his mind. Curse or not, he was going to marry Beth in front of that altar someday. But before he could take his bride to heaven, he had to send two brothers to hell.

The pounding inside Beth's head reached a deafening level as the van stopped. A minute later, the vehicle slowly crept forward.

"Where are we?" She prayed her question sounded demanding instead of terrified like it did in her ears.

"A building guarded by an army, where we can talk in private before we head to Mexico." The enforcer hauled Beth up and handed her to his brother.

She winced as he cupped her elbow. "I heard about what your mother wants for Christmas. I'm no present."

"But you are, *querida.*" He lowered his head to her ear. "You're the gift I've been waiting for. I know you love Christmas. By tomorrow, you'll be sitting under the largest tree you've ever seen."

Tomorrow? That meant she had time before she left the country. She didn't know how long she'd been out in between the tunnel and regaining consciousness in the van, but they'd arrived at this destination only a few minutes after she'd woken up. "Is it midnight yet?"

"It's not even six."

"Glad I didn't miss Santa."

Her stalker dipped his head to her ear. "There's plenty of time to tell me what you want for Christmas when we get home."

She jerked her arm away from him. "You're not my home."

Kane was her home. He, along with the nation's strongest and smartest, was looking for her. She'd fight with everything she had to buy Kane and her friends precious minutes to storm in with their V-Strikes blazing.

The back of the van opened. The devil brothers hauled her out of the vehicle and into a dimly lit warehouse. Little light shone through the high windows that touched the ceiling. The cold air sharpened her will to fight.

Biceps and his buddy pushed Evangeline out of the van. Another thug appeared from around the side. Beth thought Biceps was big, but this guy looked like he snacked on steroids.

He caught Evangeline with one hand before she fell face-first onto the concrete floor. "What do you want me to do with this one?"

"Merry Christmas." The enforcer extended his arm with the flourish of a game host presenting the grand prize. "Have fun and then kill her."

Evangeline's scream echoed through the long, cavernous space.

"Don't touch her." Beth coiled her thigh muscles. "If anyone is going to kill her, it's me." She pulled away from her stalker and charged. Evangeline's breath huffed out as Beth's shoulder rammed into her ribs. Steroids jumped back as they fell to the ground. With speed and agility born from desperation, Beth managed to straddle Evangeline's waist.

"Please," Evangeline cried.

"You psychopath," Beth snarled as she punched her with bound hands. Evangeline didn't try to fight back. Grabbing Evangeline's neck as best she could, she leaned closer to her. "If you want a chance to live, fight me."

A heartbeat later, recognition flashed in Evangeline's eyes. With a grunt, she headbutted Beth and reared up her hips.

Beth went with the movement and rolled off. She allowed Evangeline to straddle her chest. Panting, she called her ex-friend every nasty name she could think of and meant every one as she pulled her hair and scratched her face.

Loud shouts and hoarse whistles sounded over the name-calling and grunts of pain. The more the thugs encouraged violence, the harder Beth fought to entertain.

"Enough."

Somebody pulled them apart. Beth wiped blood from her cheek where Evangeline had sunk her claws. She was sure her forehead had the impression of Evangeline's skull, along with the imprint of the enforcer's hand on her cheek. She'd endure more pain if it bought time for Kane to find her.

The enforcer yanked her to him and glared at the thugs. "This one isn't here for your amusement, but have a merry time with the one I gave you."

Beth struggled in his grip. As much as she wanted to drive a knife through Evangeline's dark heart, she deserved to face justice for her sins, not die. "No. Don't kill her. I'll tell you everything you want to know." She'd figure out how to avoid that last part later.

Chavez dragged her to one of the metal doors set in the dingy white wall. "She's not the one whose life hinges on your cooperation. I have men standing by to make your boyfriend number four at my command. Shooting at him at the cemetery was fun, but this time, my bullet will find his flesh."

Beth's jaw dropped. Kane had been right. Someone had known exactly where to shoot him.

The enforcer snickered. "Surprised I know about his bionic leg? Henry Richardson was more than happy to share his firsthand knowledge about VIPER. And we learned a lot more about what your boyfriend's capable of last night. He took out six of my men without raising a gun, according to my driver, who witnessed the fiasco going down."

No. If they knew VIPER's secrets, they could exploit them. She quickly masked her bone-deep worry with false bravado. "I shot two of your men, you know."

Fury darkened the enforcer's eyes. "I underestimated both of you. That won't happen again. You have five minutes to tell us every Triple X secret you know, or Kane Darren will be the next member of your Dead Boyfriends Society."

Beth kicked and clawed the entire way through the door and down a long hall to the back of the building. Her actions cost her another slap across the face, but it bought Kane and the VIPER team another thirty seconds. The enforcer wouldn't kill her until he got the formula, and he wouldn't kill Kane as long as he needed him for leverage.

Well, he could try to kill him. Even if he knew some of VIPER's capabilities, he didn't understand the full extent of their power. After the show Kane put on at headquarters, she did. He truly was invincible.

And so was her love.

Nobody with eyes as soulless as Chavez could understand that.

Despite her impossible circumstances, the black shroud she'd been dragging around lifted as the enforcer yanked her down the hallway. She'd never been a black widow. She was just a girl who'd had the privilege of loving three wonderful men who were called to heaven way too early. She had to let Kane know she truly didn't believe in the curse any longer. That if something happened to him, she'd grieve but wouldn't stop living, and there wouldn't be any guilt because it wouldn't be her fault. She'd divulge the formula to the Diablos and risk dying to keep him safe. She loved him that much, that deeply and wished she had told him.

The enforcer shoved her through a doorway in the rear of the building. Her stalker steadied her. Blinking against the harsh overhead light, she shook off his touch and fought for balance. Her ribs screamed in pain from a hard kick Evangeline had landed.

Her stalker grabbed her hands. "That's no way to treat your fiancé, *querida.*"

She tried to pull back, but he was stronger than she'd given him credit for. "I'm not anything to you."

"Give it time, *mi amor.*" He tugged her to the center of the small space facing another door in the back of the room. "Soon, you will call me your love."

"The hell I will." Other than a scarred desk and the laptop waiting for her to betray her country, the room held nothing else besides a wooden chair too bulky to wield as an effective weapon. The laptop and the power cord plugged into the wall might be effective though.

The enforcer pressed her to sit and pushed her to the desk. He hit a key on the laptop. A screen with a blank document came up. "Type everything you know about Triple X, and don't think about making shit up. Once you're done, I'm going to send this to *mi madre.* You don't want to know what will happen if my mother suspects you're fucking with us."

Crap. There went her plan to share everything she knew about ibuprofen. She'd give up the Triple X formula to save Kane's life, but that was a last resort. She needed to stall until the VIPER boys busted in and neutralized every Diablo in the building.

She held up her hands. Blood dripped from where the zip ties cut into her flesh. "I can't type with my circulation cut off. And I'm shaking too much because you're scaring me." She swiped her wrists along her cheek and let hot tears fall into the smears of blood on her skin.

The enforcer snapped a photo with his phone. "I'm happy to give you a few minutes to collect yourself." He walked to the door in the back of the room and shoved it open with his boot. "Maybe hanging out with your friend might help."

Thick, hot vomit erupted up her esophagus as she took in the scene. This time, she couldn't stop it from spewing out of her mouth and onto the floor.

FORTY-ONE

Kane gripped the dashboard of the SUV and stared at the photo. The text he'd received moments ago from an unidentified number hadn't come with a taunting message. No demands. Nothing but an image of Beth's bloody and swollen face. "Motherfucking fucker."

Nic reached from the back and grabbed the phone from Kane's hands. He cursed the devil in Spanish.

"We know she's alive," Linc said. "And we know they're waiting for us."

Linc was right. That text wasn't just a taunt. It was bait.

Kane gripped the dashboard tighter. If Chris didn't drive faster, he'd jump out and cover the remaining blocks on foot. Lacing his hands on top of his head, he fought to control his emotions. Impulsive decisions would get them killed, but shit, if he didn't get to Beth quickly, everything he'd learned in training would be moot. At least she wasn't on her way to Mexico—yet. That was a small miracle. But American soil didn't make the Diablo cartel any less deadly.

"One minute out." Chris glanced his way. "Hold on,

brother. We didn't let Scarlett get kidnapped to another country. We won't let that happen to Beth."

Kane nodded. Beth had better hold on too. He didn't want to spend Christmas, or any day after that, without her.

"I got surveillance," Ryan said through the mind comms. *"But I can't pinpoint any hostiles."*

Kane cursed. "The Diablos must have figured out that we have weaponry they can't combat or explain. The pussies are hiding so they don't get hit with our cyborg voodoo magic."

Nic laughed. "Cyborg voodoo magic?"

"Yeah. It's what Beth calls our superpowers."

Linc shrugged from the back seat. "We don't need superpowers to fight. And if they want to hide, we'll take the fight to them." He cracked his knuckles. "Mexico was fun when I got to bust some noses in between shooting V-Strikes."

Sweat broke out on Kane's forehead despite the cold temperature. Mexico hadn't been fun. When he'd seen Jenna nearly dead and beaten…

He slammed that thought down hard. Jenna's battered and bloody image slid away. His sparkly sugarplum dancing under the Christmas tree took her place.

No regrets.

He finally understood what that meant. He regretted keeping his distance the past few weeks from Beth, of not holding her when she needed him. Of skulking in the shadows to watch her when he could have been in her arms. What he didn't regret? Asking Beth to marry him. He should have confessed his love too.

He'd fucking remedy that as soon as he held her again.

FORTY-TWO

Beth spat out the remaining vomit in her mouth. The smell from the puddle of puke she left by the desk engulfed the room. "I'll give you anything you want. Just tell them to leave her alone."

But was it too late? Evangeline didn't move as she hung there from the hook in the ceiling her arms were tied to. The toes of her heeled boots scraped the concrete floor. A fluorescent light directly overhead illuminated the blood gushing from her nose. More stained her pink sweater. Steroids and Biceps surrounded her as if deciding who would get the next shot.

"Please stop," Beth cried. Nobody deserved to be brutalized like that. The leers on the thugs' faces said hitting her was just the beginning of their sadism.

Evangeline whimpered behind the dirty gag in her mouth. Steroids pulled out a knife.

The enforcer slammed the door. "Do you still need a break, *Cazampulga?* There's another hook in the ceiling. Your friend might want some company."

Evangeline's muffled scream echoed like a prelude of worse to come in Beth's ears.

"Please, *querida*." Her stalker hissed at his brother as he knelt next to her. "Do as he says. I don't want you harmed."

A whimper squeaked through her lips as she turned back to the computer. The classified data she swore she'd never reveal threatened to burst through her fingertips. She curled the fingers on her uninjured hand to keep from typing. There had to be another way to stall for time until Kane and the VIPER team arrived.

The enforcer pressed the tip of his knife into the top of her arm and dragged the blade down an inch. She gasped as her sweater tore. A half second later, she screamed as red-hot agony bled through her skin.

The stalker slapped the weapon from his brother's hands. "You promised you wouldn't cut her."

"I know you're too smart to let a woman come between us, brother."

Beth breathed through the pain in her arm. Her wrist. Her head. Her heart. But she refused to let the Chavezes scare her into submission. There was only one man she'd relinquish control to, and it wasn't the alpha devil brother. It wasn't his obsessed brother either. He may be as brilliant as Scarlett, maybe more since he'd eluded her, but based on the sibling dynamic she'd witnessed, he was the weaker of the two.

And weakness made a prime target.

She turned up the tears for her stalker. "Are you going to let him do that to me?"

"No, *querida*. Just give us the formula and we can be on our way home. *Mi madre* is eager to meet you and start planning our wedding."

She touched the cut on her lip. "Your mother is going to have to wait. I can't walk down the aisle looking like this."

She looked away from the brothers, unable to mask the contempt in her gaze, and slowly scanned the room. "Where are we anyway?"

The enforcer waved his hand. "In a building owned by an associate of the cartels."

"Let me guess? Richardson?" The silence confirmed her suspicion. Apparently, his immorality spread all over the globe.

Her stalker gently caressed her cheek. "Please type so we can get out of here."

She tensed at his touch. Panic pumped through her veins. She knew Kane would find her, but God knew what waited for him when he arrived. The Diablos would likely kill him even if she did give up the formula. And if she got on a plane to Mexico…

The enforcer shoved the tip of his gun into the bruise on her cheek. "Do you need more incentive?"

She bit her tongue, but another whimper escaped.

The enforcer grabbed his brother's wrist. "Stop."

"Our plane takes off in thirty minutes. I want that information before we get on it. I'm not taking any chances of missing Mama's deadline. You know how much beating the other cartels means to her. You know what this formula means to the family business, and you know I need to prove myself to Mama before she'll let me lead the Diablos."

"I wouldn't know, since she kept me locked in a bunker for years so I could hack her enemies." He waved his hand. "That's an issue for another time. Right now, we are doing this my way." He glanced at Beth. "Please, *querida*. Do what he says."

Sweat dripped onto her raw cheek. "Please," she whispered to her stalker. "If I'm yours, then get the two of us out of here." She didn't stand a chance with the enforcer, but she might with just him.

The enforcer turned the gun to his brother. "Need a reminder where your loyalties lie?"

Without warning, her stalker executed a martial art maneuver she'd never quite mastered and stole the gun from his brother's hand.

Holy shit. Her stalker had other skills besides hacking, it appeared.

"I'm loyal to my future wife." He looked at Beth. Ragged breaths scurried through his lips as he teetered in his boots. "Are you loyal to me, *querida*?"

Beth choked back a sob as she stared into his gaze. An unstable kaleidoscope of obsession and insanity swirled in their brown depths. Or maybe that was his concussion. Either way, feeding his delusions might be her only hope of escape. "Yes. I'm yours. Take me home."

He knelt by her side with the gun still trained on his brother. "Seal it with a kiss."

Fighting revulsion, she leaned into him and hoped she tasted like puke.

Kane's comms unit beeped with a biofeedback alert as he and the team fanned out to their positions around the warehouse. The surrounding buildings appeared quiet. Hopefully, any innocent bystanders had gone home to celebrate Christmas and wouldn't get caught in any cross fire.

He glanced at his wrist. Shit, it was warning him that his heart rate was dangerously high.

Chris slid next to him behind a dumpster. *"Calm down, brother."*

Kane scanned the desolate street. *"You weren't calm when Scarlett was at the mercy of a psycho a few weeks ago."*

"Point taken."

As if on cue, Scarlett's voice came over the mind comms. *"The building belongs to my freaking stepfather."*

A collective "what" sounded over the brainwaves.

"It's registered under a dummy corporation. I'm sending the layout now. And there's a plane that's headed to Mexico at the airstrip. Guess whose name was on the registration at the end of a long paper trail?"

Kane's leg bounced like a jumping bean. *"Can't they just lock Richardson in solitary already?"*

"We'll deal with him another time," Chris said. *"Let's get your girl first."*

Kane nodded as the schematics appeared on his comms unit. *"What are we working with?"*

"There's a wireless signal coming from the easternmost room with three heat signatures. Three from the room behind it. There are a dozen men positioned at the front entrance and another dozen at the back, all with clear shots. Cameras are situated throughout the exterior. Once you leave your cover, you'll be a target."

"Can you take the cameras out?" Linc asked.

"Don't." Kane patted the weapon strapped to his chest. New protocols required them to carry backup in the unlikely event their V-Strike weaponry failed. *"Let's use good old-fashioned firepower to draw out as many assholes as possible."* He'd given the Diablos a taste of what a super soldier could do. Now, he'd demonstrate the lengths a desperate, lethal man in love would go to rescue his woman. *"Before we go high tech on their asses, let's light the fucking place up."*

A minute later, they had a plan.

"Ready to do this?" Chris raised his weapon.

Kane pulled out his own gun, aimed, and wrapped his finger around the trigger.

Beth pulled back from her stalker's clammy lips. "I swear, I'll go with you wherever you want and give you the information. Just please get me away from your brother before he—"

Gunshots erupted outside. Her stalker pushed her to the floor. A moment later, shots rang from inside the building in rapid succession as she landed on her knees and pitched forward onto her hands. Pain lanced up her injured arm and she screamed.

The door to Evangeline's torture chamber swung open. Biceps barreled past her. Steroids followed and slammed the door behind him.

"Kane," she whispered. Dread flooded her system as she cradled her arm against her stomach and shook. He was here, but something was wrong. She stopped breathing as more gunshots pealed from the front of the building. Why were Kane and his team using guns instead of voodoo magic? Ryan and Scarlett wouldn't let them come into battle without their superpowers unless…

Voices shouted in the hallway. She strained her ears for Kane's. More shots boomed closer and closer and drowned out every other noise but the pounding of her heart.

The enforcer pulled her by the hair and shoved her to his brother. "Head to the airfield. Once you're on the plane, use your gun to control your woman and make her give up the formula."

The firefight intensified as the enforcer ran into the hall. She spun to her stalker. "Did you mess with VIPER's network?" If anyone could compromise it, he could.

He grabbed her injured wrist and tugged. "Come."

Pain so intense she couldn't even scream doubled her over. She had to think. Giving up the formula wouldn't protect Kane any longer. He could be dead by the time she divulged it at the airfield. He'd said he was protected from head to toe, but every part of him couldn't be bulletproof.

And Chris was out there. And Nic and Linc. All the gunshots could only mean that VIPER's technology had been compromised and they were fighting superpowerless to save her.

She couldn't let them be numbers four through seven. Not because she thought she was a black widow but because they were her family.

If she could get her hands free…

Her stalker tugged her toward the room where Evangeline hung unconscious.

"I'm sorry." His yell carried over the shots still pounding from the front of the building. "I didn't mean to hurt you, but when my brother gets angry, I get angry too."

She caught the exasperation in his pitch and dug in her heels. She almost pitied him for having a big bully as a brother. Almost. "Do you always let him make your decisions?"

Anger and embarrassment flashed in his muddled eyes as he wobbled.

She ignored the battle raging down the hall and steadied her shoulders. "Stand up to your brother." She stepped closer, her throat raw from puking and yelling over the raucous and held out her wrists. "Take these off and let me leave here as your bride, not your prisoner."

She held her breath, praying he'd grow a pair of balls and accept the challenge.

He touched his bandaged face. "I've endured so much for you. Do you love me, *querida?*"

She touched his cheek as tenderly as he touched his broken nose instead of punching it. "No, but I can learn to." The words felt as wrong on her tongue as having a conversation about love with her stalker in the middle of a gunfight. Her next words felt even more wrong. "Kane is going to die out there. He wasn't just my boyfriend. He was my bodyguard. You can't leave me unprotected and helpless until we're safe at your house in Mexico."

The tears coursing down her cheeks weren't forced for his benefit. She clamped her teeth together to stop her jaw from shaking as he retrieved his brother's knife from the floor and placed his gun on the desk. The zip ties rubbed against her bloody skin as he slid the blade under her bonds.

Unbearable seconds passed until the last piece of unforgiving plastic broke free. She lifted her hands to her face. Blood dripped from her angry flesh. She forced a choking sound from her throat and clutched her stomach. "I'm going to barf."

As she clamped a hand over her mouth, she doubled over beside the laptop. From the corner of her eye, she caught the gleam of his gun on the edge of the desk. Pain ricocheted up her injured arm as she gripped the weapon. Slowly, she tucked it against her belly.

FORTY-THREE

"*All clear in back,*" Ryan said over the mind comms.

"*Roger that.*" Kane stole from the shadows of the neighboring building to the rear door of the warehouse. Their simple plan to draw the Diablos out with gunfire proved to be a success. One by one, the hostiles positioned at the back had abandoned their positions to join the fight up front, leaving an unguarded infiltration point.

"*The rear room you are entering has one heat signature. The room it leads into has two.*"

Kane nodded to himself as he fired a V-Strike into the lock on the door handle. It took less than five seconds for the metal to melt. He could assume Beth and one of the Chavezes, or maybe a guard, were in the second room. They'd be stupid to leave her alone.

Unless she was dead.

No. His sugarplum was strong. She'd not only survived but flourished when most would have deteriorated into a shell of the person they used to be. Instead, she'd become the person he'd fallen head over combat boots for.

The tempo of the gunshots from the front of the building

slowed but didn't stop. If this had been any other mission, he wouldn't have appreciated hiding outside while the others engaged with guns and V-Strikes, but he'd do whatever it took to achieve his goal.

Tell Beth he loved her.

Marry her.

Make supersmart babies.

If Ryan's intel was correct, his new life plan of serving his country while he loved the most incredible woman in the world was only two rooms away.

He pushed the outer door open with his boot far enough to enter. A woman hung from the ceiling. The blinding light from above cast her in a flaming, distorted aura. His flesh-and-bone knee buckled. His super leg held him up.

No.

He ripped off his helmet. Nausea tore through his gut. Tears blurred his eyes as the wind whipped through the open door. The body shifted. Straight blonde hair, not brown curls, came into focus. He breathed again.

Evangeline.

He ran to her as an image of Jenna's beaten, lifeless face morphed into Beth's. For so long, he'd feared leaving someone behind if he died. He didn't like the tables being turned.

He checked her pulse. It beat steady beneath his fingers. *"Evangeline is bound and unconscious in the rear room. Heading into the second room. Status?"*

Ryan confirmed there were still two heat signatures as Kane skirted around Evangeline and headed for the door. As he gripped the handle, Evangeline moaned behind him.

He spun and froze again.

A slim man in black held Evangeline by the throat. His knife pressed into the hollow of her neck. Kane didn't need to ask how he'd evaded the thermal imaging. He recognized the head covering and tight clothes that cloaked heat signatures.

Kane itched to take him out with a V-Strike, but if Beth wasn't in the room behind him, he needed him to talk. "Stop hiding like a pussy and tell me where the Black Widow is."

The pussy pulled off the head covering. Dark hair spilled out in waves. "Why don't *you* tell me about whatever it is you did last night at the safe house that nobody can explain?"

Kane didn't answer. He just stared at a miniature, feminine Chavez. "You must be the other dead twin."

"I'm very much alive, but if you hurt me, she'll be dead." She pressed the tip of her knife into Evangeline's neck. Evangeline moaned but didn't open her eyes.

Kane shook off the shock. "I don't care about her."

The female Chavez laughed. "But you do care about the *cazampulga,* and she's on the other side of that door with my brother. Answer my questions and maybe I'll—"

Fire!

The V-Strike Kane aimed at her shoulder found its mark. She dropped her knife and howled in pain.

He spun to the door to the second room and lunged for it. As it swung open, another surprise rooted him to the ground.

Beth spun and kicked her stalker square in the gut. As he sailed across the room, she squeezed the trigger. The bullet plunged into the center of his forehead. She held her breath as the life left his eyes and *he* became number four.

"Beth."

She spun to the voice that sounded sweeter than church bells.

Kane was here.

Alive.

Tears streaked down her cheeks as she drank in every living, breathing detail of the beautiful, lethal man she loved.

He slid over the desk as if he couldn't waste precious seconds walking around it. Instead of pulling her to him, he gently cupped her cheeks and held her as if he'd never let her go. What she felt in her heart—fear, relief, respect, love— shone in his gaze.

"My God, Beth." His lips brushed her temple. "That was incredible. Are you hurt?"

She tucked her injured arm under her breasts and gripped one of the biceps she loved so much with her good hand. "Yes, but I'll be okay. I killed my stalker. He was Chavez's brother and Henry Richardson—"

He held up his hand to silence her. A moment later, he smiled. "Nic reported all hostiles are down, including the other Chavez. The FBI just arrived. The team is helping them sort the mess out."

"Thank heavens." All the emotions she'd struggled with the past two years—fear, tension, anger, despair—along with the freedom to love gathered behind her eyes. The onslaught pushed more tears over her lashes. "Can we go home and celebrate Christmas now? I have so much I want to tell you and so much to—"

A shot peeled from behind her. Kane's hand flew to the side of his head. She screamed his name as his eyes rolled back in their sockets. Another deafening shot from the same direction rent the air. She launched herself at Kane and dropped them to the ground.

"Oh, God." More pleas streamed from her lips in torrents as she rolled off him. Blood peppered his face. She heard Chris shout over her screams. Heard a woman's voice over the pounding of her heart, but Kane didn't open his eyes. Sobbing harder, she clamped one hand over the blood and cupped his cheek with the other as her nightmare hurtled to reality.

More people rushed into the room, but she didn't look away from the blood seeping through her fingers. Battling the panic seizing her rib cage and the organ beating erratically inside it, she begged the rational part of her brain to assure her it was only a flesh wound. The rational part was nowhere to be found.

No, she couldn't do this again. Danny had been hard enough, but God, the thought of losing Kane ripped a hole in the heart he'd healed. "Please. Don't die. You're supposed to be invincible." She pressed her palm harder to his wound.

Chris pried her hands away from Kane's head.

She heard his words, but they didn't register over her pleas. "Wake up, dammit, so I can yell at you about not wearing your freaking helmet."

Someone tried to pull her away. She held tight to the man she loved and dropped her lips to his. "You are not number four. Do you hear me, cowboy? Not. Number. Four."

The side of Kane's head burned like he'd hugged a blowtorch, but he slogged through the fire toward the sound of Beth's voice. Each desperate plea, each rise to her hysterical demand that he not be number four, brought him closer until his mouth stirred against hers.

"I hear ya, sugarplum."

"Kane." She bolted upright. Relief and a dozen other emotions he felt in his own heart shook her so hard her lips fought to form another word. She sniffed back tears as more flowed. "Thank God. I was so afraid you'd—"

He gripped her cheeks in his hands. "Don't even say it."

He never wanted to hear her say number four again. "A flesh wound may hurt like hell, but not even a nuclear missile could take me away from you."

Nothing would. Not a curse. Not his fears. Not any enemy the world might throw at them.

She swatted him lightly on the chest. "It could if you're not wearing your helmet, asshole."

His heart sang at her snark. Man, she was tough. And she was all his. "I only took it off because I thought you were the one hanging from the ceiling back there." He wrapped his hand around her neck and pulled her to him. "Christ, Beth, I thought I'd lost you." He'd also thought he'd understood the meaning of "no regrets." Apparently, it took taking a bullet too close to his brain and the woman of his dreams begging him not to die to make him understand the true meaning. As he held her to his chest and absorbed every inch of the incredible woman he'd almost lost, he vowed never to forget this lesson. "No more wasting time, Beth. Got it? You're mine and I'm yours."

"*Dios Mio*. Will you two just get a room?"

Beth lifted her head and swung it to the woman sandwiched between Nic and Linc. She pointed to the feminine-looking Chavez. "You must be my stalker's twin."

"I'm Valentina, the weak female, locked safely away from my family's enemies." She snorted. "That didn't work out so well for Mama." She cocked her head to a beefy body on the floor. "I saved your boyfriend's ass from my cousin's second bullet. He's always been a crappy first shot, but for some reason, he gets the hang of it with the next one."

Beth peered at Steroids. The bullet hole in his forehead matched the one she'd delivered to her stalker. "He's your *cousin?*"

Valentina shrugged. "*Was* my cousin a few times

removed. That didn't make him any less of a douchebag than my brothers."

Nic snickered. "Are you sure we have to turn her in to the FBI? I like her."

Of course, Nic liked the exotic sprite with a badass attitude.

Kane accepted a towel Chris pressed into his hand and sat up. "Thank you, Valentina."

Beth helped ease him to a sitting position. "Yes. Thank you. You have no idea how much we appreciate what you did."

"You're welcome."

Sincerity shone in her mischievous eyes as she linked one arm through Nic's and the other through Linc's. "Come on, boys. Take me to your leader so I can ask for asylum from my fucked-up *familia*."

Chris laughed. "And Scarlett thinks dealing with Henry Richardson as a stepfather is tough."

Valentina cursed. "That man is almost as evil as my mother."

"No wonder you want to defect." Chris patted Kane's shoulder. "I'll send in an EMT for you two." As he rose from the floor, he pulled something out of his pocket and dropped it in Beth's lap. "Based on the puddle of puke over there, which I'm guessing came from you, you're going to need that."

Beth looked down at the pack of spearmint gum as she brought her hand to her mouth. "Does my breath smell that bad?"

"Yeah, it does." Kane leaned his head toward hers. "But I'm going to kiss you anyway."

She put her hands between their faces. "Not yet." She tore into the pack, stuffed a stick in her mouth, and chewed. A moment later, Kane claimed her lips. The mint, the tender way she held his face in her hands, careful not to touch any of his wounds but a whisper away if he needed her to soothe them, erased the aftertaste of his fears.

Beth pulled back. He tugged her back down to him, but she resisted. "Give me a second to stare into those eyes I plan to get lost in forever now that you've helped me find myself." A smile reached her watery gaze. "I'm not a black widow. My curse is dead."

"Thank fuck." He swiped his finger over a patch of dried blood on her chin. "How did you kill it?"

"With the invincible love of a marvelously incredible superhero."

He laughed. The rich sound rumbled through his body like a healing massage. "Well, sugarplum. I am all those things, but I'm not as invincible as I'd like to be." He linked his fingers through hers. "Neither are you, but we'll be okay. Together." He kissed her lightly on the lips. "I heard there's a midnight mass tonight, and I may have promised a kid named Madalynn she could be our flower girl. Want to have a Christmas wedding?"

She shook her head. "Seems like I'm going to have to be the sensible one in the relationship. You're going to the hospital, and we are not getting married tonight."

A newfound fear flamed the burning in his head. "Why the hell not? Gran says you're the woman for me. She has a weird sixth sense about stuff like this, and she's never wrong."

Beth kissed him until his lips perked into a smile again. "I've been afraid to fall in love for two years because of my so-called curse. Now that I've killed and buried it, I don't want to miss a thing about being in a relationship. I want the whole shebang. Besides, Scarlett and Chris need to get married. I can't be the best maid of honor ever if I'm planning our wedding. In the meantime, you can ask me on dates, woo me with flowers, take me dancing, teach me to ride Holly Jolly, let me drive Gran's Buick…"

He touched his fingers to her lips. "Don't forget tell you each and every day how madly I've fallen in love with you."

"Good, because I'm madly, deeply in love with you too."

"No regrets, Beth. That's how we live."

She raised their linked hands and kissed their entwined fingers. "That's how we live. Forever."

EPILOGUE

One Year Later

Beth shivered as she gazed at the Washington Monument from the steps of the church. The bright Christmas Eve moon shone above the tip of the tower.

She didn't wish for snow this year. She didn't wish for anything at the moment.

Kane and the VIPER boys were home unscathed from their latest mission. Triple X had already saved thousands of lives. Evangeline was in a court-mandated mental health facility. Henry Richardson awaited trial, and Valentina Chavez was working with the feds in exchange for asylum from the Diablos.

And this morning, she and Kane had returned from his family's farm in West Virginia, where she'd gotten an early Christmas present. They hadn't planned to visit again until after the new year, but Holly Jolly had gone into labor early, so they'd rushed out west. They got there in time to witness her gift, a beautiful foal she named Noel, come into the world.

Now, she couldn't wait to wake up with Kane on Christmas morning. She may have gone over the top with a big tree in every room, but Kane took her demand that he woo her quite seriously and indulged her every desire. Now she couldn't wait for him to get here with her parents and Gran. The three of them had gone on a cruise together. Kane left a couple of hours ago to pick them up at the airport.

Scarlett slid next to her and pointed to the monument. "That sight never gets old."

"Still my favorite." But Beth's gaze wasn't on the landmark.

Linc sidled to her other side and pointed to the curb. "About fucking time your man got here. Let's get this church stuff over so I can have some moonshine."

"Merry Christmas to you too." She rose on her toes and kissed him on the cheek as she watched Kane exit the baby-blue Buick. As he opened the doors for her mom and dad and then helped Gran out of the car, her heart glowed as bright as the moon.

Nic elbowed Linc out of the way and wagged his finger at Beth. "Listen here. No sneaking away with cartel members into tunnels. I don't want to be late for my date with the Santa's helper I met at the mall yesterday with Gage and his daughter."

"Promise." Kane was the only person she wanted to sneak away with tonight, but she wasn't in any rush. Everyone she loved stood outside the church.

Chris chatted with Hudson and his wife, Tessa, who held their baby boy in her arms. Gage stood close, alert as always, even when there was no imminent threat, as his adorable daughter Lucy made funny faces at the baby. Even Dr.

Patience Fairbanks, VIPER's surgeon, was here with her twin boys. Beth had gotten to know Tessa and Patience well and considered them dear friends.

Smiling bigger than the monument, Beth closed the distance between her and Kane and kissed him. As she whispered, "I missed you," she turned to her father. "How was traffic?"

"Good, but not as good as the Buick. I drove until we stopped a few blocks back for wine. That baby drives like a dream."

"Seriously? He only lets me drive it around the block." She turned her pouty lips to Kane. "Not cool, cowboy."

Kane laughed as he adjusted his hat. "Is that what you want for Christmas, sugarplum? To drive Gran's car all the time?"

"No, I want to drive *your* car all the time." Gran gave him the ownership papers on his birthday and said his grandfather would have been proud of him. Kane had teared up. Beth had full-on bawled.

Her heart skipped a beat as he tugged the lapels of her sugarplum coat and laid a kiss on her lips. Somehow, he'd found a replica to replace the one she'd lost in the fire. She'd be eternally grateful for that thoughtful gesture, along with everything else she found sweet and sexy and incredible about her man.

"Miss Beth."

Madalynn scurried up the stairs ahead of her parents. Her body jittered like Kane's leg under her deep-green jacket. "Can we play hide-and-seek after mass? I know we can't go in the tunnels anymore, but playing in the church is just as fun."

Kane ruffled the girl's blonde hair. "Miss Beth already said yes to playing with *me* tonight." He reached into his pocket and pulled out a purple velvet box. The keys to the

Buick dangled from his pinkie finger. "I'm hoping she'll say yes to driving my car, and say yes to *me,* for the rest of her life."

The first strains of the organ music pealed through the doors behind her as he flipped the lid open. A round diamond surrounded by amethysts caught the moonlight.

Kane took off his cowboy hat and handed it to Madalynn as he stepped back and bent his knees.

Beth pulled him up before he hit the stone and wrapped her arms around him. "Yes. Yes."

He captured her face between his hands. "Are you sure you won't regret that you didn't give me the chance to properly ask you to marry me?"

"No regrets, remember?"

"You got that right, sugarplum. No regrets."

The End

ACKNOWLEDGMENTS

Oh crap! Now that book two in the Project VIPER Series is out, I need to write the third.

Starting a new book is the hardest part of the process for me, but the high of knowing someone will read it someday keeps me going. This time I have the added high of knowing there are readers waiting for it. (Excuse me while I step away and do a happy dance with lots of squeals.)

Thank you, thank you, thank you to my readers for taking a chance on this indie author. I sincerely appreciate your support.

And now on to the people in my life who deal with me through the writing process.

My husband, **Gary Clement** - Yes, honey, you are still the inspiration for my steamy scenes. Thanks for not batting an eye when I spend money on inappropriate stickers.

My son, **Alexander** - I can't wait to hear your stories about Navy boot camp and use them in a book someday. My daughter, **Charlotte -** Thanks for letting me tell your English teachers about my books even though it embarrasses the hell out of you.

My parents, **Kathy and Al Wolf** – Who do I turn to when I need tiny holes punched in two-hundred bookmarks and tassels looped through? My awesome parents, of course. Thanks for your unconditional support.

Linda Lenahan (okay, Luongo, but you'll always be Linda Lenahan to me.) – Here's to more fun times in Seaside and more memories on the boardwalk. And let's never talk about that insane night in our twenties again. (Unless I write it into a book. Then we can talk.)

My author bestie, **Aria Wyatt** – I promise I'll get to that book you keep bugging me to finish, just as soon as I finish up with my super soldiers. In the meantime, thanks for your thoughts and friendship. Love you!

My business manager, **Samantha Heil** – thanks for organizing me, for beta reading, and for being my friend. I can't wait to see what the future holds for both of us.

Shannon Holtz - To my sorority sister, dear friend, awesome assistant at events, and the only person besides my mom to read the first book I ever wrote – thanks for your friendship and support from day one.

Beth Prellberg – Thanks for being my real-life bestie.

Jaymee Diviacchi - Mexican anyone? Our author dinner dates with Samantha are the best!

Jen Graybeal – Thanks for editing another VIPER story. Your patience and understanding this time around are most appreciated.

Kimberly Hunt of Revision Division – I'm so glad I met you at the library!

Rosa Sharon of Fairyproofmother Proofreading – Thanks for your magical skills. Don't give up on teaching me grammar rules. I may grasp the concepts one day.

Laura Hidalgo of Spellbinding Design –Thanks for another cover of my dreams. Can't wait to see what you do with my next super soldier.

Kayla Dieckman – Thanks for making my books sparkle with your gorgeous hand-sprayed edges.

Mary K. Tilghman – Thanks for your friendship and support. Looking forward to many more book signings with you.

Jenn Bloch– Thanks for everything you do at work so I

can pursue my passion, and thanks for being there when I need to talk to Alexa.

Tammy Ward – Thanks for your eagle eye again.

The Hosky Clan – Tom, Claudia, and John Hosky – Thanks for supporting my writing dream and being the best cheerleaders. I know Peg is sitting on a cloud, knitting something for her angel friends, and reading over Claudia's shoulder.

Hana Kabashi – Thanks for your support and for playing along in my Facebook group and naming Madalynn. Hope you like her.

To my readers – Thanks again for reading my books. I'll make you a deal – you keep reading and I'll keep writing.

Lots of love,

Kristie

ABOUT THE AUTHOR

Kristie Wolf is an award-winning author of steamy romantic suspense. When she was a teenager, she read her first romance novel and connected with it so deeply that she immediately told her mother she was going to publish one. Many years later, she did just that.

While her career as a marketing professional in the government technology space hasn't taught her to troubleshoot a computer, she's fascinated with what happens when technology spectacularly fails. The chilling stories she's heard from the nation's tech leaders are the catalyst for plots about maniacal terrorists but don't worry. Her military and law enforcement alpha heroes and badass heroines always save the day while burning up the pages and finding happily ever after.

Kristie resides in Maryland with her husband - aka her tech support - and her two teenagers who participate in nearly every sport or activity ever invented. Many of her words are written on the pool deck, on the sidelines and in the bleachers, or in her car. When she's not behind her computer, she can be found:

• Walking her Vizsla and her Pittie-mix rescue while listening to her favorite authors.

• Watching cheerleading videos on her phone because she misses being a coach.

• Learning everything she can about Elvis Presley because she's going to write a novel based on him someday.

• Making space in her closet for another pair of cowboy boots she doesn't need but has to have.

Want to be notified about Kristie's upcoming releases? Sign up for her newsletter at https://www.kristiewolf.com/

Kristie loves to connect with readers. Drop her a note on social media.

facebook.com/KristieAWolf

instagram.com/kristiewolf_author

tiktok.com/@kristiewolfromance

Project VIPER Series

They're the nation's strongest and smartest, but their dangerous attractions could be the death of them.

Book One: *Too Dangerous to Love*

Book Two: *Too Lethal to Love*

Book Three (Coming 2025)

Blood Snow Series

Welcome to Red Snow, Colorado, where heroes emerge from the shadows, and love and danger entwine on every snowy slope.

Book One: *Knife to the Heart*